roadside assistance

Also by Amy Clipston:

A Gift of Grace

A Promise of Hope

A Place of Peace

A Plain and Simple Christmas

roadside assistance

Amy Clipston

ZONDERVAN.com/
AUTHORTRACKER
follow your favorite authors

We want to hear from you. Please send your comments about this book to us in care of zreview@zondervan.com. Thank you.

ZONDERVAN

Roadside Assistance
Copyright © 2011 by Amy Clipston

This title is also available as a Zondervan ebook.
Visit www.zondervan.com/ebooks.

Requests for information should be addressed to:
Zondervan, Grand Rapids, Michigan 49530

ISBN 978-0-310-71981-6

Cover design: Faceout Studios
Cover photography: Corbis
Interior design: Tina Henderson

Printed in the United States of America

11 12 13 14 15 /DCI/ 22 21 20 19 18 17 16 15 14 13 12 11 10 9 8 7 6 5 4 3 2 1

For my precious motorheads,
Joe, Zac, and Matt, with all of my love.

chapter one

My dad's twelve-year-old, burgundy Chevrolet Suburban roared down the winding streets, pulling a U-Haul packed with our remaining belongings past sprawling brick McMansions with perfect, manicured yards. The humid August air whipped wisps of my curly brown hair across my face, tangling the long strands that had escaped the ponytail I'd stuck through the back of a ball cap.

Frowning, I yanked off the hat and tried in vain to capture the offending strands and wind the rubber band around my thick mane. "I wish you'd just fix the air-conditioning so we could close the windows," I bellowed to Dad over the classic rock blaring through the speakers. "How much does Freon cost?"

While singing off-key to Aerosmith's "Angel," my dad winked at me. After the song ended, he said, "You know it'll take more than Freon to fix this ol' hunk-a-junk, and we can't afford the parts I'd need. I'm just happy it still runs with all the miles on it." He tapped the dashboard and shook his head. "She got us here safe and sound at least."

I adjusted my cap and settled back in the seat, peeling my sweaty legs from the faded tan leather. Our rebuilt Suburban looked like a junk pile reject in comparison to the shiny European SUVs lining the concrete driveways surrounding us.

My dad maneuvered around the corner, passing more oversized brick colonials. I had to hold back a groan. Our tiny three-bedroom ranch could've fit in the downstairs of any of those homes.

"This neighborhood is still classy. Looks the same as it did seven years ago." He turned to me. "Do you remember coming down here for Christmas when you were ten?"

I shrugged. "I remember bits and pieces. I had fun, right?"

"Oh yeah." He nodded, a smile cutting across his face, weathered by long days spent in the sun working on cars. "You and Whitney always had fun together as kids, the few times you saw each other. I always wished we could spend more time with my sister and her family, and I guess now that wish is coming true." He got quiet for a second and then added, "Isn't it funny how life works?"

Yeah, real funny.

I bit my lower lip, wondering if Whitney and I could possibly have any fun together now. We had nothing in common, aside from being born less than a month apart. From the stories Grandma recounted during her tedious phone calls, Whitney ruled the high school with her court of perfect friends. She did everything—from cheerleading to church youth group to the honor society. Grandma's perfect little princess.

The latest visit with Grandma, as well as with Whitney, her parents, and her little brother, Logan, was a blur of raw emotions. Eight months ago, they'd come up north for my mom's funeral and stayed four days. And I'd counted the minutes until they went home.

My aunt Darlene, my dad's younger and only sibling, showed up and took over our house, coordinating the funeral and reception down to the color of the tablecloths. She also dictated what I would wear to the funeral, dragging me around the mall and insisting I try on dress after dress, probably two dozen total, before she declared the perfect fit. It was an uncomfortable, short dress, not my style at all.

But that was the root of the problem—Aunt Darlene didn't like my style. She didn't approve that I preferred to wear black pants and a nice blouse to the funeral instead of a dress. Darlene didn't approve of any of the clothes in my tiny closet, not even my jeans and T-shirts. In fact, she'd started in on me when she walked in the door of our house, chastising me for oil stains on my hands, insisting I was too pretty to be a grease monkey, and ordering me to pull my messy curls back from my face.

"Check that out," my dad gushed, pointing at a restored 1966 Mustang sitting in the driveway of another huge house. "That's what I had when I started dating your mom. She loved that car. In fact, she said she used me just to get to ride in that car." He chuckled and glanced at me. "Maybe you and I can build one of those someday."

"Yeah, sure, Dad," I said, staring out the window at another enormous home as we drove by.

I had a feeling I wouldn't be working on vintage cars anytime soon. The minute we arrived, Darlene would probably stick me right back into her Boot Camp for Beauty Delinquents. The morning of the funeral, Darlene insisted I get my hair and makeup done, subjecting me to three hours at the salon, including having a woman wash and straighten my hair, a painful and tedious process. After the hair-straightening torture, another woman plucked my eyebrows, painted my fingernails and toenails, applied lotions to my hands, and caked my face with makeup. Normally I would've protested, but I was too emotionally distraught after losing my sweet mother to fight with my drill sergeant aunt. Plus, when I'd expressed my resentment to my dad the night before, with a pained expression he'd told me to just go along with it.

When we arrived at the church for the service, I looked like a completely different person. If my mother had looked down from heaven that day, I doubt she would have recognized me. My best friend, Megan, and my boyfriend, Tyler, had both walked right past when they entered the church, and I had to wave them down, insisting I was Emily Curtis and not some cousin visiting from out of town. Megan was stunned by my appearance and said I looked like a movie star, but I felt more like a clown with all of the makeup and my hair full of spray. Tyler, on the other hand, was speechless when he saw me.

Since my cousin Whitney graduated from Darlene's beauty camp with honors, she wasn't much support either. Whitney hadn't said much to me at the funeral, except that I looked beautiful. Then she hugged me hard, making it difficult to breathe. I wasn't sure if her hug was sincere, but I didn't really care. I'd been too busy trying to figure out how I could possibly get through the next day without my mom. Other than the hug, Whitney had her eyes trained on her phone, texting friends constantly. I couldn't even imagine what she was telling them. Maybe she felt so uncomfortable with me she used her friends as a distraction.

After the funeral and torturous reception filled with more awkward hugs, as well as condolences from strangers and acquaintances, I'd bagged the black dress, shoving it to the back of my closet. I put on jeans and a sweatshirt and retreated to my dad's garage to drink Coke and talk cars with Tyler, Logan, and Megan. It was the most relaxed I'd been during the visit.

The Richards family went home after the funeral, to my relief. I was tired of being told what to wear, how to style my hair, and how to behave like a "nice young lady." My mother had never ordered me around that way, and I wasn't about to let Aunt Darlene do it. She just didn't get me. Aside from Megan and Tyler, Logan seemed to be the only one who understood me.

But then again, I doubted Tyler ever really "got" me. Two weeks ago, he'd broken off our relationship with two simple sentences: "You're really cool, Em, but I'm just not attracted to you *that* way. Let's be friends."

Thanks for the love, Ty.

But my failed relationship with Tyler was only a fraction of the train wreck that I now called my life. Since we'd lost Mom, my dad's business, Curtis Collision Center, had tanked; our house was ripped from us due to foreclosure; and we were left with only a rented trailer full of boxes and bags containing the remaining pieces of our former existence.

"Check out that brand-new Lamborghini," Dad said, pointing to a canary yellow car in a driveway. "Wow. That's what money looks like, Baby Doll."

Crossing my arms, I stared at the cracked and faded tan vinyl dashboard and frowned. *We'll never fit in here.*

"Well, this is the place," my dad said, steering into a horseshoe driveway winding in front of a huge, two-story, dark-red brick colonial.

Although I'd been here seven years ago, I was still taken aback. The house featured huge windows, an attached three-car garage, and a wraparound porch. As our truck crept around the curve in the driveway, I noticed that the concrete snaked to the back of the house, where I caught glimpses of a cabana, a wrought iron fence surrounding the Olympic-size in-ground pool, and a detached three-car garage.

I took my first thought back—our house could've been someone's *garage.*

I looked over at my dad. His dream, aside from his collision repair business, had always been to have a huge garage to tinker in at home. Chuck had two garages—a total of six bays counting the one attached to the house—but I doubted he even knew how to change the oil, let alone build a car.

Two shiny Mercedes M-Class SUVs sat next to each other in the concrete driveway like a his and hers set. Were they issued upon entrance to the neighborhood? Both were new models, and both vehicles were also evidence Uncle Chuck was still raking in the dough with his high-powered job at the bank. My fingers itched for a chance to look under the hood of those two machines, to see what made them tick. Maybe my dad and I could take them out to the interstate and blow the cobwebs out of the engines to see just how quickly we could get from zero to seventy. But I doubted Chuck would let me get behind the wheel. Based on how clean the cars were, I wondered if he ever pushed them beyond forty miles per hour.

Behind the SUVs was an older-model Honda Accord SE with a faded red paint job, which had to belong to Whitney. Maybe the Suburban wouldn't be so out of place ... I briefly wondered how Miss Perfect dealt with driving such an old car and parking it next to the SUVs.

My dad brought the truck to a complete stop, and the U-Haul groaned in response. Turning to me, his lips formed a reluctant smile as he patted my leg. "Well, Baby Doll, we're here. Time to begin fresh."

Before I could respond, a voice rang out behind us.

"Welcome!" Aunt Darlene yelled, trotting down the steep front steps. "We're so glad y'all made it here safe."

Pushing the door open, I slid from the seat and leaned back against the truck.

"Hey, little sister!" My dad rushed from the driver's seat, slamming the door and enveloping my tall, slender aunt in one of his famous bear hugs.

Darlene laughed and smacked his arm before stepping back and assessing him with her big, brown eyes. Her platinum blonde bob was perfectly manicured, much like the lush, green landscaping. While her style was impeccable, my stare was drawn to the hint of her black roots.

Dressed in white shorts and a collared shirt, she looked

like she'd just returned from playing tennis at the country club. "You're looking well, Brad," she said. "It's so good to see you. I hope you'll be comfortable here and stay as long as you need."

He smiled. "Thank you." He then made a sweeping gesture with his arm and motioned for me to join him at his side. "Get over here, Emmy."

Taking a deep breath, I stepped over to him and forced a smile. "Hi, Aunt Darlene." I held out my hand for her to shake.

"Oh my!" Aunt Darlene tugged me into a tight hug. "You're still pretty as a picture, despite that messy hair. I can't believe how much you've grown up in the past year."

I gasped for air and tried in vain to escape her crushing embrace.

"Let me look at you." She pushed me back, her hands still gripping my shoulders like vices. "My goodness. You look just like your mama." Her smile turned to a grimace, and she quickly added, "Lord rest her soul." Studying me, her eyes filled with concern. "You must miss her so. How are you doing, Emily?"

I shrugged. "I'm fine." I was *not* going to open up to her. She'd never understand how I felt.

She frowned, her eyes moving down to my hands, streaked with grease stains from last-minute fixes on the Suburban this morning.

Oh no. Here come the lectures. Why didn't I scrub my hands with Gojo before we left? I swallowed a sigh.

Darlene clicked her tongue. "You got yourself back into that grease again?"

I leveled my glance, not backing down. "Dad needed some help with the truck this morning, so I pitched in."

She took her hand in mine, running her fingers over my dry skin. "You know it's not very ladylike to play with engines. Boys tend to like girls who dress and act like girls."

I swallowed a gasp. The words stung almost as much as when Tyler broke up with me.

"Yeah, well, someone has to help him get the truck running, right, Dad?" I glanced at my dad, who grinned while nodding. "Besides, it's not very ladylike to be broken down at the side of the road with a packed U-Haul, right?"

"That's right," Dad chimed in.

Darlene frowned, her eyes focused on my hands. "I guess you're right. Why aren't you using that lotion I bought you? You've got some seriously dry skin, young lady. The goopy stuff is not very good for your hands."

So when did she become my mom? I bit my bottom lip, censoring my words. "I ran out." It wasn't exactly the truth, but Darlene wouldn't have been happy to hear I'd given the frou-frou-smelling lotion to Megan a month ago. The scent of lilac didn't appeal to me.

"Well then," Darlene said with a smile. "We'll just have to take you out shopping and get you some more. Oh, and look at those nails." She clicked her tongue. "Emily Claire, we've got to get you back to the salon too."

"Absolutely," I muttered. "I can't wait."

My dad placed a hand on my shoulder. "I think the nail salon may have to wait until we're all moved in."

I breathed a sigh of relief when Uncle Chuck appeared on the stairs, taking the focus away from me.

"You made it!" he announced, taking the front steps two at a time. He definitely looked the rich banker part. His graying brown hair was cut short and his smile was bright against his tanned skin. I'd bet the tan was courtesy of the golf course.

My mom once called Darlene and Chuck "Barbie and Ken," and I could totally see that now. They were perfect standing in front of their "dream house" with their designer clothes and brown tans. All they needed was the pink Corvette. Maybe there was one in the back garage.

I suppressed a smile at the thought.

"Good to see you, Brad," Chuck said, shaking my dad's hand.

The backfire of a loud engine drowned out my dad's reply. I turned toward the street just as a dark-haired boy my age piloted a 1970 Dodge Challenger into the driveway next door, the motor ticking with an irregular sound. Obviously a project car, it was faded green and peppered with gray primer spots.

I could feel the thump of the engine reverberating a deep, low drone against my chest. I bit my lower lip, squelching the urge to run over to the garage and help him fix that tick. My interest and specialty had always been Chevrolets, an affection I'd inherited from my dad. But rebuilding a Dodge would be a fun challenge. One I could use right now.

My dad's brown eyes flashed with a question, waiting for me to diagnose the car's thumping problem as I always did when I helped out at his shop back home.

"I hear a bad tick," I said. "Bet he's got to tear it apart and rebuild the whole top end of the motor. Sounds like a big block."

He smacked my back. "Good girl."

I grinned with triumph. I still loved impressing my dad. Lately it seemed like cars were all we talked about. But at least we still talked.

As the thundering engine died in the distance, I turned toward the sound of the front door slamming shut. Tall, slender Whitney negotiated the front steps like a runway model. At five foot ten, she topped me by three inches. A faint hint of black roots lined the symmetrical part on her blonde head as well, and I wondered if she and her mother made a girls' day out of their salon appointments to take care of those pesky roots.

With a pink, sequined cell phone pressed to her ear, she spoke, gesturing with her hands. Her fingernails and toenails were painted a deep red, matching her lipstick. I wondered if *Teen Vogue* had ever considered her for one of their covers. Surely Grandma must've sent them at least one photograph.

"Exactly, Kristin," she was saying as she headed toward us, all business. "I'm having a small pool party at my house tonight. Come over around seven. Call the rest of the girls. This is our last chance for some fun before school starts Tuesday." She nodded, listening. "Okay. Gotta go. My cousin is here. *Ciao*."

Snapping the phone closed, a smile grew on her rosy lips. "Uncle Brad! Emily!" Arms extended, she pulled my dad and me into a hug, and I nearly choked at the stench of her flowery perfume, without a doubt the latest designer fragrance.

She stepped back and grinned. "It's so wonderful to see you again. You look great!"

"Thanks." I adjusted the baseball cap on my head. Whitney was a good liar, seeing as she'd nodded in agreement when her mother criticized my attire during their last visit.

"Well, I guess we better start unpacking," my dad said, stepping to the back of the trailer. "We're loaded down." He pulled keys from his pocket and unfastened the lock. The metal rods squealed in response, and the doors groaned open. "I hope you all ate your Wheaties this morning. We brought a lot of junk."

Embarrassed, I wished I could hide in the backseat of the truck. I couldn't even imagine what Whitney and her family would think of our possessions.

Chuck snatched a duffle bag and suitcase from the pile in the trailer. Slinging the bag over his arm, he headed up the stairs. "Whitney, put the phone down and grab something. If we all pitch in, we'll get it unloaded quickly."

"Logan can help too. You'll just have to surgically remove him from his controller." Whitney's gaze swept over my attire.

"Do you have your bathing suit? A few of my friends are coming over later to swim. I thought it would be nice to have one last girls' night before classes start Tuesday."

"Oh." I glanced down at my faded blue T-shirt and denim shorts and then back at the trailer. "I doubt I can find my suit in that mess."

Whitney shrugged. "No worries. You can borrow one of mine."

I bit back a snort. As if I could fill out one of her bikinis. "That's okay," I said. "I have plenty of unpacking to do. I'm sure I'll meet your friends at school."

"Emily." She touched my shoulder, her expression serious. "Have some fun. You have the rest of the year to unpack."

"Girls," Darlene called, heaving two large tote bags onto her slight shoulders. "You can get caught up later. Let's unpack now."

Saved by Darlene of all people. I threw a backpack onto my back and grabbed a suitcase with wheels and then followed my aunt up the steep front steps and into the large foyer. In front of me, a sweeping open staircase unfurled to the second floor.

To my right was a large living room, complete with a baby grand piano, matching brown leather sofa and love seat, and curio cabinets filled with expensive-looking figurines. The doorway behind it led into the kitchen, as I recalled. To my left was a spacious formal dining room, with a long dark wooden table that would comfortably seat eight. Alongside it sat a huge matching hutch filled with formal dishes. The furniture alone was probably worth more than our old house. I wondered if Whitney knew just how lucky she was to have all of this.

"This way, dear," Darlene called while walking up the stairs.

At the top of the stairs, we stepped into a long hallway lined with doors on either side. A bookshelf packed with books, framed photographs, and knickknacks sat at the end of the hallway.

"I'll give you a quick tour before we head into your room." Darlene nodded as we walked by a row of doors. "This is Logan's room." She stopped and popped her head in. "Logan, turn off the game. Emily is here."

Logan glanced over and grinned. "Hey, Emily." He stood and clicked off the television. At ten, he was tall for his age, much like his parents and sister. He had sandy blond hair and deep brown eyes.

"Hi, Logan." I glanced around his room, which was twice the size of what I'd had back home. Star Wars and car posters cluttered the deep-blue walls. A bunk bed, the top unmade with Star Wars sheets hanging over the side, took up the far wall.

"Logan, go down and help your father and uncle empty the trailer," Darlene said, heading back down the hallway.

"This is Whitney's room," Darlene said as we passed a room decorated in all pastels and white furniture. She then pointed toward the end of the hallway. "I thought I'd put your father in the room over the garage since there's a flat screen and a sofa along with the bed. It's sort of a suite."

She pointed toward another door, this one at the other end of the hall. "That's our room." Then she nodded across the hall to two doors. "That's the bathroom, and this is your room. It's a guest room, as you can see."

She opened the door to a large room, probably three times the size of my old one, with a couple of bookshelves, a double bed, a love seat, a triple dresser, and a bureau holding a flat-screen television. The walls were a light peach, and the bed contained matching decorative pillows. Four paintings of seascapes and lighthouses graced the walls.

She opened a door to a huge walk-in closet. Empty hangers cluttered the rod, and shelves lined the far wall.

"I moved all of the clothes to my closet so you have plenty of room." She placed my things on the bed and pointed toward the bureau and dresser. "Those are empty too. You can unpack everything and feel at home."

"Oh, I won't need all this space," I said, shaking my head. "I probably won't fill half of the closet or dresser, but thank you."

She waved off the comment with a smile. "Oh, you don't need to thank me." Then she hugged me. "We're family, Emily. If you need anything, just let me know."

"Thanks," I said, glancing around the room, trying to process it all in my brain. Yesterday I was standing in my tiny room with my single bed. Now I was moving into a peach guest room with decorative pillows and paintings of beaches and lighthouses.

As nice as the space was, I knew my boxes of car manuals and magazines would never go with the décor. It would remain a guest room.

Whitney appeared in the doorway with a brown suitcase. "Does this go in here?"

"Yeah." I gestured toward a hope chest that had been made into a seat complete with padding, which sat in front of two large windows. "Right there would be great. Thanks."

"Let's get some light in here," Whitney said, drawing the long peach curtains back and raising the white blinds. Sunlight flooded the room.

I stepped to the window and peered out over the backyard, which was even bigger than it had looked from the street. A deck, complete with a long table, several chairs, and an umbrella, stretched from the back of the house to a concrete patio. In the center of the yard was the pool, surrounded by more concrete lined with chaises. Various pool toys bobbed in the crystal blue water, which sparkled in the sun. The long driveway that snaked around from the front of the house ended at the garage.

The car I'd heard earlier roared and sputtered again, and I

glanced toward the fence separating Whitney's yard from the neighbor's.

A larger, four-bay detached garage sat on the other side of the fence. The doors were up, revealing a cluttered mess of toolboxes and engine parts with the Dodge in the center of it all. The boy I'd seen earlier emerged from the driver's seat. I absently wondered if he'd figured out the engine needed to be rebuilt. A hunter-green Jeep Wrangler, the top removed, was parked in the driveway outside of the garage. This guy was a Chrysler fan, all the way.

"Who lives there?" I asked once the engine noise died.

"The Stewarts," Whitney said, pulling her phone from her pocket, checking the screen, punching buttons. "That garage is always noisy, but I guess you're used to that." Her phone chimed and she grinned. "Awesome. Tiffany's coming too."

Chuck burst through the door with an armload of boxes. "These go here?" he asked, panting as if he'd run up the stairs double-time.

I spotted my name scrawled on the side in black Sharpie. "Yes, thanks. Drop them anywhere."

"Let's go, girls," Darlene called from the hallway. "I'd like to get the trailer unloaded so I can start supper."

Part of me wondered if she also wanted to get our stuff out of their driveway before all the neighbors saw our belongings, and I hoped that wasn't the case.

Three hours later, the trailer now empty and parked in front of the detached garage, I sat across from my dad and between Logan and Whitney at the large kitchen table. The center of the table was cluttered with platters and serving bowls full of baked chicken, mashed potatoes, mixed vegetables, rolls, and salad. While it smelled heavenly, my appetite had evaporated the moment we'd pulled into the driveway.

"Logan, would you like to say the prayer?" Darlene asked.

I glanced at my dad, who shrugged and then bowed his head. Who knew Aunt Darlene was religious?

I bowed my head and studied my faded denim shorts while Logan recited something quickly, ending with the word "Amen." I looked up just as arms began reaching across the table, grabbing at the serving dishes. Utensils clinked and scraped as food filled the plates surrounding me.

"Emily," Darlene said, "how's your boyfriend doing? He was such a nice young man when we met him."

I swallowed a groan and took a deep breath. "We broke up," I said, with a shrug, hoping to look casual.

"Oh dear." She shook her head, frowning. "I'm so sorry."

"What happened?" Whitney asked, looking concerned.

It took every fiber of my strength not to kick her under the table. What did she think happened? I considered telling them the truth, but the humiliation would be too much to bear. Besides, I still had a hole in my chest when I thought about Tyler, and I didn't want to risk getting emotional in public.

Hoping I looked unaffected by the failed romance, I shrugged again. "You know, what usually happens when someone moves away."

Darlene gave me a condescending expression. "Well, you know long-distance relationships don't usually work."

An uncomfortable silence filled the air, followed by another chorus of cutlery tinkling.

"So, Whitney, are you excited about your junior year?" my dad asked.

Silently thankful for the change in subject, I snatched the bowl of salad and scooped some onto my plate, smothering the green, leafy pile in buttermilk ranch dressing.

"Absolutely." Nodding with emphasis, Whitney grinned.

"You can show Emmy here the ropes." He winked at me.

Whitney shrugged. "Sure thing." Her phone chimed and she snickered at the screen and then began typing.

"Whitney Jean," Darlene scolded. "You know the rules. No texting at the table. Turn it off, please, and hand it to me."

Sighing dramatically, Whitney hit a few buttons and surrendered the phone. "Fine."

Darlene dropped the phone onto the counter behind her and then shook her head. "Kids these days. It's all about technology. I remember when we had to call our friends from the kitchen phone, and Mom wouldn't allow us to make or take calls after nine o'clock. Right, Brad?"

My dad nodded, chewing. "That's right."

"Now they call and text each other at all hours," Darlene continued, stabbing her salad. "It's very intrusive." Her gaze met mine. "I imagine your dad doesn't allow you to text at the table either, right, Emily?"

"Uh." I looked at my dad, hoping he'd save me more embarrassment, but he was studying his glass of Coke. "Actually, I don't have a phone."

Darlene looked confused. "You don't?"

"No." I fingered the condensation on my glass. "I don't see the use for one." Truth be told, cell phones were one of the first luxuries we relinquished after my mom was diagnosed with cancer and the doctor bills started clogging our mailbox.

"Really?" Darlene smiled. "We'll have to take care of that. We can add another line for next to nothing, right, Chuck?"

My uncle nodded with a mouth full of chicken.

"That's okay," I said. "I'm fine without it. It's nice being able to come and go as I please." *And I sure don't want to be your charity case.*

"That's right," my dad chimed in. "There's nothing wrong with leaving a message on the machine."

Frowning, Whitney shook her head. "I would die without my phone."

I refrained from rolling my eyes by lifting my glass of Coke to my lips and taking a long drink.

"What was so important that it couldn't wait until after dinner anyway?" Chuck asked.

"It was about cheerleading," Whitney said. "We have to wear our uniforms on Tuesday."

I glanced out the window and thought about Megan back home. Was she eating dinner? Certainly she wasn't listening to a cheerleader discuss her excitement about the new school year revving up.

I began to wonder what Tyler was doing and if he even knew I'd moved already, but I pushed thoughts of him from my head. No need to pine for a guy who didn't care about me.

"Maybe you should go out for cheerleading, Em," my dad said, breaking through my thoughts. "I bet you could jump and yell with the best of them."

I blinked, shaking my head. Had my father completely lost his mind? Was the humidity seeping into his brain? "I don't think so," I said, trying to keep my voice even.

My dad shrugged. "You might want to try something different this year."

I stared at his smile, my mouth gaping with disbelief. Was he joking? *Different* wouldn't be the word. Certainly he'd not forgotten the loner I'd been back home. Aside from Tyler, who'd turned out to be a waste of my heart and my time, I'd been happy to spend most of my nearly nonexistent social life with Megan.

"There's plenty I wish I could've changed," he added.

"Like studying instead of working on cars at all hours?" Darlene asked with a chuckle.

"Did you fail out of school?" Logan asked.

"No, no," my dad said with a laugh. "I didn't fail."

Darlene bumped her shoulder on my dad's. "But he almost did. He managed to graduate by fixing his English teacher's car."

"No way!" Logan beamed, impressed. "What was wrong with your teacher's car?"

While the conversation turned to my dad's and aunt's fond high school memories, I picked at my salad. When everyone was finished eating, I helped load the dishes into the dishwasher, smiling and nodding while Darlene chatted about the beautiful summer they'd enjoyed with very few rainy days.

Once the kitchen was clean, I headed for the stairs, hoping to make a clean getaway to my room, which was a sea of boxes, bags, and suitcases. Just as my flip-flop hit the bottom step, I heard my name.

"Emily," my dad called, and I swallowed a groan.

"Yeah," I said, craning my neck to look into the kitchen.

"Are you going to try out the pool?"

I shook my head. "No, thanks. I have tons of unpacking to do."

"Why don't you just relax tonight?" He shrugged. "You don't have to swim. You can just sit on the deck with me."

Didn't he know that I needed some time alone to sort through all of the emotions that were threatening to overtake me? "I think I just need some quiet time alone," I said slowly, hoping he would get it.

"Oh, I see. No problem. Let me know if you need anything." He smiled and then turned to my uncle and said something.

Relieved that he finally took a hint, I schlepped up the stairs and headed into my room, locking the door behind me. I then dropped onto the floor in front of a box and began digging through it, searching for something, anything, that would connect me to my old life, the life I'd always known, the life where I felt like me, not some misfit stuck in a superficial world.

I pulled out the small, pink, leather-bound journal that the school counselor, Mrs. Whitehead, had given me. She insisted that writing down my feelings was the best form of therapy. I tossed the journal onto the bed and kept digging through the contents of the box.

My hands clamped onto a photograph wrapped in tissue paper. Unwrapping it, my throat dried, and my eyes filled with tears. I held the frame in my lap and studied every detail, running my finger over the glass.

My dad's best friend, Ross, had snapped the photograph on Christmas Eve two years ago, the last one I'd shared with my mom. My parents and I were posed in front of our small Christmas tree, and I was seated between them with my arms wrapped around my mother. She looked beautiful, despite the cancer that was eating her up inside. A mint-green scarf covered her bald head, bringing out her bright emerald eyes, the same eyes she'd bestowed on me. Her skin was pale, yet she glowed in the photograph, her smile electric. I also smiled, as did my dad, and we looked happy, so very happy. We had no clue that it would be our last Christmas as the complete Curtis family.

I wiped away an errant tear from my cheek and sniffed. "I miss you, Mom," I whispered. "How am I going to make it here without you?"

Placing the frame on the bedside table, I stood, took a steadying breath, and surveyed the boxes containing all I had left in the world. The most logical place to start unpacking seemed to be clothes. I stepped over to the largest suitcase and opened it.

I was hanging up my jeans when a screech followed by a splash sounded outside. I glanced out the window and spotted Whitney and three bikini-clad girls splashing around in the pool. I opened the window and then sat on the window seat, inhaling the strong scent of chlorine while watching the girls splash each other and giggle.

My father sat at the table with a can of Coke in his hand while he chatted with my uncle. He seemed so at ease, so comfortable on the deck with his brother-in-law, as if he spent every Saturday here. How had he managed to adjust to this new, strange life so easily? Was he hiding his pain or was he truly happy here? Sadness and anxiety churned in my gut.

The sputter and hiss of an air compressor drew my eyes to the garage next door. As if pulled by a magnetic force, Logan hopped from the deck and raced down the concrete path and through a gate, making a beeline into the garage.

The Stewart boy stood up from under the hood, dropped his air ratchet onto the bench next to him, and gave Logan a high five. He then lowered himself onto a creeper across from Logan, who sat on the floor. The boy wiped his hands off on a red shop rag and grinned while Logan spoke. He then leaned back and laughed, running his hand through this hair. From my view, I could tell he was tall, lean, and had thick, dark brown hair cut in one of those messy, trendy styles that fell below his ears. He was clad in jeans and a white T-shirt, both covered in grease spots.

Part of me wanted to join them in the garage and find out what was so funny. I longed to grab that ratchet, lean under the hood of that car, and help the Stewart kid tear apart the engine while giving him my opinion of Dodges.

But I knew that running over to a strange boy's garage probably wouldn't sit well with Whitney and her friends. They could form the wrong impression of me, which was not how I wanted to start my first day at Cameronville High.

Besides, did I really want to open myself up to a friendship with another high school mechanic?

Tears welled up in my eyes, and Mrs. Whitehead's voice

echoed in my head: *Whenever you feel like you're so full of emotion that you want to cry your eyes out or scream your head off, just open up this journal and write, Emily. Write everything down—every thought, every feeling. Nothing is too big or too small. It'll help you sort through your feelings and ease the weight of the world from your shoulders.*

I flopped onto the bed and fished a pen from the backpack I'd thrown there earlier. Reaching up, I grasped the gold cross I'd put on the day my mom died. My mom had worn the necklace every day since she'd been diagnosed with cancer, and she said the little gold charm gave her hope. Although the necklace hadn't given me any hope, it made me feel closer to her. Closing my eyes, I tried to whisper a prayer for strength, like my mom used to do, but nothing came to my mind. Instead, I recited a prayer I'd learned in Sunday school when I was a kid, but the words felt forced instead of sincere.

I let the cross fall to my collarbone and, turning to a new page in the journal, I began to write a letter to my mom:

Saturday, August 20
Dear Mom,
Dad and I arrived at Whitney's this afternoon. I feel like I'm trapped in an alternate universe. Everything here is perfect—from the houses to the landscaping. Classes start Tuesday, and I can't fathom starting my junior year without Megan.

I'm afraid I might suffocate here if I stay too long. I hope Dad finds a job soon, so we can get our own place. He seems totally unaffected by this move. He's still smiling and joking like usual. Doesn't anything get to him?

I'm still wearing the cross you wore while you were sick. I wish it gave me the strength that it gave you. You always said that God was your strength and your rock. Apparently he's not mine. I want to talk to God and tell him how I feel, but lately when I lay in bed at night, I can't seem to form the words, no matter how hard I try. Isn't that crazy? I was raised in a church, but now I've forgotten how to pray. You were the one who taught me how to talk to God. How will I remember now that you're gone?

I've never felt so alone before. It's going to be a horrible junior year.

And more than anything, I miss you, Mom.

I closed the journal, laid it and the pen on the nightstand, and leaned back on the pillows. Closing my eyes, I held the cross tightly in my fingers and fell asleep.

chapter two

○○○

"Yꝏ ready?" Whitney bellowed from somewhere in the house. "I've got to pick up Kristin in, like, ten minutes."

"I'm coming!" I called back, taking one last look at myself in the bathroom mirror. I frowned at my hair, which was a curly mess to the middle of my back. Megan, who was blessed with sleek, pin-straight black hair, once told me she'd kill to have my natural wave. I told her that if she'd ever spent an hour trying to run a pick through my curly knots, she'd change her mind.

Fearing my hair might frizz in the humidity, I snatched a rubber band from the bin on the counter and forced my hair into a ponytail at the nape of the neck. I then studied my reflection once last time, smoothing my plain gray T-shirt and denim shorts. I smeared on some lip gloss just to give my fair complexion a little color.

Then, with a deep breath, I grabbed my green camouflage book bag and raced down the stairs to where Whitney stood scowling in her maroon, yellow, and white cheerleading uniform. A matching maroon bow in her golden ponytail completed the Cameronville Barbie look.

"We gotta roll, Em," she said, jingling her keys and heading for the back door.

I followed her through the living room to the kitchen, where my father, uncle, and Logan sat at the table eating heaping piles of pancakes while my aunt stood at the counter.

"Are you going to eat?" my dad asked, glancing up from the classified section of the paper.

"No time," I said, fetching the lunch bag I'd packed the night before from the refrigerator. I slipped my lunch into my book bag.

My aunt shoved a bagel and a napkin at me. "It's the most important meal of the day."

"It's okay," I said. "I'm fine."

Darlene opened my hand and placed the bagel in it. "Take it."

"Thanks," I said.

"Are you sure you don't want me to take you to get registered?" my dad asked.

"I have everything I need in here," I said, smacking my bag. "I can register myself."

"All right." My dad stood and kissed the top of my head. "Have a good day. I'll see you tonight."

"Thanks, Dad."

"Let's go," Whitney said with a huff, opening the back door. "Kristin is waiting."

I followed her out to the red Honda in the driveway and opened the rear passenger door.

"What are you doing?" she asked, wrenching open the driver door.

"Getting in the car." I dropped my bag onto the floor.

"Don't be silly," she said, climbing in. "Sit up front with me."

"But Kristin—"

"She doesn't care." She waved off the comment. "Just get in."

I grabbed my bag and slipped into the front seat. A cross, similar to the rainbow-colored one on Whitney's keychain, swung back and forth from a gold cord on her mirror. I wondered how much stock she put in the symbol. Was she truly a Christian or was it for show, like the cheerleading uniform?

As I pulled off a piece of bagel, a big glob of white cream cheese plopped into my lap. "Oh man," I groaned. I'd spent the weekend worrying about how things would go on my first day at Whitney's school, and this wasn't the start I'd been hoping for.

"I have napkins in the glove compartment," Whitney said, jamming her key, which was on a ring filled with a dozen different keychains with various sayings, happy faces, and the cross, into the ignition switch.

I considered warning her that the weight of those key chains could break the ignition. Instead, I kept my thought to myself, opened the glove compartment, and pulled out a couple of napkins. I then tried in vain to clean my shorts, succeeding at only rubbing the white blob deeper into the fabric. "Great. I'll be known as the new girl with the cream cheese spot on her shorts."

"It's hardly noticeable." Whitney turned the key, and the engine turned over but didn't catch. "Stupid car," she grumbled. She turned the key again with the same result.

I raised an eyebrow. "Does this happen a lot?"

"Like only every day!" She tried the key again, and once more it only turned over. "I've told my dad, and he keeps promising to take it to the shop." She turned the key a fourth time, and it caught. "Finally!" She slammed the gearshift into drive and my neck snapped back as we roared down the driveway.

"Well, it sounds like you need— "

Out of the corner of my eye, I saw movement. I turned my head just as we hit the end of the driveway—at the same time that the green Jeep from next door hit the end of the parallel driveway. And the two cars were about to bounce onto the street at the same time.

"Stop!" I screamed.

She slammed on the brakes, bringing the Honda to a stop inches from hitting the Jeep. "Sorry," she whispered.

The boy in the Jeep grinned and moved his arm in a cranking motion.

As I rolled down my window, I was mesmerized by his deep blue eyes, which were a startling contrast to his dark brown hair. "In a hurry to get to class?" he asked with a laugh.

Whitney leaned over me, and her cheeks blushed a bright pink. "Sorry about that. I wasn't thinking."

"It's no problem." He made a sweeping gesture. "Ladies first."

"Thanks!" she called with a wave before steering out onto the street. "Good grief. That was almost a disaster."

I watched in the side mirror as he pulled out behind us. He drummed his steering wheel and sang as he drove. He was so good-looking that I couldn't stop staring at him for a few moments. He had athletic good looks, with facial features that seemed to be chiseled from fine tan granite. But there was something sweet about his face and his smile. And those blue eyes. Wow.

"Who was that?" I asked.

"Zander Stewart," Whitney said, checking her eye makeup in the mirror. "He's the guy building that big, ugly gas-hog car."

"Dodge Challenger," I corrected her, still studying him in the mirror. "Zander's a unique name."

"His real name is Alexander, but he prefers Zander."

"Oh," I said. "So he likes cars?"

"That's an understatement," she said. "He spends all of his free time in that garage. Logan goes over there to talk to him. Logan says he wants to be a mechanic, which doesn't make my father happy at all."

My eyes snapped to hers, and she blushed again.

"Sorry. I didn't mean anything about your dad," she said, slowing at a stop sign and slapping on her blinker.

"It's okay." I glanced back at the mirror. Zander was still drumming the steering wheel and singing, and I couldn't help but think he was adorable. "He's good with cars?"

"Oh yeah. I've been meaning to ask him to look at this old thing, but I've been so busy." She turned left, and he beeped while going right.

"It needs a good tune-up. Spark plugs for sure," I said, watching the Jeep disappear around another corner. I wondered if he would be in any of my classes. If he was, would I find the nerve to talk to him?

"Huh," she said, nosing the Honda into a driveway and beeping the horn. "Maybe I can get your dad to do it."

"I'm sure he would," I said. "Or I can. I did a few tune-ups at his shop."

The front door opened, and a bottle blonde dressed in the same cheerleader uniform with the same matching bow in her ponytail bounced down the front steps and grinned all the way to the car.

She bounded into the backseat, dropping her pink backpack onto the floor. "Hi," she said. "I'm Kristin. You must be Emily!"

"Hi," I said, thinking she was way too perky for this early in the morning.

"It's great to meet you," Kristin said, her gaze sweeping my attire. "We missed you at the swim party." She turned to Whitney. "How are you?"

"This morning was nearly a disaster." Whitney backed out of the driveway and steered down the street. "I just about took out Zander and his Jeep when we were pulling out of the driveway."

"That wouldn't have been so bad." Kristin raised her eyebrows. "I wouldn't mind giving him mouth-to-mouth."

"Oh, stop it!" Whitney said, and Kristin squealed.

"So, did you hear the latest about Holly Lloyd and Rob Myers?" Kristin said.

"No! What happened?" Whitney said, meeting her gaze in the rearview mirror.

"Well, you won't believe this! Tiffany called me last night to tell me the news." Kristin launched into a long, convoluted story involving beer, betrayal, and a secret rendezvous.

I stared out the window and finished the bagel while wondering how long the ride would last.

When we pulled into the parking lot behind the sprawling Cameronville high school, I spotted the green Jeep and then Zander standing with a group of jock-looking types a few cars away.

Whitney parked the Honda one row over and I hopped out of the car. She and Kristin joined a group of girls clad in the same uniform, and I headed for the door with *Administration* written above it. As I moved past the group of jocks, I locked eyes with Zander, and he nodded, causing me to quicken my steps.

Forty-five minutes later, I negotiated my way through the hallway just in time to make the last few minutes of homeroom. After showing my paperwork to the teacher, I moved to the back of the room, ignoring the questioning stares. I vowed to keep a low profile and stay anonymous, which would be better than being known as Whitney Richards' Cousin with the Cream Cheese Stain.

At the front of the room, I spotted Whitney giggling and flipping her ponytail back while chatting with a group of cheerleaders. I bit back a groan at the sight. Whitney was so pretty and made friends so easily that it made my stomach roil. And even if I wanted to, there's no way I could make myself fit into her group. Her eyes met mine and she waved. I forced a smile as she approached.

"How did it go?" she asked, leaning over my desk.

"Fine," I said, ignoring the curious looks her friends threw our way.

"Let me see your schedule." She lifted the piece of paper from the desk and studied it. Looking up, she smiled. "I'll see you in gym and at lunch."

"Cool," I said.

The bell rang, followed by a scramble for the door with bags and backpacks flying. Whitney rushed back to her desk, and her friends continued to watch me, causing my cheeks to flare with embarrassment. I hated how I blushed so easily.

The halls were packed with kids that bumped and nearly tripped me on my way to my English class. After checking in with the teacher, I took a seat all the way in the back. My thoughts turned to Zander and the Dodge, and I busied myself with doodling a Challenger on my spiral notebook. I was adding details when a girl dropped into the seat beside me.

"Hi," she said.

I kept shading, certain she wasn't speaking to me.

She leaned over. "Hi," she repeated. "I'm Chelsea."

I looked up and found her grinning in my direction. I glanced behind me to see if she was speaking to someone else.

She snickered. "Yeah, I'm talking to you. You're new, right?"

I nodded.

She held out her hand. "I'm Chelsea. And you are ...?"

"Emily." I gave her hand a quick shake. "Nice to meet you." I turned my attention back to my drawing.

"Where are you from?" she asked.

"Up north," I said.

"Where up north?"

I looked up at her and she smiled. She wore a colorful peasant-type shirt with splotches of primary colors on it. A matching headband held her deep red hair back from her pale face. Her makeup was perfect—as if a makeup artist had spent hours on her face. The colors brought out the gold in her brown eyes, but it wasn't overdone.

"Outside Philly," I said, placing my pencil onto my spiral notebook.

"Then this is a change for you, huh?" she asked.

"Yeah."

She pressed on. "Where did you move to?"

"Castleton," I said.

"Wow." Her eyes were wide. "That's a nice part of town. Huge houses. I'd love to live there. I live on the other side of town in Rock Creek."

I nodded, even though I had no idea where that was.

"My best friend, Eileen, lived in Castleton and moved to Philly last year. Kinda funny, huh? Her dad's in banking. Is your dad a banker?"

"No." I twirled my pencil in my fingers. "He's in the automotive industry."

"Oh." She smiled. "Cool."

I nodded, not sure what to say next.

"I moved here in the middle of seventh grade," she began, "so I know what it's like to be new. It's a total drag. Let me know if you need anything."

"Thanks," I said, overwhelmed by her welcoming smile.

Chelsea opened her mouth to say something, but the teacher interrupted, calling the class to order and handing out a syllabus.

When class was over, I gathered up my books and started for the door.

"Emily!" Chelsea came up behind me. "Where are you headed?"

"Gym," I said, following the line of students out to the hallway.

"Cool," she said, falling in step with me. "Me too."

She made small talk about the weather as we weaved through

the cramped hallway to the gymnasium. I scanned the area hoping for a quick look at Zander, but he was nowhere in sight.

I pushed through the double doors of the gym, and my stomach clenched when I spotted Whitney in the corner surrounded by a group of girls in matching cheerleading uniforms. How many of these girls were there?

Hoping Whitney wouldn't spot me, I turned to Chelsea, who was yammering on about how hot it'd been all summer.

"Hey," I said, interrupting her. "Want to go sit over there?" I pointed to a spot on the other side of the gym.

She shrugged. "Sure."

I dropped onto the floor next to her and pulled my knees up to my chin while she continued on about spending the summer babysitting. I was only half listening to her while my thoughts returned to Zander and his Challenger. I wondered how he would react if I showed up in his garage one afternoon and offered to help him with his car. Would he dismiss me as a strange girl or would he welcome the help? I'd met Tyler when he started working part-time at my dad's shop. Although our relationship made me wonder if I had any sense at all when it came to guys.

"What about you?" Chelsea asked.

"Huh?" I glanced over at her, and immediately felt guilty when she frowned, looking hurt. "I'm sorry. I was a million miles away thinking about my best friend back home." It wasn't a complete lie; I'd been missing Megan all day. And, actually, at one point I had considered Tyler my best friend. That is, until he dumped me.

She smiled. "It's okay. I miss Eileen too." She touched my leg. "I'm just glad I have you to talk to."

And at that moment I knew she was genuine, and I was glad she'd chosen me.

The coach called the class to order and spent the next

forty-five minutes lecturing about the intricacies of badminton. Who knew it was such a complicated sport?

When the bell rang, the crowd of students murmured while heading toward the double doors.

"I guess I'll see you later," I said, following Chelsea to the door.

"Yeah." Chelsea pulled out a piece of paper and studied it. "I've got to head clear to the other side of campus, so I better run. Have a good one."

"You too." I moved through the door and fished my schedule from my pocket. Turning the corner, I came face-to-face with Whitney.

"Hey," she said. "I looked for you in gym."

"Oh, I was sitting in the back with a friend," I said. "I didn't see you."

Whitney eyed me with suspicion. "Oh. So, how's your day going?"

"Fine." I hiked my bag strap further up on my shoulder. "How's yours?"

"Great." She smiled. Someone called her name, and she turned and waved. "Sorry, I gotta go. See you later."

"See ya." I watched her run off toward another group of girls and wondered if she'd ever lamented, "So many friends, so little time."

After Spanish, I headed toward the cafeteria. Choosing a table in the back corner, I emptied my turkey sandwich, apple, and bottle of water from my lunch bag and, needing something to do, fetched my journal from my bag. Taking a bite of my sandwich, I began to write.

Tuesday, August 23
Dear Mom,
First day of school has been pretty uneventful. While the

high school population is about half the size of my old one,
the people seem to be the same. I made a friend in English
class, a girl named Chelsea. She seems really nice. Her best
friend moved away last year, so I think she may be a kindred
spirit. But she's not Megan.

I keep wishing I could talk to you and tell you how scared
I am to be alone. I used to feel so sure of myself because I
knew I could always go to you and get your advice. Now I'm
flying solo, and I can't stop thinking about how much I miss
our old garage. When I was out there working on a proj-
ect, I felt like I could solve all of the problems in the world.
Sometimes I would pray out loud, and I could almost feel
God answering me, and

"Hey," someone said. "Is this seat taken?"

My heart leapt into my throat at the sound of the voice. My first reaction was to slam my journal shut. Glancing up, I found Chelsea grinning at me while holding a bright-orange lunch tray balancing a burger, fries smothered in ketchup, a piece of chocolate cake, and a bottle of water. Quite the healthy meal.

"Oh," I said. "Hey." I pushed an errant curl behind my ear, hoping to appear casual despite my pounding heart.

"Sorry. I didn't mean to scare you." She nodded toward the chair across from me. "So, can I sit here?"

"Oh, yeah." I shoved my journal into my bag. "Have a seat."

"Thanks." She lowered herself into the chair.

Movement behind her drew my eyes to Whitney's table. A tall jock with sandy blond hair walked up to where she was sitting, leaned down to her, and kissed her. It wasn't a short kiss either. It was a long, meaningful kiss.

My eyes widened and my mouth gaped as I processed the sight.

Chelsea followed my gaze and gave a knowing smile. "Oh, you've spotted the homecoming king and queen."

"Who?" I asked.

She jerked a thumb toward Whitney's table. "Whitney Richards and Chad Davis."

"Chad," I said, lifting my water bottle. "Huh."

"I guess the rumors aren't true," Chelsea said, drowning a fry in the pool of ketchup on the plate. "They didn't break up over the summer."

"I guess not." I bit into my sandwich. "So Whitney has a boyfriend," I grumbled. "Imagine that."

"You know her?" Chelsea stuck a fry into her mouth.

"You could say that." I took a long drink. "She's my cousin."

"Really?" Chelsea's eyes were wide. "I had no idea."

"What do you mean?" I batted my eyelashes and flipped a curl off my shoulder. "You don't see the family resemblance?" I glanced down at my shirt. "Oh, that's right. I forgot my cheerleading uniform and matching hair bow today."

Chelsea laughed, and I chuckled along with her.

"You're a hoot," Chelsea said. She pulled her wallet from an overstuffed, colorful quilted bag that looked homemade. "Want to see a photograph of my twins?"

"Your twins?" I studied her.

She held out a wallet-sized photograph of two boys dressed in matching red sweaters and grinning while sitting in front of a background that showed Santa. Their red hair and smile matched hers. From my limited knowledge of kids, I guessed they were about three years old.

"They're adorable," I said, handing her the photograph.

"Yeah." She studied the photograph. "Everyone thought I'd resent them, but honestly, they're a blessing. We had a fun summer together. I miss them."

"Oh," I said, trying to piece her story together. "So you babysit them."

"As often as I can." She slipped the photograph back into her wallet and dropped the wallet into the bag.

I knew I'd missed something, but I didn't want to admit I wasn't listening to her in gym. "What are their names again?" I asked, hoping to piece the story together with leading questions.

"Justin and Jason Jr., after my stepdad." She bit into her greasy cheeseburger.

I almost choked on my sandwich. "After your stepdad?"

"Yeah. My stepdad always wanted to have a junior, so my mom caved."

"Oh! They're your brothers."

She gasped and threw a fry at me. "Of course they are. Did you think they were mine?"

I laughed so hard that my eyes watered, and it felt like some of the weight on my shoulders magically lifted.

Laughing as well, she shook her head. "Good grief. I don't even want to imagine what you were thinking about me."

"I was wondering." I wiped my eyes with my napkin and then finished my sandwich. "They're adorable, and it's really cool that you love them so much."

"How could I not?" Chelsea chewed another fry.

Behind her, I spotted Zander standing by Whitney's table. He pulled a chair up to the table, straddled it backward, and snatched a fry off another guy's plate. The guy said something to Zander, and he leaned his head back, laughing.

"Do you know him?" I asked, nodding toward Zander.

"Which one?" Chelsea asked, turning around.

"The guy straddling the chair." Biting into the crisp golden delicious apple, I pretended I didn't know his name just to see what information she would share about him.

"Zander Stewart," she said, snatching another fry. "He's a senior. Cute, huh?" She waggled her eyebrows.

I nodded. "What's he like?"

"He seems nice from what little I know of him. He used to play football, but he tore up his knee pretty bad last year and had to have surgery." She wiped her hands and opened her bottle of water. "That ruined his football career. He's not like Andrew but he's just as hot. If not hotter."

"Who's Andrew?"

"His older brother. He goes to the university now." She sipped the water. "He dated my sister for a while. They both graduated together four years ago. My sister was a cheerleader and all that, and he was captain of the football team. They were similar to the king and queen over there."

"Huh." I watched Zander steal a few more fries from his friend's plate while he grinned, listening to a story one of the other guys was telling. "Did your sister tell you anything interesting about the family?"

Chelsea shrugged. "Not too much. I just know that Andrew is following in their dad's footsteps. He's premed."

"Their dad's a doctor?"

"Yeah, a surgeon, I think." Chelsea bit into the burger and then wiped her mouth with a napkin. "You like him?"

I shook my head. "I don't even know him."

She grinned. "He makes for nice eye candy."

We both laughed.

She pulled a cell phone from her purse. "You need to give me your number."

"Oh." I wiped my hands and cleared my throat. The stupid cell phone issue had come up again. "I don't have a cell phone."

"Seriously?" She lifted her eyebrows.

"I don't like being tied down to technology." I sipped the water, hoping I sounded convincing. In all honesty, I missed the convenience of having a cell phone, but I knew it wasn't a priority right now since Dad was out of work.

"Really." She took a bite of her chocolate cake and then glanced at her watch. "How is it that lunch goes by so quickly and classes move at a snail's pace?"

"Because lunch is fun," I said with a smile. "Thanks for sitting with me."

She grinned. "You're welcome. Same time tomorrow?"

"Absolutely."

The bell blasted through the conversations in the cafeteria, and we both stood.

"Have a good afternoon," she said, balancing her bags on her arm and her tray in her hand.

"You too." As she walked away, I smiled, thankful to have at least one friend at Cameronville High.

chapter three

After school, I was leaning against the Honda when Whitney approached.

"Hey," she said, pushing her ponytail off her shoulder. "I'm sorry, but I've got a cheerleading meeting and I can't miss it."

"Oh." I stood up and adjusted my bag on my shoulder. Glancing across the parking lot, I spotted a line of yellow school buses. "I'll just take the bus home. Which one goes to your neighborhood?"

"Oh no." She yanked the keys from her Coach shoulder bag. "Here." She held them out and the wad of key chains jingled. "Just pick me up at five."

I studied the keys as if they were foreign objects. There was no way I was going to drive her car. I'd be lost for days in this town. "Well, I don't think—"

"Don't be silly, Em. I know you can drive." She grabbed my hand and slapped the keys into my palm, like a surgical nurse handing a scalpel to a doctor. "Just pick me up."

"I don't even know how to get to your house, Whitney. I'd be driving in circles around town like some idiot tourist." I handed her the keys. "I'll take the bus and be perfectly fine. Which one is it?"

She turned and pointed to the green Jeep, and my stomach clenched. "Zander's still here. I'll just ask him to—"

"No," I said with more force than I intended. "I'll take the bus."

She laughed. "Zander is harmless, probably the most harmless guy at Cameronville High. Trust me."

What does that mean? "I don't care if he's a priest, I'm not going to get in the car with him. I don't even know him." In all honesty, I knew that if I got an anxious feeling in the pit of my stomach that overcame me every time I imagined speaking to him, I'd likely pass out the moment I got into his car. But I wasn't about to admit that to Whitney. "Just tell me the bus number."

She threw her hands up in surrender. "Fine. It's 176, but I don't want to hear it if you get hit on by freshmen or pelted with spitballs."

"Thanks. See you later." I jogged across the parking lot and hopped onto the bus.

By the time the bus reached my stop, I'd been offered phone numbers from four freshmen and actually had several spitballs lodged in my curls. I walked around to the back of the house and saw that the U-Haul trailer was gone and the Suburban was backed up to the detached garage. My dad must've made a trip to town today. I entered the house through the back door and found Logan sitting at the table chewing an apple while leafing through *Hot Rod Magazine*.

"Hey," I said, dropping my bag onto the chair next to him. "How was school?"

He shrugged. "Okay. We're supposed to read for forty-five minutes every night." He made a face accompanied by gagging noises.

I snickered, crossing to the counter. "Reading's not so bad. It makes you smarter." I swiped a pear from the bowl on the counter and took a bite, savoring the sweet juice.

"I'd rather read stuff like this article on this awesome

restored Barracuda." With a toothy grin, he held up the magazine, displaying a deep orange 1970 model.

Leaning back against the counter, I nodded. "Is that what you want to build someday?"

"Yeah. Someday." He flipped the page and then looked at me again. "Do you like Plymouths?"

"Sure." I shrugged. "They're pretty cool."

He grinned. "You prefer Chevys, right?"

I laughed, taking another bite of the pear. "Am I that transparent?"

"All you and Tyler talked about when I visited you was Chevys, so yeah, you are."

I ignored his reference to Tyler. "It's in the Curtis blood, I guess. My dad loved his Mustangs, but he preferred to race Chevys."

"I would love to race, but I probably never will," Logan said. "Dad says I should concentrate on school and think of cars as a hobby."

I bit back my frown, the comment Whitney made in the car this morning echoing through my mind. "That's a good idea. School's important." I nodded toward the magazine. "Is that the newest issue?"

"It came today. Want to see it?"

"Thanks." I pushed off the counter. "When you're done. I have a ton of homework."

Just as I grabbed a bottle of water from the refrigerator, Darlene emerged from the laundry. "Emily! How was your day?" Her eyes moved to my shorts and she sucked in a breath. "What on earth happened to your shorts?"

I glanced down at the spot. "I had a run in with cream cheese this morning in the car." I shrugged. "No biggie."

She studied my curls. "And what is stuck in your hair, dear?"

I reached up and pulled a few pieces of paper from my locks. "Oh, probably spitballs from the bus."

She looked confused. "The bus?"

I nodded. "Yup, the bus was my mode of transportation this afternoon."

"Hmm. Well, take those shorts off and I'll treat them right away." She flitted across the kitchen to the sink, where she added dish soap and pushed on the hot water. "I have this fabulous stain remover pen that works wonders. It got ketchup out of one of Logan's white shirts last week."

"I'll bring them down in a bit. Thanks." I gathered up my bag and water and started for the stairs.

"Wait," she called, catching up to me. "You didn't tell me how your day went."

"It was good. Oh, Whitney had to stay for some cheerleader meeting."

"Right." Darlene smiled. "I'm glad you had a good day." Her brow furrowed. "Let me know if you want me to help you straighten your hair. You could pull it up in a cute clip tomorrow if you'd like. And I bet Whitney has a cute dress you could borrow too. You could even think about wearing a little bit of makeup."

"Thanks," I said with a tight smile. "I'll think about it." Did the woman sit around all day and think of ways to criticize me? And for a second there I'd thought she was actually interested in me. Groaning, I trotted up the stairs and dumped my bag in my room before tapping on my dad's door.

"Come in," he called.

I pushed the door open, and it creaked in response. The room over the garage was T shaped. At the top of the T was a love seat in front of a flat-screen television, and behind the love seat sat a computer desk and chair. A double bed, two bureaus, and nightstand were in the long part of the room.

My dad sat at the computer desk staring at his résumé displayed on the screen in front of him. He leaned back in his chair and grinned. "Hey, Baby Doll. How was your day?"

"Pretty good." I sat on the back of the sofa and opened the bottle of water. "How about yours? I saw that the trailer is gone."

"Yup." He laced his fingers behind his head. "I took care of that this morning and also scoped out the dealerships around town. I hope to start distributing my résumé around tomorrow. I want to polish it just a little bit more. Would you proofread it for me later on?"

"Of course I will." I took a sip of water. "I bet it'll be hard for you to go from being the boss to being an employee again, huh?"

He shrugged. "It doesn't matter. All that matters is that I get a job, and we rebuild our lives." He smiled. "So, tell me about your day."

Now it was my turn to shrug. "There's nothing to tell. Cameronville High is just another high school, and I'm just another student."

"No, you're not. You're special." He leaned forward in his chair. "Tell me, did any boys fall in love with you today?"

I rolled my eyes. I know he meant well, but I hated discussing my nonexistent love life with my dad. He liked to tell me I was this great beauty and would knock all of the boys' socks off at school, but I'd had a whole lot more experience with cars than I'd had with boys.

Before Tyler, I'd dated Bobby Matthews for about five minutes at the beginning of my sophomore year. He took me to the movies a few times and to one school dance. Our only kiss lasted about a half a second. Thinking back, I wondered if our lips had even actually touched. Megan insisted I intimidated guys with my car knowledge, and maybe she was on to something. When Bobby's car broke down the night of the home-coming dance, I was the one who got it running again—all the while clad in a hunter green dress I'd been talked into wearing. He never called me again after that night.

Megan's theory hadn't worked with Tyler, but thinking back on our relationship, I wondered if he'd only ever considered me as a friend and never considered me his girlfriend. We'd spent much more time under the hood of cars than we did kissing. Truthfully, he'd rarely kissed me, and he'd never said the words "I love you," even though I was certain I loved him. Perhaps I needed that makeover Darlene had offered.

"Dad, please." I shook my head. "If any guys fell in love with me today, they didn't bother to tell me."

"Don't worry. Your time will come." He crossed one leg over the other. "So, did Whitney give you a tour of the school?"

I sipped my water. "I didn't get to see her much."

He raised an eyebrow. "Did you make any friends?"

"Yeah." I nodded.

"Good." He smiled. "Do you have lots of homework?"

"Oh yeah." I stood. "Tons. I better get on it."

"I'll see you at dinner," he said.

"Okay." I headed back into my room and moved to the win-dow. I spotted the green Jeep pulling up to the garage next door. Zander hopped from the driver's seat and loped over to a key-pad mounted by the side garage door. After punching numbers on the pad, the garage door lifted up. He then crossed back to the Jeep and hoisted his backpack on his shoulder before disap-pearing into the garage.

I bit my lower lap and fought the urge to run over to the garage to see if he'd torn down the engine yet. I knew the whole idea was crazy. Most guys didn't understand why I'd rather work on cars than get my nails done or go shopping, and I didn't expect Zander to understand me either. Besides, he might not want a girl's help. My abilities could threaten his masculinity or something.

I flopped onto the bed and concentrated on my homework until I heard Logan bellow my name from the bottom of the stairs.

I helped my aunt serve the meal of lasagna, breadsticks, and salad, and then took my seat next to Logan at the table. Logan once again uttered the prayer and then we dug in. I picked at my salad, while Logan gave one-word answers to his mother's cross-examination about his day.

The back door opened and slammed with a bang, and Whitney appeared carrying her backpack with her cell phone pressed to her ear. Perhaps one of those handsfree ear jobs would be more convenient for her.

"Okay," she said. "Love ya. Bye!" She dropped her bag on the floor and placed her phone on the counter. "Hey, everyone!" She bounced over to the table and sat beside me. "Oh, lasagna! Yum." She lowered her head and closed her eyes, apparently praying. She then began to fill her plate.

"How was your day, dear?" Darlene asked.

"Great!" Whitney's brown eyes sparkled with excitement. "Oh my gosh, Mom. We had such a good meeting. The girls have great ideas for Spirit Week."

"How were your classes?" Chuck asked, in between bites of lasagna.

"Fabulous." Whitney flipped her ponytail back behind her shoulder and then cut up her lasagna with the side of her fork.

"Do you have any homework?" Darlene asked.

Whitney nodded. "Yeah, I do." She forked her lasagna again and moaned. "This is awesome, Mom."

"Thank you." Darlene looked at me. "So, are you girls in any of the same classes?"

"Homeroom, gym, and lunch," I said, swiping a breadstick.

Whitney glanced at me. "That reminds me. I didn't see you at lunch."

"I was sitting in the back with a friend." I bit into the breadstick.

"Who?" Whitney asked.

"Chelsea."

"Chelsea Morris?"

"Yeah," I said with a nod, hoping that was Chelsea's last name. I couldn't admit I had no idea what my new friend's last name was.

"She's nice."

"Yes, she is."

"You know you can sit with me, right?" Whitney's eyes studied mine. "My friends will like you."

I nodded. "Yeah. Sure."

"So aren't you in any other classes together?" Darlene asked.

"No," Whitney said, cutting up another bite with her fork.

"I'm surprised," Darlene said. "I was hoping you'd be in more classes together, so you could study together."

"I'm in the 'average' classes, not the honor and AP classes like *Whitney*." My comment was laced with more resentment than I'd planned.

My father frowned, and I studied my plate. The conversation turned to Whitney's busy schedule of practices and meetings, and I finished my dinner while avoiding my father's stare.

After helping with the dishes, I retreated to my room and sat on the window seat. I split my time between homework and staring out the window at Zander, who was busy under the hood of the Dodge next door. Even though I realized I was obsessing, I wondered if he had any homework tonight. Did he bother to complete his assignments or was he one of those wonder kids who got straight As and a perfect SAT score without even cracking open a book?

A soft knock drew my attention to the door.

"Come in," I said, drawing my legs up under myself and placing my history book on the bench beside me.

The door opened with a squeak, and my dad stepped in. By the frown on his face, I knew he wanted to discuss something serious. I bit back a sigh as he lowered himself onto the end of my bed, facing me.

"Hi," I said, hoping to sound at ease.

"So, Emily," he began, placing his right ankle on his left knee. "How did your day really go today?"

"Fine." I shrugged. "I already told you that."

His brown eyes studied mine. "Are you sure?"

I fingered my mom's cross. "Dad, I don't know what you want me to say. My life has been turned upside down, and I had to start over today in a brand-new school. If you want me to, I'll tell you that I've never been happier in my life, but it would be a lie. Starting over is a drag." I surprised myself by quoting Chelsea. "But I made a friend today and that made the day a little better. I'll be okay, but you can't expect me to be all happiness and smiles on my very first day. You have to give me time."

"I know that it's hard and I don't expect you to do cartwheels." He paused, gathering his words. "But you need to stop making little sarcastic comments like you did tonight at supper. We're lucky Darlene and Chuck took us in."

I turned toward the window and took in the sight of Zander standing in the driveway with a cell phone pressed to his ear. I absently wondered if he was talking to a girl on the other end of the line. And if so, why did I care? And why couldn't I stop thinking about him?

I looked back at my dad. His disappointed expression both angered and embarrassed me at the same time. "I didn't make a sarcastic remark. I simply stated the truth: Whitney's in all honors and AP classes, and I'm in the average classes, which is why we're only in homeroom, gym, and lunch together. I don't see how that can be considered sarcastic."

He looked unconvinced, and I knew he'd seen right through me.

"Emily Claire," he began. "I know when you're trying to pull the wool over my eyes, and it won't work. I was the king of sarcasm when I was your age. Just watch your attitude, that's all I ask. I understand that this is hard for you, but your aunt and uncle are doing all that they can for us. They're not even charging us rent, which is above and beyond anything I could've ever asked for."

A glimmer of hope twinkled within me. "If they're not charging us rent, then that means we can save our money and move out soon, right?"

He shook his head. "It's not that easy. I'm knee-deep in debt from all of your mom's treatments and hospital stays, and that means my credit is pretty much shot. I'd have to find a landlord who would make an exception. It may be awhile."

"Like a few months?" I bit my lip, hoping for good news.

He sighed and touched my knee. "It may be longer than that, but you need to look at the bright side." He gestured around the room. "You have a gorgeous room and a pool." He nodded toward the window. "We'll never have a place this nice."

"Never give up on your dreams, Dad," I whispered. "That's what Mom always said."

He gave me a sad smile. "You're right, Baby Doll. She did say that."

The sputter and hiss of an air compressor drew our eyes to Zander's garage.

My dad stood to get a better view of the action in the garage and snorted. "That boy is trying like the devil to get that car running, isn't he?" He smiled at me. "You should go show him how it's done."

"Me?" I shook my head. "I don't think so. He'd probably fall on the floor laughing if I told him I could help him."

My dad looked confused. "Why would you say that? Tyler was happy when you got his Nova running."

"Please don't say that name," I grumbled.

"That breakup was Tyler's loss, not yours."

I frowned.

Sitting on the edge of the bed, he studied me again, and his expression made me want to crawl under the bed. "Why are you playing the part of the loner all of a sudden?"

"What do you mean?" I grasped the cross tightly in my fingers. "I made a friend today."

"You seem shyer than you used to be." He touched my arm. "I guess the change happened after ..."

He let the thought trail off, but I knew what he was trying to say, and he was right. I had become more of an introvert after we lost Mom.

I glanced back toward Zander's garage to avoid his concerned stare.

He stood and stretched. "This isn't getting my résumé done. I better get back on it so I can start printing copies. I went by the store and picked up some overpriced professional paper, like that will help me find a job."

"It just might." I pulled my history book back into my lap. "Think positive."

The air compressor hummed, and an air tool whizzed like an imaginary voice beckoning me to the garage. I missed working on cars and wished I had the guts to run over there, introduce myself, and get under the hood of the car.

But I knew what was really holding me back, and it wasn't my apprehension of what he would think of my abilities with a car. Even from here his eyes were dazzling.

"I think you should go help that poor kid," my dad said with a grin as if reading my thoughts. "I bet you could teach him a thing or two."

Looking out the window, I shook my head. "Who knows? He may have a thing or two to teach me."

chapter four

During the rest of the week, I fell into a routine. I drove to school with Whitney and Kristin every morning, pretending to do my homework while they analyzed what their friends had worn and said the day before. Then I rushed off to homeroom alone while they chatted with their friends in the parking lot.

Chelsea and I met in the hallway after homeroom and walked to English together. After English, we sauntered to the gym and were partners for badminton practice. We met at the cafeteria and ate, chatting and laughing through lunch. I shared little tidbits about my personal life, but even though I liked Chelsea a lot and trusted her, there were some things I preferred to keep to myself.

Chelsea and I were on opposite sides of the school at the end of the day, so I often didn't see her before I left. And since Whitney had an after-school event each day, I continued to ride the bus home, ignoring the freshmen Casanovas and spitball battles.

But on Friday afternoon, I crossed the parking lot and spotted Whitney leaning against her car with her phone attached to her ear, as usual. I gave a wave as I approached, and she disconnected from her conversation.

"Hey," she said, all business. "I've got an honor society meeting."

"I figured you were busy." I nodded toward the line of buses. "I'll see you at the house."

"You can take my car, you know," she called after me.

I faced her, walking backward. "It's okay. I like the atmosphere on the bus."

She shook her head and shrugged. "Whatever you say."

As I stepped past the green Jeep and crossed in front of an old silver Nissan Sentra wagon, Chelsea approached, waving.

"Hey," she said. "Did you forget something?"

I pointed toward the line of buses. "Uh, I'm bussing it today. My ride has a late meeting."

She gestured toward the Nissan. "Hop in. I have to run an errand for my mom in town, so I can drop you off on the way."

I shook my head as my mind raced. One of the things I'd kept from Chelsea was the fact my dad and I lived with the Richards due to our financial situation. I didn't want her to know the truth—at least not yet. "It's okay," I said. "I don't mind the bus."

She grimaced. "Please. I remember those days, and they weren't fun. Get in."

I hesitated, and she pulled out her keys. Across the parking lot I spotted Zander, flanked by two guys I recognized from his lunch table, moving through the crowd toward the sea of student-owned vehicles. I didn't want Zander to see me clambering onto bus 176.

I climbed into the passenger seat while Chelsea slipped behind the wheel.

I dropped my bag at my feet and fastened my seat belt. Glancing around the car, I spotted gray cloth interior and a cassette deck. I was certain it was a mid-1980s model, maybe even an 1987 XE, based on the body style. I remembered a tech at my dad's shop fixing a faded red one that had been rear-ended last year, and he said they were great project cars ... Suddenly I realized Chelsea was looking over at me.

"I appreciate the ride," I said.

"It's no biggie," she said, turning the ignition and bringing the old car to life. "Like I said, I've got to go to the pharmacy for my mom, so I'll drive right by your neighborhood."

She made small talk about the weekend, and I stared out the window, wondering how I was going to explain the tremendous house. I wanted to tell her everything, but saying that my father and I were destitute and sponging off our relatives was humiliating. I directed her through the neighborhood, and she pointed out the houses she liked.

Chelsea whistled as she steered into the driveway. "Nice place," she said.

I unbuckled my belt while she parked near the back door.

"Thanks for the ride," I said, grabbing my bag from the floor. "Have a great weekend."

"You're welcome," she said.

The Jeep roared up the driveway next door, and Zander blasted his horn before parking in front of the garage.

"Zander Stewart lives next door?" Chelsea asked.

I nodded. Wrenching the door open, I climbed out. "I'll see you Monday."

The back door opened and slammed, and Darlene came down the deck stairs to the driveway. Great. "Hi, Emily!" she called. "Where's Whitney?"

"She had to stay for an honor society meeting," I explained, closing the car door.

"Who's your friend?" she asked, approaching the car.

Chelsea climbed from the car and extended her hand. "Hi. I'm Chelsea Morris."

Darlene shook her hand. "I'm Darlene Richards. It's nice to meet you."

"You too, Mrs. Richards." Chelsea looked between us, obviously trying to figure out what I was doing at the Richards' house.

"What grade are you in, dear?" Darlene asked.

"I'm a junior, like Emily." Chelsea glanced around the yard. "This is a beautiful house."

"Thank you," Darlene said with a smile. "We like it. So you're in Whitney's grade too."

Chelsea nodded. "You're Whitney's mother?"

"That's right, dear." Darlene gave me a sideways glance, as if asking why I hadn't explained this critical piece of information.

"Mom?" Logan asked, popping his head out the back door. "Dad's on the phone."

"Be right there, sweetheart," she called to him and then turned her attention back to us. "Would you like to stay and have a snack, Chelsea?"

"Oh, no, thank you. I have to run an errand for my mother," Chelsea said. "My brothers are sick, and I have to go to the pharmacy."

"Oh goodness," Darlene said, looking concerned. "I hope they feel better. Well, I better run back inside. It was nice meeting you." She started up the path and then turned around once more. "Oh, Emily. Whitney's having a pool party Saturday night. You can invite your friend to join you. The more, the merrier!" She then rushed back into the house.

I swallowed a groan. I didn't want to go to Whitney's party and inviting Chelsea stuck me between a rock and a hard place. I turned to Chelsea. "I wasn't planning on going to the party Saturday night. I have plans with my dad."

"Oh." Chelsea frowned. "So, this is Whitney Richards' house."

"Yeah," I said, my cheeks heating.

Looking confused, Chelsea hugged her arms to her chest.

I cleared my throat. "My dad and I are living here until we can get our own place."

"That's cool." Chelsea gave a sad smile, opening the driver's side door again. "I guess I better run. I'll see you Monday."

"Thanks again for the ride," I said.

"You're welcome." She fastened her seat belt and started the car. "You have my number. Feel free to call me."

"Okay." I stood in the driveway and watched her drive off, wondering if she was hurt to find out the truth about where I lived, and how I hid it from her.

I was still pondering Chelsea's expression Saturday night while I sat up in my room and stared down at her phone number, written on the small piece of paper she'd given me at lunch Friday.

Screeches and splashes sounded outside, and I sank onto the window seat and opened the window. The strong aroma of chlorine wafted up from below, where several girls clad in string bikinis lounged around the pool, chatting and giggling with tanned and athletic guys in swim trunks. Whitney sat dangling her feet in the water while Chad pulled her close and kissed her.

I fingered Chelsea's number and glanced toward the cordless phone at the other end of the room. I knew I should call her, apologize for not being up front with her, and invite her to the pool party. But the truth was that the idea of parading in a bathing suit in front of Whitney and her friends scared me to death.

Conflicted, I opened up my journal and began to write:

Saturday, August 27
Dear Mom,
I need you more than ever right now. I've really made a mess of things since I came here. I'm afraid I've really hurt my new friend, and I need to find the strength to reach out to her and apologize. You always told me to tell the truth, but sometimes the truth is just too painful. I know it's not Dad's fault that we're in this mess, but it's difficult to admit it to other people without being embarrassed.

This had gotten me thinking of everything you taught me about being a Christian. You always told me that you would pray whenever you felt scared and alone. I might try to pray again tonight. But it seems like every time I try, I don't know what to say. I'm not good at talking to God. I feel like I have spiritual laryngitis when I try to open up to him. It's like since you've left us, I've lost part of myself. I don't remember how to reach out to others and give myself. I find myself clamming up and hiding who I really am.

Maybe I'll try to call Megan. She knows what Dad and I went through with your illness. She would understand how I'm feeling right now and help me sort through it all.

I set the journal on the bedside table and grabbed the phone. After dialing Megan's number, I flopped back on the bed and stared up at the ceiling fan. When Megan's recorded voice filled my ear, I groaned and hung up.

Rolling to my side, I picked up Chelsea's number and stared at it again. Closing my eyes, I thumped myself on the forehead.

Don't be stupid, Emily. Call Chelsea. She likes you. She's your friend.

My stomach clenched as I dialed her number.

"Hello?" she asked.

"Hey, Chelsea," I said, sounding a little too cheery. "It's Emily."

"Oh," Chelsea said, her voice the opposite of mine. "Hi, Emily."

I tried to ignore the frost as I pushed on. "What are you up to tonight?"

"Not much," she said. "Just sitting here watching TV."

"How are your brothers feeling?" I asked.

"Better, thanks." Chelsea paused. "How's the pool party?" Her usually sweet and upbeat voice seeped with hurt.

Way to get right to the point, Chels.

I swallowed. Now was the time to fix this. "I didn't go. I've been up in my room most of the night."

"Right," she said. "Look, I've got to go. I think I hear my brother cry—"

"Wait!" I cut in. "Don't hang up. Let me explain."

"Fine," she said with an I-mean-business-tone. "Just level with me. And I want the *truth*."

"Of course," I said.

"Do you even like me?" Chelsea asked.

"Yes." I nodded with emphasis even though she couldn't see me through the phone.

"So explain why you didn't tell me you were living at Whitney's." Her voice pleaded with me.

"I was embarrassed to tell you the truth."

"Why?" Chelsea voice softened.

I shook my head and blew out a sigh. "I didn't want to admit my dad and I moved here to get a new start. We lost everything when his business failed."

"Emily, no one would think badly of you for that." I could feel the warmth and compassion through the phone.

I frowned. "I don't want pity either. I want someone to like me for me, not because I'm a charity case or because I'm Whitney Richards' cousin."

"I'm not into pity or using someone to get popular. I just want a good friend."

I smiled. "Me too."

"So why didn't you want to invite me to that pool party?"

"Because, honestly, I didn't want to go. I don't fit in with Whitney and her friends, and I didn't think you would want to either." I grabbed my water bottle and took a sip. "Look, I should've been up front with you, but honestly, I'm not good at friendships. I'm not good at relationships, period."

"Don't be silly. I'm sure you had friends back in Philly."

"I had a few but not many." I looked down at my lap and took a deep breath. For a split second I considered telling her about Tyler, but then thought better of it. "Look, I'm sorry. I should've told you everything from the beginning."

"You're right," she said, her voice bright again. "You should've told me the truth, but it's okay. I understand now." She paused for a moment. "Can I ask you one question? It's a personal one."

"Sure," I said.

"Where is your mom? Did your parents get divorced?"

"My mom died last year," I said softly. "Cancer."

She gasped. "I'm so sorry. That has to be hard. If you ever need someone to talk to, I'm here to listen. I mean that."

"Thanks." I smiled, thankful.

"Listen, what are you doing right now besides avoiding the pool party?" she asked.

I shrugged. "Nothing."

"Why don't we go to a movie? There's that new romantic comedy that just came out with the cute blond guy."

"Oh." I grinned. "I know exactly what you're talking about."

"So, what do you think?" she asked. "I can pick you up in twenty minutes. It starts in about an hour. I checked the times because I was thinking of going by myself."

"Going to the movies by yourself?" I asked. "That's no fun."

"Yeah, tell me about it," she said. "Who's going to share the big bucket of popcorn with me? That's why I'm glad you called."

I could hear the smile in her voice, and it caused my smile to widen.

"How about this?" I asked. "I'll pay for the tickets and you pay for the popcorn?"

"Hey! No fair!" Chelsea said with a laugh. "The tickets are cheaper!"

I chuckled as I crossed the room and grabbed my purse. "I know! That's why I said it."

"Pick you up in twenty minutes?" she asked.

"I'll be out in the driveway." I hung up the phone and trotted down the hall to my dad's room. I knocked on the door, and then pushed it open, finding him staring at the computer screen where his résumé was displayed.

He leaned back in his chair and laced his fingers behind his head. "What's up, Em?"

"Can I go to the movies?" I asked.

He raised his eyebrows. "With who?"

"My friend Chelsea," I said. "She's going to pick me up in twenty minutes. We're going to see that new romantic comedy."

"No problem. Just come home right after." He yanked his wallet from his back pocket and started to open it.

"Oh, thanks, but I have money." I held up my purse as I backed out the door. "I'll see you later."

"Don't bring home any guys," he joked with a wink.

I groaned and shook my head on my way to the stairs.

I found Logan in the kitchen, sitting at the bar while studying his handheld video game, which tweeted and beeped.

"Where's your friend who was supposed to sleep over?" I asked, plucking a fresh bottle of water from the refrigerator.

"His mom called and said he has the stomach flu," Logan said without looking up from his game.

I leaned over the island in the center of the kitchen. "So you're going to sit here by yourself and play your game all night?"

"Probably." His eyes stayed fixed on the screen. He frowned, smacking his hand on the counter and muttering something about Darth Maul and light sabers.

I shook my head. I had never understood the appeal of video games. *Must be a boy thing.*

"Are you going to swim?" he asked, his eyes trained on the miniature screen.

"Nope." I turned toward the sliding glass doors leading to the deck.

A few soaking-wet guys stood by the railing while holding cans of soda and talking. I recognized two of them from Whitney's lunch table.

"Do you know how to swim?" he asked.

"I do." I opened the bottle and took a drink of water.

"But you don't like to swim."

Three of Whitney's friends pranced by the edge of the pool. They reminded me of those contestants on Miss America, arching their backs and smiling. I could never compete with their curves.

"I don't like putting on a bathing suit in front of strangers," I said.

"Oh." He shrugged. "Must be a girl thing. I wouldn't care who sees me in my swim trunks."

"You're a boy and not in high school."

"I'm sure you look just as good as those other girls."

Smiling, I mussed his hair. "You're sweet. I'm actually going to the movies with my friend Chelsea. She's going to pick me up in a little bit."

"Oh." He looked up. "Are you going to church with us tomorrow?"

My hand fluttered to my cross and my mouth dried. Since Mom had died, the thought of stepping into a church made me feel uneasy. "I guess. I haven't asked my dad about it."

"You should come. Pastor Keith and Jenna are cool."

I fingered the cross. "Who's Jenna?"

"The youth director. She's really nice." His eyes moved back to the screen while his fingers moved about the keys.

A *woot!* sounded, and I faced the sliding glass doors just as a male body in black swim trunks ran across the patio, flew through the air, and landed in the pool with a tremendous splash, soaking Whitney and Chad, who were sitting with their feet dangling in the water. Screeches and shouts followed.

Grinning, Logan moved to the door. "Who was that?"

The boy bobbed up in the center of the pool and then pulled himself up onto the patio. He smoothed back his hair and I immediately recognized the culprit.

"Zander!" Logan laughed.

I was drawn to Zander's wiry and muscular chest and his wide, lopsided grin. My stomach fluttered and my pulse skittered at the sight of him. Why did he always have that effect on me?

Two of the guys moved over to him and pushed him back into the water while the crowd surrounding the pool cheered. Zander bobbed up to the surface of the pool and splashed everyone within the water's reach.

"He's so funny," Logan said, snapping his game shut and placing it on the counter. He laid his hand on the door handle and looked back at me. "I'm going to go say hi to him. You coming?"

"In a minute." I held up the bottle of water. "I'm going to finish this before Chelsea gets here."

He rushed out the sliding glass doors, and I stood by them while I drank the water.

Logan approached the crowd, and Zander emerged from the pool, his tan skin sparkling with beads of water. Around his neck, a gold chain glittered in the dim lights surrounding the pool. Whitney grabbed Logan's arm and Zander took the other one before they dragged him kicking and screaming with delight over to the side of the pool. Zander motioned like he was going to throw Logan in and then let him go. Logan jogged back toward the deck, unscathed and still dry.

The group laughed in response.

A flash of headlights glowed in the driveway, and I tossed the bottle into the recycling bin and then stepped out onto the deck.

"Hey!" Whitney called. "Where are you going?"

"To the movies," I said, my cheeks heating as the group of kids focused on me.

"Oh," Whitney said with a smile. "Have fun."

Zander grinned and nodded at me, and I gave him a weak smile before trotting off to Chelsea's car, with my face on fire and my stomach in knots.

chapter five

For the first time in probably six months, I found myself biting my nails. I didn't realize I was doing it until the nail tore off between my teeth. Grimacing, I discreetly fished it out of my mouth and dropped it onto the ground while following my dad up the stone steps of Cameronville Community Church. I hadn't been to a church in eight months.

I jammed my hands in the pockets of my white sweater, which I'd pulled on over a green sundress I'd found stuffed in the back of my closet. Since I rarely bought or wore dresses, I felt gawky and awkward, like a little girl wearing panty hose and heels for the first time. I'd thrown my hair up in a French braid and brushed on a little bit of lip gloss. I'd hoped that my outfit would fend off Darlene's criticism. Luckily, we were running late, so she barely gave me a once-over before we dashed to Darlene's SUV and my dad's Suburban.

In comparison to me, Whitney looked confident and put together, clad in her gray designer skirt and satin camisole top and jacket. It must've taken her hours to form the perfect French twist at the back of her head and get her makeup just right. Whitney entered through the doors to the church first, followed by her parents and brother.

My dad hung back and faced me, frowning. "You all right?" he asked.

"Yeah," I said, examining the straps on my white sandals.

"I just wanted to be sure." He looped his arm around my shoulders and steered me up the stairs. "You look beautiful."

"Thanks," I mumbled. Truthfully, I wasn't even close to all right. Being at a church brought back memories I wasn't ready to face.

We stepped through the doorway and into a large hallway crowded with families dressed in their Sunday best. A man who I'd guess was in his midthirties wearing a white robe with a colorful stole weaved through the knot of people, shaking hands and sharing pleasantries about the beautiful weather. The pastor approached my aunt, and she gestured toward my dad and me and then waved us over.

"This is my brother, Brad, and my niece, Emily," she said, with a proud smile.

"Welcome," the pastor said, shaking my dad's hand. "I'm Pastor Keith. We're so glad you've joined us today." He turned to me. "It's nice to see you, Emily. We have some youth programs you may enjoy. Whitney could tell you about them."

"Cool," I said with a nod. Out of the corner of my eye, I spotted Whitney chatting with a group of high school girls.

The pastor moved to another family, and the crowd in the hallway began to file through the large doors to the sanctuary.

My aunt, uncle, and father followed the line of people, stopping to receive a bulletin from the usher, a friendly looking gentleman in a nice suit.

I moved through the line and took a bulletin. Stepping through the doorway, my knees wobbled. I hung back, trying in vain to stop the images swimming to the surface of my mind.

My eyes moved to the altar and I shuddered at the memory of the casket sitting up front at our church back home. The sanctuary had been packed with the hundreds of people who'd been touched in some way by my mother. The overwhelming crowd had spilled out into the hallway.

During the service, the sound of sobs and sniffs had echoed in my ears, drowning out the pastor's description of my mother's short life. I'd sat numb between my dad and grandma, studying the poinsettias lining the altar behind the Christmas tree dotted in white decorations my mother had called Chrismons. The tree and flowers seemed to mock me with the ultimate irony—Christmas decorations on the altar at my mother's memorial service.

"Emily?" Logan asked, touching my arm. "You all right?"

"Yeah," I said with a nod.

Logan pointed toward the middle of the sanctuary. "My parents and your dad are sitting over there."

I spotted my dad near the end of the pew. "Where's Whitney?"

He jerked his thumb toward the very back row. "With her friends over there. All of the girls sit together."

I turned and found her grinning and chatting with four girls.

"Are you going to sit with them?" Logan asked.

"No." I walked down the aisle and slipped in next to my dad, who glanced up from his bulletin and smiled.

His focus returned to the order of worship, and I studied his warm brown eyes, wondering if being back in a church was as painful for him as it was for me. His expression during my mother's funeral was burned into my brain—the dark rings under his puffy red eyes, the tears that didn't stop throughout the service. I was certain he'd wanted to be strong for me. He'd told me that morning that he and I would be an unstoppable force, despite losing Mom. We'd take care of each other, and he promised to be strong for me. Yet I was the one who'd held it together throughout the funeral. I'd grasped his hand and swallowed my tears until I was alone in the privacy of my room with my door locked later that evening after Tyler and Megan had gone home.

I wasn't disappointed in my dad. I was glad he could express his feelings for my mom, the love of his life, who he'd met and married shortly after they'd graduated from high school. I was simply surprised I'd managed to be so strong for both of us.

Logan sank into the seat next to me and waved to someone across the aisle. "Zander's here," he said.

Before I could stop myself, I found Zander sitting directly across from us and next to a well-dressed middle-aged couple who I assumed were his parents. His mother was dressed in a deep navy, perfectly tailored suit with her short, dark hair styled in a precise bob.

His father wore glasses, along with a black, expensive-looking suit and a bland gray tie. He was clean shaven, and his brown hair was all business, short and sensible.

Zander seemed to represent his father's alter ego. While he shared the same brown hair and blue eyes, his hair was almost messy, but stylish. He was clad in tan Dockers and a sky-blue collared shirt that made his eyes even bluer, if that were even possible. He gave Logan a cheesy grin that caused Logan to snicker.

Zander met my gaze and his smile changed to warm and honest. My eyes locked with his. I tried to smile in return, but my lips were cemented in place. And then I felt my cheeks heat and wished I could crawl under the pew.

But I knew that I really didn't want to disappear. I wanted to know him, and I wanted him to know me. And that truth caused my heart to race even more.

The pastor appeared at the altar and welcomed everyone, and I buried my eyes in the bulletin. The organ began to play, and the service commenced. I went through the motions, reciting the prayers and singing the hymns, but it all felt forced. Although I tried, I once again couldn't feel the connection with God I'd enjoyed before I lost my mom. I felt eyes on me and glanced over to find Zander watching me a few times during the service, and I absently wondered if I had a hair out of place or if my slip was showing.

During the sermon, I covered my cross with my hand and lost myself in memories, contemplating the Sundays my family and I had spent at our home church. My mother had a deep faith that had been ingrained in her as a child. She read her Bible and prayed every night, like it came easily to her. She never missed a service—until the week before she died.

Some nights I would curl up in her arms while she held me and I cried to her, asking her why God had given her that wretched disease. She told me all things happen for a reason, and it was all part of his plan. She insisted that even though we don't understand why God chooses certain people to be ill and others to be healthy, we have to trust him and believe he'll take care of us.

The words offered me no comfort. It still didn't make sense why he'd bestowed the incurable disease on *her*. I'd continue to cry and she'd tell me that her love for me would live on forever and would hold me close with invisible arms whenever I was sad. She'd kiss my cheek and say, "Now Emily, just remember my favorite verse, and it will get you through."

That verse was Hebrews 11:1. She recited it often and even requested we have it engraved on her headstone. The verse floated through my mind: "Now faith is being sure of what we hope for and certain of what we do not see." I understood what it meant, but I couldn't put any stock in it.

She also told me that if I was ever sad, or angry, or lonely, I could open my heart to God and he would get me through. And when the waves of grief threatened to drown me, I tried to open my heart. I tried with all my might.

But I couldn't.

It was as if my faith had evaporated and I was left an empty shell of the Christian I used to be.

Music from the organ brought me back to the service. I lifted a hymnal from the pew pocket and flipped it open. The series of chords flew together in my mind, and I realized what hymn was playing: "Beautiful Savior."

My mother's favorite.

At her request, it had been the last hymn the congregation sang at her memorial service.

My eyes filled, and I gnawed at my lower lip, trying in vain to stop the tears. A hand covered mine and I looked up at my dad, who gave me a sad smile as if to tell me he understood. I cupped my mouth with my hand to stifle a sob, but the tears flowed, betraying my efforts and rolling down my hot cheeks.

Consumed with embarrassment, I slipped by Logan. As I started down the aisle, I felt dozens of eyes focused on me. For a split second, I met Zander's gaze and thought I saw a concerned expression.

My body shuddering with sobs, I pushed through the ladies' room door and locked myself in the handicapped stall at the far end of the restroom. I leaned against the wall, hugged my arms to my chest, and cried, silently cursing myself for losing it in public. What was my problem?

The restroom door opened and slammed shut, and I held my breath, willing the tears and sobs to stop.

"Emily?" Darlene called. "Emily, dear? Are you in here?"

"Yeah," I said, my voice thin. I snatched a handful of toilet tissue and wiped my eyes and nose.

"Are you okay?" she asked, alarmed.

Clearing my throat, I unlocked the door, and it swung open with a groan. "I'm fine."

She clicked her tongue and pulled me into a hug. "Oh, honey. I'm so sorry. I wish I'd known we were going to sing that."

"It's okay." I held onto her, thankful for her warm, comforting arms, despite her past criticisms. At that instant, I just needed a hug, and she provided it. "I should've kept it together."

She pulled back, her eyes serious. "That's where you're wrong. You don't need to be strong. Let God do that for you."

I resisted the urge to roll my eyes. I'd been hearing phrases like that since my mom was diagnosed, and each time the words were like a placebo the speaker believed would cure me. If it were only that easy.

The door opened and banged shut again, and Whitney rushed over, looking panicked, with two girls about our age in tow. *Leave it to Whitney to make this a social event.*

"Are you all right, Em?" Whitney asked.

Her friends looked on, their eyes assessing me.

"I'm fine, thanks." I moved to the mirror and examined my reflection. My eyes were red and puffy, leaving no way to hide I'd been crying. I ripped a paper towel from the roll and dabbed my face, hoping to conceal some of the emotion.

Darlene placed her purse on the counter and then rooted through it until she pulled out a compact. "Don't you worry about the tear stains." She opened it, producing a powder puff that she began to wipe on my face.

I stepped back. "No, thanks. I don't wear makeup."

Frowning, she shook her head. "Oh, but you should, sweetie. You're a beautiful girl. You should accentuate those gorgeous eyes God gave you."

"She's right," Whitney said, and her friends nodded in agreement. "You look great. That dress is fabulous. Green is your color."

"Thanks," I said.

The door opened and banged shut, and line of women filed in, glancing at me with worried expressions before disappearing into the stalls. I saw Darlene looking at them with an expression that read, "I know, poor thing," like she was apologizing for me.

Anxious to exit this humiliating scene, I nodded toward the door. "Well, we better get back out there before my dad thinks I ran away."

Darlene looped her arm around my shoulders and gave me a squeeze. "Whitney and I are here for you. And if you want help with your makeup later, just let me know."

"Thank you," I whispered. But yet again, she'd shown her understanding was limited to a few seconds before she peppered with me unsolicited advice and criticism.

We stepped out into the hallway and were swallowed into a crowd moving from the sanctuary toward the large meeting room at the other end of the hall.

"Where's everyone going?" I asked.

"Fellowship Hall for coffee hour," Darlene said, steering me toward the room. "You should get something to eat."

"I think I just want to go home. Where's my dad?" I tried to turn around, but she pulled me forward.

"Nonsense." Darlene steered me into the Fellowship Hall and over to a table with a white tablecloth covered with an array of cookies, pieces of chocolate cake, bowls of fruit, bite-size pieces of bagels smothered in cream cheese, small slices of sticky buns, and a pile of napkins. "You should eat something, Emily. It will make you feel better."

In order to appease her, I fixed a small paper plate with a few pieces of fruit and a bagel and then smiled politely while Darlene introduced me to a few of her church friends, who discussed the weather at length. I frequently glanced toward the door in search of my dad. I wondered what on earth could've caused his journey from the sanctuary to the hall to take so long. Perhaps he'd gotten sidelined by a conversation with someone. My dad was one of those social types who made a friend wherever he went.

Darlene touched my arm and pulled me over to a young,

pretty woman with warm brown eyes and dark hair that fell past her shoulders.

"Jenna, this is my niece I was telling you about." Darlene gestured toward me. "Emily, this is Jenna, our fabulous youth director. Whitney is very active in the youth group, and you should join her."

The woman held out her hand. "It's nice to meet you, Emily. Welcome to our church family."

"Thank you," I said, shaking her hand.

Jenna's smile was kind. "I hope we'll see you at youth group when you're ready to join us."

"Sure," I said with a shrug, even though I doubted I would ever join the youth group. I was certain I would never fit in— my inability to pray would probably get me placed on the missions list.

Darlene looked across the room. "Oh, there's Marilyn." She glanced between Jenna and me. "Excuse me. I must catch up with her about our women's circle potluck." She took off, her heels clicking across the tile floor.

I gave Jenna a forced smile, wondering what on earth I could chat about with this woman.

"We do have fun at youth group," Jenna began. "You might be surprised if you check us out. We're very laid back."

"Sounds good." I spotted my dad walking into the hall with Pastor Keith. "Oh, there's my dad. Well, it was nice meeting you."

"Wait." Jenna touched my arm. "If you ever need someone to talk to, you can call me." She pulled a business card from her pocket and held it out to me. "Call me anytime, and I'll listen, no matter what you want to share."

Surprised, I examined the card and then looked up. "Thanks," I said.

Her eyes were serious. "I mean it, Emily. Call anytime." She then turned and joined a group of teenagers standing near the soda machines.

I shoved the card into my purse and weaved through the crowd. I finally sidled up to my dad, who was standing at the door with the pastor.

"Hey, Emily," he said, resting his hand on my shoulder. "Have you met Pastor Keith?"

"Yes," I said, nodding. "We met before the service, remember?"

"Are you doing okay, Emily?" Pastor Keith asked, concern clouding his face. "You looked upset during the last hymn."

"I'm fine, thanks." I forced a smile.

He looked skeptical. "Okay. Good to hear. I was concerned."

"I'll see you Thursday," my dad said, shaking the pastor's hand. "Thank you again."

"It's my pleasure," Pastor Keith said. "Call me anytime you need to talk." He looked at me. "I'm here if you need me too, Emily."

"Thanks," I said, wondering if he could truly help me find my way. Did he know how to instantly fix everything that was wrong with me?

"Take care." My dad steered me toward the door, and we hit the hallway just as Logan and Zander approached the door.

They both looked concerned, and my cheeks flared with embarrassment. Maybe I should have touched up my face in the bathroom after all.

"Are you okay?" Logan asked me.

"Yeah, I'm fine." I smiled. "I'll see you at the house."

"Hi," Zander said. He opened his mouth to say something else, but was called to the other side of the room by his father. "I'll see you later. My dad's calling me." He hurried off, and I felt a huge sense of relief. Having his eyes focused on me made me nervous.

Logan looked confused. "You're not going to J2A with Whitney?"

"What's J2A?" I asked.

"It's like Sunday school for high school kids," he said. "It stands for Journey to Adulthood."

"Well, I—," I stammered, glancing at my dad, who shrugged.

"It's up to you," my dad said.

"I have a lot of homework, so I'd better not," I said quickly. Logan frowned.

"Remember, I blew off my homework to go to the movies with Chelsea last night." I glanced at my dad. "Let's go, okay?"

My dad and I walked out to the Suburban in silence. I wondered if he felt the same overwhelming grief I did after sitting through that service.

"What were you and Pastor Keith discussing?" I asked as he steered out of the parking lot.

"I'm going to start meeting with him this week," my dad said, his eyes focused on the road.

"Why?" I asked.

"I guess you could call it counseling." He tapped the steering wheel to the beat of the music serenading us through the speakers.

I turned down the radio and studied him. While my dad insisted I see the counselor at school after my mom died, he'd never spoken with anyone. This sudden change shocked me. "How did that come about?"

He shrugged, his eyes still on the road and avoiding mine. "I feel like I may need to work through some stuff, I guess."

"About Mom?" I asked, wanting to hear him say the words.

"I guess." He glanced at me sideways. "How are you doing?"

"I'm fine." I smoothed my dress over my thighs.

"Do you want to talk about anything?" he pressed on. "You know I'll always listen. You can say anything to me."

"I know," I whispered.

"If you'd rather talk to someone else," he continued, "you can always meet with a school counselor or talk to Pastor Keith or the youth director at church."

"Yes, Dad." Facing the window, I rolled my eyes. I was tired of counseling. Tired of being told what to do, what to wear, what to think. I wanted to disappear into our tiny old garage back home and work on a car. No, I wanted to work on *my* car, the Camaro I was forced to sell before we moved.

We drove in silence back to the neighborhood.

"It was the hymn, wasn't it?" he whispered as we pulled into the driveway. "That's what got to you."

Tears filled my eyes as I looked at him. I nodded.

He patted my knee. "Me too."

"Do you miss her?" I asked, my voice quavering.

"All the time, Baby Doll," he said with a sigh. "All the time."

"But you don't talk about her. You never say her name." My voice was thick and shaky.

His brown eyes were sad, and I had to hold my breath to keep from crying again.

"I think about her," he said, "but I can't always say it out loud."

When we got inside the house, I ate a quick lunch with my dad and then retreated to my room. After changing into denim shorts and a blue tank top, I unbraided my hair, since the braid was so tight my scalp was throbbing. My hair fell in a mess of curls and frizz, more wild than usual. I sprayed it with water, finger combed it, and then pushed it back with a thick, black headband.

Later, I turned down Whitney's offer to join her and Kristin for an afternoon at the mall, including manicures and pedicures. Instead, I spent the afternoon in my room doing homework, unpacking the remaining boxes, and alphabetizing my

CDs. I was straightening the books on my shelf when a knock sounded on the door.

"Emily," my dad called. "Supper's ready."

"Coming." I stood and followed him down to the kitchen, where Darlene was placing platters on the table. "It smells delicious, Aunt Darlene."

"Thank you, dear." She brought a large bowl of salad from the refrigerator. "I love making chicken cordon bleu."

I went for the cabinet containing the glasses. "I'll get the drinks."

"Actually," she said, "it would be helpful if you tracked down Logan."

I glanced toward the deck. "Is he outside?"

"He's probably next door at the Stewart's." She pulled a glass pitcher full of iced tea from the refrigerator. "He likes to go over there to pretend to work on cars with Zander."

"Oh." I stood at the sliding glass doors and stared out. My brain was telling me to just march over to Zander's garage and introduce myself, but my legs were stuck, nervous about making a fool of myself after my display in church or intimidating him with some car comment.

"Go on, Emily," Darlene called. "I don't want the chicken to get cold." She glanced toward the driveway. "I hope Whitney gets home soon. I told her supper was going to be at six."

I stepped out onto the deck and my hands absently flew to my hair, smoothing any renegade curls. Why was I worried about how I looked? I was only stopping over to collect Logan. Right?

I took a deep breath and followed the path to the gate, my flip-flops smacking the concrete. The gate opened with a squeal, and as I stepped over to the garage the air compressor sputtered and hissed, followed by the whirling of an air ratchet. I scanned the garage, taking in the row of toolboxes and workbenches scattered with tools. The walls were dotted with posters and calendars featuring sports and muscle cars of various eras and makes. Zander Stewart was a true car lover.

Was he a kindred spirit? Maybe even a true friend? Did I want to risk finding out?

Logan sat on a stool by the front end of the Dodge while Zander leaned under the hood, ratchet in hand, taking apart the top end of the motor. The air compressor rattled and hummed, vibrating off the surrounding walls.

I stepped over to the hood, crossing my arms over my chest. I tapped Logan on the shoulder, and he jumped, screeching with a start.

Zander saw me and smiled before placing the ratchet on the toolbox and killing the air compressor. "Hi," he said, pushing his sweaty hair back from his forehead. He wore a grease-spotted T-shirt featuring a drawing of a Pontiac GTO, along with jeans that were also stained.

His eyes mesmerized me for a moment, but I fought through it and cleared my throat. "Hi." I turned to Logan. "Your mom sent me over to get you. Supper's ready."

"Already?" Logan glanced at Zander. "I gotta go."

"No problem, dude." Zander grinned. "Mom's meals are always the best." He glanced at me. "I'm Zander, by the way. We haven't been introduced, but I've seen you around." He glanced down at his hands and wiped them on his jeans. He then looked up at me. "I'd shake your hand, but I'd cover you in grease."

"I'm Emily," I said. "And I don't mind grease."

He raised his eyebrows. "You don't?"

I nodded toward the car. "Have you fixed that tick yet?" The question escaped my lips before I could stop it, and I wanted to kick myself. I hoped he wasn't put off.

"How'd you know about the tick?" He continued to look surprised.

I laughed. "Are you kidding me? I could hear it plain as day when you drove by the house last week. It was hard to miss." I craned my neck and examined the engine, resisting the urge to move next to him and help with the project. "You'll have to completely rebuild the top end of the motor. There's no way around it."

Nodding, his eyes widened. "That's what I'm trying to do."

Logan slipped off the stool. "She's a total motorhead."

Zander looked intrigued.

"I know an easier way to fix it, though," I said, a smile curling up the corners of my lips.

"Oh yeah?" Zander snatched a red shop towel off the workbench and began to wipe his hands. "I'm all ears, because it's giving me a fit."

"Trade it in for a Chevy," I said.

Zander gave a bark of laughter. His laughter was authentic, and his smile was contagious. I couldn't help but grin along with him.

"You got told!" Logan yelled, laughing along with us.

"Logan! Emily!" Darlene's impatient voice rang out over ours. "Supper!"

"We better go," Logan said, heading for the door. "Bye, Zander." He waved before disappearing down the path.

"See ya," I said, heading out the door.

"Hey," Zander said, coming up beside me. "Wait."

I faced him, his proximity causing my mouth to dry. He tossed the shop towel onto the workbench, and I spotted the glimmer of the gold chain around his neck. I felt myself reach for my own necklace.

"I saw you rush out of church today," he said. "Is everything all right?"

"Oh, that?" I asked, waving off the question. "It was nothing. I had something in my eye. I think it was an eyelash. You know how painful those can be."

"An eyelash, huh? They are painful." He nodded but didn't look convinced. "Well, I just wanted to check. It's none of my business."

"I'm fine, thanks." I absently twirled a ringlet around my finger, a nervous habit I'd developed as a child.

"Emily!" my dad's voice shouted. "Hurry up or I'm going to eat your cordon bleu!"

Zander nodded in the direction of the Richards' house. "You better go, Chevy Girl. He sounds serious about his supper."

I blinked, stunned by the nickname. "See you around," I finally said, starting toward the house.

"Yup, you will," he called.

Stepping through the gate, I glanced back and found him watching me, a grin adorning his handsome face. My heart skipped a beat as I smiled at him in return.

Later that evening, I curled up on my bed with my journal and a bottle of water. Opening the journal to a blank page, I began to write:

Sunday, August 28
Dear Mom,
Today Dad and I went to church for the first time since your funeral. It was gut-wrenching to walk into that sanctuary. I couldn't help but remember the day we said our last good-byes to you. What made it even more difficult was that we sang your favorite hymn.

I keep thinking of your strong faith. I still don't understand how you maintained your relationship with God up until your last days. How did you do it, Mom? How did you continue to talk to God and invite him into your heart even though you knew you weren't going to make it? I have to admit, what you told me isn't helping. I know you meant it and believed it, but it feels ... hollow to me. I wish I could ask for your help in person. I wish you could lead me back to my path. I'm afraid to admit out loud that I've forgotten how to talk to him.

I met the pastor today, and the youth director. They were really nice to me, and they both offered to listen if I ever needed to talk to someone. Jenna, the youth director, gave me her card, but I don't know if I'll call. Dad, however, made an appointment to talk to the pastor, which really shocked me since he refuses to talk about you, even when I ask. In the car, all I got was a few sentences before he shut down. What can he tell a pastor—a stranger—that he can't tell me, his own daughter?

I don't want to go back to counseling, and I especially wouldn't want to talk to the youth director or the pastor. What would they think of me? They would never understand how confused I am. A real Christian wouldn't lose her faith like this, right?

Enough heavy stuff. Mom, I have to tell you something funny too. I finally met Zander today when I went next door to get Logan for supper. Zander was working on his Dodge. He seems nice and he asked me if I was okay after seeing me cry in church. And that was <u>after</u> I started spouting off car stuff—which makes me hopeful he's not at all like Tyler. Not that I'm thinking anything romantic, or even want something like that ... Zander's blue eyes are amazing though. I keep finding myself staring at them. Oh, and he called me "Chevy Girl." The weird thing is that I actually like the nickname. It makes me feel special. How corny is that?

I glanced at the clock and saw that it was nearly eleven. I closed the journal, placed it on the nightstand, and then turned off the light.

Snuggling under the covers, I closed my eyes. Taking a deep breath, I tried to pray, but nothing came to my heart or my head. I rolled onto my side and hugged my blanket. Soon, I fell asleep.

chapter six

Monday afternoon Chelsea and I walked out to the parking lot together after school. I was so glad I'd called her Saturday and we'd gone to a movie together, because I felt that our friendship had grown from acquaintances to almost best friends since Friday. We'd chatted before our English test and then were partners in gym, where we did more talking than actual racquet work. Chelsea and I spent lunch laughing and discussing the movie, and we talked about going to see another one soon.

During lunch I'd spotted Zander sitting with Chad, and when Zander caught my eye he'd waved at me. Despite my surprise, I waved back and hoped we'd run into each other again soon.

"Do you need a ride home?" Chelsea asked as we crossed the parking lot.

"Whitney has a cheerleader thing, so I was planning to take the bus," I said.

"Don't be silly. I can drive you," Chelsea said, adjusting her bag on her shoulder. "I'm free today, but I have a theater meeting tomorrow."

"Theater?" I asked, stopping and facing her. "You act?"

She laughed. "No, I do costumes and makeup. I dabble in hair too."

"Really? I'd noticed your outfits are always so coordinated. You have an amazing sense of style."

Her smile was wide, proud. "Thank you. It's my dream to actually design clothes someday. I want to go to school in New York City."

"You'd be good at that."

She nodded toward me. "I'd love to get my hands on your hair. I could give you a total makeover. You've got amazing features—you could make those eyes really stand out."

"Oh. Maybe someday." I started walking again, hoping to change the subject. Fashion was so not my thing. Maybe I was defensive, but she was starting to sound like Darlene. *My hair is just fine, thank you very much.* "So, back to that ride. Are you sure you can drive me today?"

"It's no biggie."

"You sure?" I asked.

She tapped my shoulder. "That's what friends are for."

I climbed into her car, and we chatted about school the entire time she drove.

Chelsea steered into the Richards' driveway at the same time the green Jeep hit the parallel driveway next door. Zander slowed down and grinned, and my stomach flip-flopped.

He stopped and motioned for me to roll the window down. "Hey, Chevy Girl!"

"Hey, Mr. Mopar," I quipped.

He laughed, putting the Jeep in gear and rolling the rest of the way up the driveway to his garage.

"What was that about?" Chelsea asked, her eyes wide with shock.

"It's a long story," I said, waving off the comment and fighting back a goofy grin.

"I got time," she said.

She parked behind the house, and I spotted my dad back by

the detached garage, leaning under the hood of the Suburban. Dad wasn't one to tinker for fun, so there had to be something wrong with the truck.

"Well?" Chelsea tapped her steering wheel with impatience. "Why does he call you Chevy Girl?"

"Because I told him that if he wants to fix his old Dodge, he should trade it in for a Chevy." I hefted my book bag from the floor and began to leave. "Thanks for the ride."

"Wait a minute." She grabbed my arm, depositing me back into the passenger seat. "You gave Zander car advice and he gave you a nickname?"

I shrugged. "Yeah. So?"

"That is so cool." Chelsea studied me. "So you know about cars?"

I pushed the door open. "My dad owned a collision repair shop, so I grew up working on them."

"Awesome. I'll keep that in mind." She tapped the dashboard. "This old thing needs some work every once in a while."

"I can check it out. Just let me know." I pointed toward my dad. "In fact, I better go see if he needs help. Thanks again."

"You're welcome." She winked. "Good luck with Mr. Mopar."

I laughed. "See you tomorrow."

While Chelsea drove down the driveway, I trotted over to the Suburban. "Hey, Dad," I said, sidling up to him. "What's going on?"

"Hey." Dad wiped his hands on a shop towel. "How was school?"

"Good." I craned my neck, examining the engine. "What's wrong with the truck?"

"Hard start." He turned to me. "The plugs look good. What do you think?"

I stood up on my tiptoes to get a better look at the engine. "If the plugs look good, it's the timing."

Smiling with pride, he nodded. "Could be."

"So you need a distributor wrench and timing light." I started toward the garage. "Is the door unlocked?"

"Don't bother. The garage is so packed with our stuff you'll never get the toolbox drawers open." He pointed toward the fence. "See if that kid next door will let us borrow his. From his setup, I'd imagine he has a timing light and distributor wrench or two. What's his name—Zane or Zac or Zeke or something?"

"It's Zander." I hesitated, too nervous to go over there. But I knew I could talk to him, and I wanted to after that friendly greeting he'd sent my way in the driveway. What was wrong with me?

"Well?" He gestured toward the fence. "What are you waiting for?"

I dropped my bag next to the Suburban and headed through the gate. I found Zander sitting on a stool in his garage, reviewing a shop manual. I stared at him for a moment, taking in his long legs, tanned skin, dark hair, and face. He was studying the book with such intensity that I wondered if it held critical government secrets.

"Hey," I finally said, crossing my arms in front of my chest and twirling a curl around my finger.

He glanced up and smiled. "Hey yourself." He placed the book on a workbench littered with tools. "What can I do for you?"

"I'm sorry to bother you, but do you have a distributor wrench and a timing light my dad can use real quick?" I jerked a thumb in the direction of the fence. "He can't get to his tools right now."

"Sure thing. It's no bother at all." He hopped down from his stool and began searching through drawers. "What's he working on?"

"The Suburban."

He faced me, the tools in his hands. His eyes were full of laughter, a grin turning up the corners of his mouth. "Really?"

I swallowed a groan. "Yes."

"You mean the *Chevy* Suburban, right?" He stepped over to me and I noticed that he towered over me by at least five inches, standing close to six feet like my dad.

"That's the one." My cheeks felt as if they would spontaneously combust. "It's having a hard time starting and the plugs look good."

"Impressive. Someone taught you well." He gripped the tools and smiled, and I noticed for the first time that he had a dimple in his right cheek. "Let's go see what's wrong with that troublesome Chevy."

We walked together through the gate and over to the truck, where my dad stood gazing under the hood and rubbing the stubble on his chin, a stance I'd seen often when he was debating fixing or kicking a vehicle. I hoped he'd choose fixing it since he'd once broken his big toe while repeatedly kicking an offending Pontiac Grand Prix.

My dad turned to us and grinned. "Help has arrived!" He stuck his hand out. "I'm Brad Curtis. I see you've met Emily."

Zander placed the timing light on the ground and shook his hand. "Nice to meet you, Mr. Curtis. I'm Zander Stewart."

"Oh, call me Brad. There's no need for formality." My dad pointed to the tools. "Thanks for helping out. I don't know if Emily told you, but I can't get into my toolbox. We unloaded it last week, but the garage is so packed I can't get the drawer open. And I can always use an extra hand for stuff like this." He rubbed his hands together. "Okay, let's get this show on the road." My dad pointed to the timing light. "Em, you grab that. You can do this stuff in your sleep."

Zander looked at me, his eyebrows arching. He was clearly impressed — again.

I hesitated, embarrassed by the spectacle Dad was making over my mechanical abilities.

"What are you waiting for?" Dad asked, jingling the keys. "I need to get this truck running or I'll never find a job."

Zander leaned over and snatched the timing light. As he stood, his gold chain flipped from beneath his T-shirt, and a cross glinted in the sun.

So he was a Christian outside of church too.

Definitely out of my league.

Zander handed me the light, and I uttered a thank you.

"You know the drill," my dad said. "I'll start it and keep my foot on the gas. You guys make the adjustment." He hopped into the driver's seat and, after I attached the timing light's terminals to the car battery and a spark plug wire, he started the truck. "I'm going to hold it at two thousand rpms," he yelled.

"I'll turn the distributor," Zander called, gripping the wrench. "What do you want it set at?"

"Put it on eight degrees before top dead center," Dad hollered back.

I held the light on the timing mark to see where the notch was.

"What's the timing mark at now?" Zander asked me as he loosened the distributor bolt two turns.

"It's at two degrees," I said.

As he slowly turned the distributor counterclockwise, the motor chugged, wheezing for air and nearly dying.

"Wrong way, Mr. Mopar," I said with a smirk.

He grinned, shook his head, and then turned it clockwise.

I watched the mark move in the flashing light and counted it down. "Two, four, six, eight," I called. "Stop!"

Zander tightened the bolt back down. "Done," he said.

My dad killed the motor and climbed from the truck. "Thanks, guys," he said. He gestured toward me. "She's good, huh?"

"Dad ..." I shot him an evil look.

"As I said earlier, impressive." Zander smiled at me, and I thought I might melt onto the pavement. I was relieved when he turned to my dad. "What kind of job are you looking for, Mr. Curtis?"

"Automotive, and I told you to call me Brad." My dad leaned on the fender. "I owned a shop before we came here. I can do collision repair or mechanical work."

"Do you have a résumé?" Zander asked.

My dad nodded. "I've applied at most of the dealerships in the area."

"Have you tried Cameronville Auto and Body out on Highway 29?" Zander asked, gesturing toward the road as if he were pointing to the shop.

My dad shook his head. "No. Are they hiring?"

"Maybe." Zander crossed his arms. "The assistant manager just quit and moved out to California, so Jack may be looking for someone."

"Management might be easier for you than starting over again with tools," I said, lifting my bag onto my shoulder.

"That's a good point." My dad nodded. "I should ask for Jack?"

"Yeah. Tell him I sent you." Zander tapped the bumper. "He's an old friend of my grandpa's. My family has known him for years. In fact, I work for him on Saturdays." He grinned. "I used to work there during the week, but my dad changed the rules last year due to my grades."

I raised my eyebrows. So Zander wasn't a wonder kid like Whitney. *He does have to study or, rather, should study.*

"Thanks for the tip." My dad slapped Zander's shoulder. "I'll go by there tomorrow. I'm anxious to get a job and get us back on our feet. But in the meantime I better finish the tune-up. I picked up some belts while I was out earlier."

"Do you need help?" Zander asked.

"Oh, no, thanks. I can handle it. But thank you for your assistance." He nodded toward Zander's garage. "How's it going with the Dodge?"

Shaking his head, Zander frowned. "Slowly."

"You'd better lock up your tools and your garage really well or you might come in one day and find your crankshaft replaced." He pointed at me. "She fixed a project while I was gone for the weekend once. She's a sneaky one."

My cheeks blazed again. "Dad!"

"Oh, I doubt she'll touch my project," Zander said, his grin wide. "I hear she only works on Chevys. Right, Chevy Girl?"

My dad guffawed, and I grimaced. I didn't enjoy being the butt of their jokes.

"I better start on my homework," I said. "Call me if you need me, Dad."

"I think I can handle some belts." My dad opened the door to the backseat and grabbed a bag from AutoMart.

I started back toward the house, and Zander fell in step with me.

"Your dad's cool," he said.

"Yeah, he is." I nodded. "He's an amazing mechanic and auto body technician too."

"He must be a good teacher, huh?"

"He taught me everything I know."

"What kind of a car did you work on when your dad was gone?" he asked.

"It was nothing. Just an old project that was sitting around." It had been more than that, actually, but I didn't want to talk about it. We reached the deck stairs, and I turned to him. "Thanks for your help with the truck."

"No problemo," Zander said with a smile.

"And thanks for the shop suggestion." I gripped the strap on my bag. "Dad's been stressed about finding a job."

"I'm happy to help. See you tomorrow." He gave me a mock salute before starting toward the gate.

I watched him disappear into the garage and I smiled. I was actually becoming friends with Zander Stewart.

chapter seven

The following afternoon, I stepped through the back door and stopped dead in my tracks when I found Zander leaning on the island, talking to my dad. They both turned and greeted me, all smiles. I was speechless for a moment, stunned by the scene.

"Guess what, Baby Doll," my dad said, rushing over to me. "I got a job, thanks to Zander!" He crushed me in one of his bear hugs, and I fought for air to breathe.

"I didn't do anything," Zander said, his hand curled around a can of Coke. "It was your experience and résumé that got you the job."

"Not true." Dad waved him off. "It's not what you know, but *who* you know."

Zander shrugged and took a swig of soda.

I dropped my bag on a kitchen chair and grabbed a pear from the fruit bowl in the center of the table. "So what will you be doing?"

"Assistant Manager." Dad looked energized, and it warmed my heart. He was genuinely thrilled. "I start tomorrow." He sat in a chair at the table.

I leaned against the counter on the other side of the island from Zander. "So that means you can order Zander around on Saturdays?"

Zander laughed. "Yup. You'll run the show on Saturdays. Jack likes to take Saturdays off."

"You'd better watch out," I said, pointing the pear at him. "Dad runs a tight ship."

Zander held his hands up. "You know you can count on me. After all, I'm Mr. Mopar."

I laughed and bit into the pear. He was adorable, and I was doomed. I was developing a crush on the guy. Not good at all.

"Where's Whitney?" my dad asked, swiping an apple from the bowl.

"She has some cheerleading thing," I said. "She'll be home around suppertime."

"Did Chelsea bring you home?" Dad asked.

I shook my head. "She has some theater meeting."

"She acts?" Zander asked, tilting his head in question.

"I'd wondered the same thing. She does costumes, makeup, and hair." I grabbed a paper towel and wiped my mouth. "She's like head of the costume team or committee or whatever, and she's really talented. Did you know she makes her clothes? They're awesome."

"Wow." Zander looked impressed.

I suddenly noticed it was really easy to talk to him. He was interested in what I had to say, and he really listened to me. I felt comfortable with him—like I could really be myself. And it felt good.

"So you took the bus?" Zander asked.

I nodded, taking another bite of the pear.

"There's no reason to take the bus," Zander said. "I drive to the same destination. There's plenty of room in my Jeep, and it's a more pleasant ride."

I shrugged. "It's no big deal. I ignore the freshmen and spitballs."

"Freshmen and spitballs?" my dad asked, his eyebrows arched.

"Don't worry about it," I told Dad and then looked at Zander. "The bus is okay. I don't mind. It builds character."

"Don't be silly." Zander lifted the can of Coke toward his mouth. "We're neighbors. We can ride together."

I hesitated. Deep down I wanted to ride with him, but there was a problem: If I drove home with him, then the crush would turn into something much deeper, and I was afraid of having to nurse another broken heart.

"Thanks," I said. "I'll keep that in mind."

Zander shook his soda can, indicating that it was empty. I snatched it from him and tossed it into the recycling bin under the sink.

"Thanks for the drink," Zander said. "I better head back home."

"Would you like to join us for supper?" my dad said. "I'm going to make tacos to celebrate my new job."

"Thanks, but my mom's making steak tonight." Zander started for the door. "I'll take a rain check, though."

"You'd rather have steak than tacos, huh?" My dad chuckled. "I'm offended."

"Sorry, but my mom's steak is out of this world." Zander gripped the doorknob. "Thanks again."

"No, thank you," Dad said. "You're a real lifesaver. You helped fix my truck and got me a job. I owe you."

"Don't be silly. That's what neighbors are for." Zander pushed the door open. "See you Saturday, Brad." He looked at me. "See you at school." Then he slipped through the door.

"Thanks again," my dad called after him, a grin wide on his face.

"I'll be right back." Without thinking it through, I tossed the pear core into the trash and rushed through the door, hitting the deck just as Zander started down the path toward the gate. "Wait," I called, leaning on the railing.

He turned around, his expression curious. "What's up?"

"I didn't get to thank you," I said. "What you did today, you know, helping my dad get the job—" I stammered, searching for the right words. "That was a huge deal. He's smiling more than I've seen him smile in a really long time. What I want to say is thank you. I really appreciate it."

He nodded. "You're welcome."

"See you in school," I said.

He grinned, revealing his dimple. "Absolutely. Have a good one."

I slipped back through the door and sat across from my dad at the table. "I'm really happy for you," I said.

"Thanks." He reached over and touched my hands. "Things are going to look up for us. It'll take some time, but we'll get there."

I gnawed my bottom lip as a plan formed in my head. "What if I got a job there too, Dad? I could work a few hours each day and sock all of the money away to pay for groceries or something when we move out. What do you think? Would that help us?"

"That's sweet, but you need to worry about school and leave working and paying bills to me." He gave me a condescending smile as if I were the cutest little girl on the planet, and it irritated me.

I glowered. "I can handle it, Dad. I used to work for you, remember?"

He shook his head. "That was different."

"How was it different?"

He frowned, and I knew what was coming. He was going to bring Mom into it, and it ticked me off even more.

"Your mom was still here, and we didn't have the pressures we have now." His voice was soft, as if mentioning her really hurt his heart. "Mom kept it together. She made sure your homework was done and you were getting enough sleep. I can't keep it all together like she did."

"I can handle it, Dad." I tapped my finger on the table for emphasis. "I'm stronger than you think. I can balance work and school. I don't get straight As like Whitney, but I get by. I could work one night during the week and then on Saturdays like Zander does and make enough money to help us find a place, Dad."

Dad wrapped his apple core in a napkin. "Emily, it's my job to support us, not yours."

"Why can't I help? I'm almost seventeen. I'm not a kid anymore."

He pushed his chair back and crossed the kitchen. "It's your job to go to school. You need to get good grades so you can get a scholarship to a great college. You know there's no money for you to go to college otherwise. Your mom and I blew through all of our savings when she got sick." Turning away from me, he threw out the core and then began searching through the cabinets and drawers, pulling out pots and utensils as he looked.

"That's not an answer." I leaned over the island, trying to make eye contact and challenge him, but he continued his search for cooking supplies. "I want to help us, Dad. I'm old enough to hold down a job. I'll still get Bs."

"This conversation is over, Emily Claire," my dad snapped. "Drop it."

"Why?" I smacked my hand on the counter. "Don't you want to have your own house and your own garage again? Don't you want to be able to open the drawer to your toolbox? Or even find a simple frying pan without having to open every single cabinet around here?" I jammed my finger into my chest. "I do! I want my own house with my own bathroom. I want to be able to go out to the garage and tinker at night so I can lose myself in a project and finally clear my head."

He blew out a frustrated sigh, and I knew I'd hit a nerve. "Don't you remember what I told you about how lucky we are to be here? Chuck and Darlene are doing more than I could ever expect. You need to just get rid of that chip on your shoulder and suck it up until we can move out. It's going to be awhile, a long while, so just make the best of it."

I shook my head, anger and hurt surging through me. "I don't have a chip on my shoulder. I'm simply trying to help." I opened the cabinet next to him and pulled out the frying pan, slamming it onto the counter.

"You can help by doing the best you can in school and keeping a good attitude." He pulled a package of chopped meat from the refrigerator and dumped it into the pan. He turned on the flame and soon the meat started to sizzle. Fetching a bag of tomatoes and lettuce from the drawer, he dropped them onto the counter with a deep sigh. "Here. Grab a bowl and knife and start chopping. Darlene should be home soon, and I told her we'd take care of everything. She's done so much for us already. It's time we started giving back."

I bit back the words on the tip of my tongue and followed orders. As I chopped, I stewed on the accusations he'd thrown at me. I didn't have a bad attitude or a chip on my shoulder. I just wanted life to be back to normal. I wanted Dad and me to have our own place. I didn't want to be a part of the Richards family, living under the shadow of their success, happiness, all-around perfection ... and wholeness.

When I sat down to supper with my dad, Logan, Uncle Chuck, and Aunt Darlene, the sting from my dad's words were still raw in my heart. I kept my eyes focused on my tacos, thankful when my dad chatted on about his new job, followed by Darlene's cross-examination of Logan's day.

I was finishing up my second taco when Whitney burst through the door and flopped down into the seat next to me.

She bowed her head in prayer and then spread her napkin across her lap.

"Sorry I'm late," she said, filling a taco shell with meat and cheese. "We had a captain's meeting after practice and it went a little long."

"How was your day, dear?" Darlene asked.

"Good." Whitney took a bite of taco and, as was becoming her routine, moaned and exclaimed, "Yum! Great job, Mom."

"Actually, your uncle made them." Darlene patted my dad's shoulder.

"It's a celebration," Dad said. "I got a job today."

"Really!" Whitney beamed and I wondered why the news made her so excited. Maybe cheerleading takes over your brain. "Where?"

"Cameronville Auto and Body," my dad said. "I'm the new assistant manager."

"That's where Zander works," Whitney said, wiping her mouth. "You'll like the manager. He's nice."

I placed my taco on my plate and stared at her. Why did she know so much about Zander's job?

"When do you start?" Whitney asked.

"Tomorrow." My dad smiled with pride.

If I weren't so angry with him, I probably would have grinned too. But I still didn't understand why he brushed off my offer to help support us. He knew I was a good mechanic and I could hold down a job and do well in school. His argument for taking it all on himself didn't make sense.

"That's fabulous," Whitney said. "I'm so happy for you."

"Thank you." Dad glanced at me and then back at Whitney. "So tell me, Whitney. What goes on during cheerleading practice?"

For the rest of supper, Whitney jabbered on about cheerleading, and my dad listened, hanging on her every word. He was positively riveted, as if she were explaining how she rebuilt her classic Corvette. I, on the other hand, wanted to be sick watching him pay so much attention to her when he had dismissed me earlier.

I was silent while my dad and I did the dishes, and then disappeared to my room as soon as I could.

Sitting on the window seat, I opened my Spanish book and stared at the words, my mind still rolling over my father's words. After several minutes, I yanked my journal from my bag and began writing.

Tuesday, August 30
Dear Mom,
I'm so upset I can't concentrate on my homework. I wish I could talk to you in person, and you could help figure out how to work through all this anger and resentment.

Dad got a job today, thanks to Zander's recommendation. While I'm thrilled for him and for us, I'm furious he won't let me get a job there as well. It doesn't make sense. Back home, I worked twenty hours some weeks, helping out nearly every day after school and on Saturdays.

Dad always told me that if I didn't use my mechanical talent, I'd lose it. Why is it different now? I always got good grades—Bs and some As too. Why isn't that good enough now? Why is Dad treating me differently? Why doesn't he trust me to do my best at work and school, like I always did?

Dad has changed so much now that you're gone. But I guess I've changed too. I'm not the same person I was, and I wish I could be. I wish I knew how to reach out to him and tell him how I feel without getting so defensive and resentful.

You always knew the right thing to say and to do. I wish I could be like you. I wish I had your strength and your faith.

I'm lost without you, Mom. I feel like a ship lost at sea without you here to guide me.

I miss you.

The sputter and hiss of the air compressor drew my eyes to the garage next door. I watched Zander work on his car for a few minutes, his cell phone pressed to one ear, and then turned back to my Spanish book, wondering how I was going to make it through this year.

chapter eight

Whitney stuck her head into my doorway Thursday evening. "Emily, get dressed. Youth group in fifteen minutes."

I glanced up from my history book. "Youth group?"

"You'll like it. Trust me." Whitney jerked her thumb toward the hall. "Let's go!"

"No, thanks." I nodded toward my book bag. "I've got a ton of—"

My dad appeared behind Whitney. "Just get ready, Emily. It'll be good for you."

Whitney's phone began to sing. "I'll be downstairs." She slipped past my dad.

"Good for me?" I narrowed my eyes. "What's that supposed to mean?"

My dad stepped through the doorway. "Look, I know you're angry with me because I won't let you get a job, but I'm not going to change my mind about that. I think you need to get more involved in the church, like you were before—" He paused. "Before we lost Mom. You used to love church and your friends there. I think this group can help you work through some of the things you're feeling. Maybe then you won't be so resentful of the changes we've had to endure."

Frustrated, I studied his expression. "So you think that if I go to youth group with Whitney I'll get rid of the chip on my shoulder."

He paused, seeming to choose his words. "Emily, everything has changed for us. Nothing will be the same ever again. All we can do is trust what God has in store for us." He glanced at his watch. "I have an appointment with Pastor Keith, so I have to run. You should go." He hurried out the door.

I glanced across the room at my reflection in the mirror. I was still clad in the denim shorts and purple tank top I'd worn to school, and my hair was pulled back into a rubber band at the nape of my neck.

"Emily?" Darlene appeared in the doorway. "Whitney's waiting for you in her car. You better hurry up." Her expression became serious, and I got the sneaking suspicion my family had staged an intervention.

Outside the Honda's horn honked.

"Just give it a try, okay?"

I stood. "Okay."

"Good girl." She patted my shoulder as I moved past her.

During the ride to the church, Whitney flipped on the radio, and Christian rock blared through the speakers. She turned it down and glanced at me. "I'm glad you're coming with me tonight."

"Really?" I asked.

"Yeah." She laughed. "Why wouldn't I be?"

"I assumed my dad and your mom made you invite me." I grabbed a handful of hair that had escaped my ponytail and pulled out my rubber band. Forming a new ponytail, I wrapped the rubber band around it and hoped it would stay secure.

She slowed at a light and turned to me. "Actually, it was my idea to invite you."

I raised an eyebrow in surprise. "Your idea?"

"Yeah." The light changed and she let off the brake. "You've been through a lot, and I thought you might like to check out the youth group. I know when I'm sad, being at church helps me." She shot me a sideways glance. "I'm not saying that anything I experience could be close to what you've faced after losing your mom. I just meant that it might help you sort through some of your feelings and all. Youth group helps me connect with God."

"Oh." I studied her while her words soaked through me. Did she really care about my feelings?

The Honda steered into the church lot, and Whitney parked next to my dad's Suburban. On our way to the youth room, we passed Pastor Keith's office, and I wondered how Dad's appointment was going. Was he talking about Mom or discussing his "issues" with me and my trouble fitting in? I shuddered at the idea of my dad revealing all of our private business.

I followed Whitney into a large classroom lined with tables. The walls were decorated with Bible verses and also familiar Bible scenes that looked liked they'd been drawn by children.

A crowd of teenagers sat at the tables while Jenna stood in front of the room by a television and DVD player on a rolling cart. The smell of popcorn permeated the air as two girls I recognized from the service entered the room with huge bowls that were filled to the brim. Two boys followed with cans of soda.

"Whitney and Emily," Jenna announced. "We're so glad you came. Whitney, why don't you introduce Emily before we start the movie?"

Whitney grabbed my arm and yanked me to the front of room. "Hey, everyone," she said. "This is my cousin Emily Curtis, who just moved here from up north. She's a junior like me, and I'm so glad she's here."

"Hi," I said, feeling like a moron as I waved to the sea of unfamiliar faces.

"Welcome, Emily," Jenna said, touching my arm. "Tonight we're going to watch a movie called *Pay It Forward* and then we're going to discuss how it relates to our faith. You may have a seat anywhere."

"Thanks." I weaved through the row of tables and found a seat in the back row near the door.

Whitney stood up front talking to a girl I didn't recognize. The bowls of popcorn made their way down the rows, and kids took handfuls and placed them on paper towels.

When a bowl got to the row in front of me, a pretty girl turned around and smiled. "Hi. I'm Mindy. Would you like some popcorn?"

"Yes, please," I said, taking the bowl. "Thanks."

A boy came around and handed me a can of soda. As I pulled the tab, I looked around the room. Other than the typical welcome wagon greetings, the kids here seemed a lot like the ones at my old church. Okay, maybe a little wealthier. As long as I could stay in the back, I might survive the night.

"Whitney," one of the girls called from the door. I was pretty sure she'd sat with my cousin in church. "Can you help us with the popcorn?"

"Sure." Whitney made her way to the back of the room, stopping at my table. "Do you want to come with us?"

"That's okay," I said, scooping a handful of popcorn. "I'm good."

"I'll be back." Whitney followed her friend out into the hallway, closing the door behind them.

The lights dimmed and soon the movie blared through the television. I leaned back in my seat and sipped my soda in between bites of popcorn. I was engrossed in the movie when I felt someone slip into the seat beside me and swipe a handful of popcorn from my paper towel.

"Hey," a voice said.

I turned and found Zander grinning at me. "What are you doing here?" I asked.

"I'm a member of the youth group." His smile was playful. "What are you doing here?"

"I think my family staged an intervention," I whispered. "I was pretty much pushed out the door."

He laughed. "You really didn't want to come, huh?"

"Shhh!" someone up front hissed.

"It's not that," I whispered, leaning closer to him and inhaling a spicy scent that must've been cologne. For a moment, the aroma made me dizzy. "I just didn't think it would be, well, fun."

"Are you having fun?" he whispered, leaning closer to me.

I shrugged and couldn't stop a smile from overtaking my lips. Sitting next to him was fun, as corny as it seemed. "I guess it's okay."

"Quiet!" someone else hissed.

"We can't hear," another chimed in.

Zander took my hand and helped me to my feet then led me through the door.

"Where are we going?" I asked as he gently tugged me down the hallway.

"Somewhere we can talk without being shushed," he said, still holding my hand.

He led me into the sanctuary, where he sank into the back pew, his hand still encircling mine. His touch made me feel as if everything was going to be okay somehow. For a split second, I hoped he wouldn't let go. Then I felt silly and pushed the thought away. I knew that feeling of euphoria brought on by an attentive, cute guy could be very misleading.

Zander let go and my hand fell to my side. "Have a seat," he said, patting the bench beside him.

I lowered myself into the seat next to him and glanced

toward the altar, trying in vain not to think about how I'd lost it during the service.

"I like to come in here sometimes to think. The sanctuary makes me feel at ease." He shrugged. "I guess that makes me a little weird, huh?"

"No." I shook my head. "That's not weird."

"Do you feel at ease here?"

Nope. I studied a few strings hanging out from the hem on my shorts while considering my answer. I didn't want to lie to him. "Not really."

"Oh," he said. "Do you want to go somewhere else to talk?"

"It's okay." I glanced up at his concerned expression.

"Would you rather watch the movie?"

"No. This is fine." *It's nice, actually.* I pulled my leg up onto the bench and hugged my knee.

"So, your family staged an intervention?" He rested his arm on the back of the bench behind me. "Why did they feel the need to do that?"

"They say I stay in my room too much." The words slipped through my lips without a filter. Had the guy given me truth serum?

I watched his expression. To my surprise, he simply smiled.

"Do you think they're right?" he asked.

I nodded. "Probably. I just don't feel like I fit in. I mean, how many girls would rather work on cars than go shopping or have their nails done?" The imaginary truth serum continued to work its magic on me as I opened my heart to this guy I hardly knew. But it felt good to be honest, and I liked talking to him. It felt as if he listened without judgment. Who knew I'd like youth group?

"Liking cars doesn't make you weird. It just makes you different." He ran a hand through his hair and glanced toward the altar. "I know what you mean, though, about being different."

"You do?"

"Yeah." He crossed his ankles and cleared his throat. "I guess you could say my dad has big plans for my future and none of them involve cars."

I studied his face, looking for regret or sadness, but his expression was unreadable. "What are those plans?"

"Medical school," he said. "Not everyone is cut out to be a doctor, but he doesn't want to hear that. He's a doctor, his father was a doctor, and his father's father was a doctor. Stewart boys are supposed to grow up to be doctors, so I'm different. Too different for his liking."

"Man." I shook my head. "That stinks."

"Oh well," he said with a sigh. "Dr. Stewart will have to get over it or die ticked off, I guess."

I studied his eyes, wondering what made Zander tick.

"Why are you a Zander as opposed to an Alec or an Alex?" I asked.

He smiled. "That was my brother's doing. Andrew was four when I was born, and he couldn't say Alexander or Alex. The story goes that he called me something sounding like Sander or Zander, and it stuck."

"So, you're never Alex or Alexander?"

"Only when my parents aren't pleased." Smirking, he turned toward me. "Last year I came home to find my father studying my report card. I knew I was in trouble. He looked up and he said, 'Alexander Lee Stewart, this is appalling. A D in Biology? How could you get a D in Biology? Andrew got straight As. He aced Biology.'" Zander folded his arms across his chest. "Then he told me I couldn't work during the week anymore. As if that would help my average."

"Does your dad compare you to your brother a lot?"

He shrugged. "Everyone once in a while. I learned a long time ago to tune it out."

"Do you resent that?" I asked. "I mean the comparison. Do you resent your brother for it?"

He shook his head. "It's not Andrew's fault he's my dad's favorite or that he chose to follow in my father's footsteps while I didn't. And he earned his straight As and worked his butt off to be the quarterback and all that. I can't resent him for that. It just wasn't what I wanted to do." He tapped his right knee. "I tried football, but my knee couldn't take it. And school isn't really my thing. I guess you could say I don't apply myself."

I grinned. "You seem to apply yourself to cars."

"Dad doesn't see it like that. He sees a lot of wasted hours and money. Whereas Andrew is going to make a difference in the world as a pediatrician."

I studied his expression but didn't find any resentment toward his brother. His words were more matter-of-fact than envious, and that fascinated me. "Are you and Andrew close?"

He nodded. "Yeah, we get along well. I haven't seen him in a while, but he calls me just about once a week to tell me what he's up to and to find out if I've gotten the car running yet."

I absently wondered if that was who I'd seen him talking to on the phone when I was looking out the window the other day.

"How about you?" he asked. "What are you called when you're in trouble? Not that you get in trouble."

I chuckled. "Oh, I tick my dad off plenty. Just the other night he said, 'Emily Claire Curtis, you need to lose the chip on your shoulder and be happy that we're here instead of out on the street.'" I shook my head. "He just doesn't get how hard this move was for me."

"Emily Claire," he repeated. "That's nice."

"Thanks." I studied the altar again. "Claire was my mom," I whispered, my voice suddenly thick.

"I'm sorry about your mom," he said, touching my arm for a nanosecond. "Whitney told me."

"Thank you." I cleared my throat and rested my chin on my knee.

"And from what I've seen, you don't have a chip on your shoulder. I can't even imagine how hard this move was for you."

He was silent for a moment, and I searched for something to say. Although the silence was comfortable, I felt like I should say something to him to keep the conversation going.

"There's something you never did answer that day we fixed the timing on your dad's truck," he began.

"What's that?" I turned toward him.

"What kind of car did you fix when your dad went out of town?"

"Nova." I held my breath, hoping he didn't ask for more details. The car belonged to Tyler.

"A Nova?" His eyes lit up. "What year?"

"Seventy." I crisscrossed my legs. "And my dad makes way too much of it. I just did the brakes."

"Yourself?"

I nodded. "Yeah. My dad went out of town on business, and my friend Tyler had something going on that weekend. So I did all of the brakes to keep myself busy. It was no big deal." That wasn't entirely true. It had been a huge, time-consuming job, but not one I was proud of completing. Looking back, I felt like a fool for all I'd done for Tyler. I'd spent two days and a full paycheck fighting to fix those brakes as a surprise for him. In the end, all I wound up with was an empty bank account and a broken heart.

"Wow." He shook his head. "That's amazing."

I shrugged. "It was just brakes." I studied my hem again, hoping Zander wasn't going to be intimidated by me or write me off as a tomboy because I'd fixed a car by myself. Working on cars was a great stress reliever for me, and the only time I could really feel like myself, but not many people understood that.

"So why Chevys?"

"What do you mean?" I met his questioning gaze. "It was my friend Tyler's car. He was having trouble with the brakes, so I took care of it as a favor for him."

"No, that's not what I meant. I mean, why do you prefer Chevys?"

"I guess you could blame that on my dad. He raced Chevys before I was born."

"Really." He leaned his arm on the back of the bench and rested his chin on his palm. "Did he race full-time?"

"No." I pulled my knees up to my chest. "He did it part-time on weekends, and he dreamt of moving up to a real league. But then I was born and he had to get a real job, or so he says. He got a loan and opened his shop. And the rest is history, I guess."

"That's cool." He ran his finger along the back of the bench. "It's a shame that you only like to work on Chevys. I sure could use some help with the Dodge."

My eyebrows shot to my hairline in surprise. "You want *my* help?" I pointed to my chest.

"Of course I do." He gave a little laugh. "You're like a mechanical genius, and the rebuild is a little more difficult than I'd imagined. I'm starting to wonder if my dad was right about how I've wasted my money on this car."

"Don't say that." I looked at him, incredulous. "A restoration is never a waste of money. It's an investment—or so we'd like to believe, right?"

"Right." His eyes studied mine. "Why are you surprised that I'd want your help?"

I hugged my knees closer to my chest. I considered dodging the question, but the truth serum won out again. "Not every guy likes the idea of a girl working on cars. Some find it, well ... intimidating." My cheeks heated at the honesty of my comment.

He shook his head with disbelief. "That would be ridiculous." Then he smiled. "Besides, if you helped me with my car, you'd be out of your room, which would make your family happy, right?"

I laughed. "Yeah, it would get them off my back."

"Cool." He nodded. "So it's a deal. You help me with my car, and I get your family off your back."

"Okay." I pushed an errant curl back from my face.

"I have another burning question for you." His expression was serious.

"Oh?"

"What was really bothering you at church last week? I know it wasn't an eyelash."

I blew out a sigh and turned back toward the altar. "Wow. You don't miss a thing, do you, Zander?"

"You don't have to answer," he said. "It's none of my business."

"It's okay." I studied my flip-flops. "It was the last hymn. It got to me."

" 'Beautiful Savior,' " he said.

"Yeah." My voice quavered and I cleared my throat. "It was my mom's favorite," I whispered, my eyes filling with tears. "It was the first time I'd been back to church since she ..." My voice trailed off.

"I'm sorry." His voice was soft and tender. "You don't have to discuss it."

"It's okay. I appreciate that you asked." I wiped my eyes. The look on his face caught me off guard, so I studied my hem again. "We sang it at her service, so it was difficult to hear it again. Brought back some stuff I was trying to put behind me."

"My grandfather used to always say that if God brings you to it, he'll bring you through it."

I bit back a frown. *Here we go.*

He gave me a little smile. "From your expression, I gather you're not buying it, huh?"

"Well ..." I hesitated. But for some reason, I couldn't be dishonest with Zander, and I found it unnerving—almost as unnerving as his obvious faith in God. "I'm sorry," I began, shaking my head, "but I'm not buying it. Not at all."

He shifted his weight and I could feel the atmosphere change. "While I'm not one for clichés, I've found that this one is actually true. I've been through some rough patches, and even when I felt like God had abandoned me, he was there all along and got me through it."

Then he was lucky.

I fingered my cross and stared at the large stained-glass cross hanging above the altar. "You really believe in God."

"And you don't?"

"I'm not sure anymore." I turned to him. "Not since I lost her."

"But you wear a cross." He nodded toward my collarbone.

"It belonged to my mother. She said it gave her hope when she was sick."

He raised an eyebrow. "And it doesn't give you any." It was a statement more than a question.

I shook my head. "No. I'd hoped it would, but it hasn't happened yet."

His expression brightened, as if I'd admitted a secret faith. "But you're not giving up."

I shrugged. "I don't know why I wear it. I guess it's in memory of her."

He paused for a moment. Then he opened his mouth to speak, but was interrupted by the sanctuary doors opening with a whoosh.

"There you are," Whitney snapped, hands on hips and impatient. "I was looking all over for you."

"We've been in here talking," I said, wondering when she became my mother. Was she filling in since Darlene was at home?

"We were tired of being shushed during the movie," Zander chimed in.

Whitney frowned. "You could've told me that you were blowing off the movie. It would be helpful if you had a cell phone, Emily. Then you could just, like, text me when you change your plans."

"You don't have a cell phone?" Zander asked, his eyebrows arching toward his hairline in surprise.

"Please, not you too," I grumbled, standing. "No, I don't have one."

"Interesting." He stood and faced Whitney. "Is the movie over?"

"Yeah," she huffed. "It's been over for, like, fifteen minutes." She scowled at me. "I was going to leave, but I wanted to be sure you got home. I called the house and your dad was home, but he hadn't seen you. Everyone was worried."

I stared at her. Was she serious? Was she really angry with me for not checking in with her? It was bad enough having Darlene on me about my attire, but being babysat by Whitney would probably send me over the edge. I opened my mouth to snap at her, but Zander interrupted me.

"It's my fault," he said with a smile, placing a hand on my shoulder. "I needed her advice on my Dodge, so I kidnapped her to pick her brain."

"Oh." Whitney looked between us. "Well, we better go, Emily. I still have homework to finish."

"If it's all right, I'll give her a ride home." Zander's hand dropped from my shoulder. He yanked keys from his pocket, and they jingled at the motion. "We still have some car talk to finish up."

I looked between them, feeling like a little kid.

"Of course it's up to you," he said quickly, looking at me. "You can ride with Whitney if you'd rather."

"Oh, well, if you need my help with your car, then I'll ride with you," I said, glancing back at Whitney, who was still scowling.

"Fine." She turned. "Would've been nice to have known that twenty minutes ago," she grumbled, starting down the hall.

"Why is she so uptight?" I asked.

He snorted. "I guess she was really worried."

I shook my head. "I felt like her child rather than her cousin."

He held the door open and motioned for me to walk through.

I fell into step with him as we headed toward his Jeep. "Thanks for saving me from a ride home listening to her complain about my behavior."

He wrenched the passenger door open. I hopped in and examined the interior. I didn't know a ton about Chrysler, but the Jeep looked to be a late nineties model, complete with a tan vinyl interior. The truck was clean and well kept, and he had replaced the stock stereo with an impressive CD changer. It was obvious that Zander loved his vehicles.

He smiled. "You may not thank me once we get on the road."

"What do you mean?" I inwardly groaned, hoping he wasn't going to start in on my lack of faith again.

"I really am going to pick your brain." Once buckled in, he started the Jeep. "I do need help with the car."

I blew out a sigh of relief. Cars were easy to discuss; relationships and God were much more difficult. I think that's why I loved cars so much. They were effortless and didn't expect anything in return, except maybe some gas, a good paint job, and a periodic tune-up.

By the time Zander parked in front of his garage, we had a

plan of attack for his troublesome Dodge, and he was all smiles, obviously pleased with my suggestions. The brief tension we'd had in the sanctuary seemed to be gone as well.

"I guess I'll see you at school tomorrow," he said as we stood in the driveway.

"I'll be there," I said. "Thanks for the ride."

"No, thank you for the help with the car."

"Don't thank me yet," I said with a laugh. "I don't know if it'll work."

"I bet it will." He grinned. "Good night, Chevy Girl."

"Night, Mr. Mopar." I smiled as I walked up the path to the deck.

I was still smiling when my dad stuck his head in my room a little while later.

"How was youth group?" he asked, stepping through the doorway.

"Good," I said, setting my Spanish book down on the window seat. "How was your appointment?"

"Good." He lowered himself onto the edge of my bed.

"Can you be more specific?" I asked, twirling my pen in my hand.

He rubbed his chin, and I knew he was censoring his thoughts, which irritated me. But I didn't want to push him too hard and have a repeat of our argument the other night.

"Pastor Keith and I talked about things, and it seemed helpful."

"Huh." I frowned at his evasive response. "Things."

"Yup." He nodded toward the window. "I saw you got a ride from Zander."

"Yeah. He and I talked about *things*." I gave him a wry smile.

"Touché," he said with a grin. "Did he finally ask for your help with his car?"

I nodded.

"I figured he would. It would be good for you to help him. I know you miss tinkering in the shop."

"Well, if you let me work for you—"

He held his hand up, shushing me. "Let's not argue tonight, Emmy. It's been a long day." He started for the door. "Don't stay up too late. You have school tomorrow."

"Yes, Daddy," I said. "Good night."

"Night." He slipped through the door and then stuck his head back in. "Oh, I forgot to tell you who called me today."

"Who?" I asked, assuming it was someone from home, like my dad's best friend, Ross.

"Your grandmother."

I groaned. I knew what he was going to say next. He'd want to go visit with her and endure endless discussions of Whitney's perfection in person. He had to be kidding me. I knew she would call eventually. I'd simply been hoping to avoid Grandma until the holidays.

"Now, now, Emily," he said, going into his father mode. "She's your only living grandparent."

I scowled. "Your point?"

"She's offended we haven't visited her yet. I told her I have to work Saturday, but she suggested you, Whitney, and Darlene come visit."

I feigned a cough. "You know, I think I'm coming down with something. It's probably best I not infect her or the other people in her assisted living facility."

"Emily Claire," he began, sounding stern. "It would be nice if you went to see her. She's dying to see you."

"Yeah, right." When his frown deepened, I sighed and waved off his expression. "Fine. Whatever."

"I told her you'll stop by as soon as you can with Whitney and Darlene, and I'll get over there as my work schedule permits." He tapped the doorframe. "Get some rest."

"I'll need it," I said after he'd disappeared. I was engrossed in my Spanish homework when a knock sounded on the doorframe.

"Hey," Whitney said. "Can I come in?"

"Sure." I closed my book, wondering if I was going to get another lecture on how thoughtless I was to run off without permission. "What's up?"

She stepped through the door clad in pink pajamas. "Sorry for being snippy earlier. I really overreacted, huh? I was just surprised when I came back to the room and you were gone. I'd thought you'd flaked out and gone home with your dad."

I snorted at her choice of words. "Flaked out, huh?"

"Well, you know." She gestured widely with her arms. "You always turn down my offers to go out, so I figured you'd snuck off at the first chance you'd gotten. Anyway, I'm sorry."

I shrugged. "It's okay."

She smiled. "You and Zander were getting pretty cozy."

I frowned, dreading any gossip she may start about him and me. "We're friends. It's no biggie."

"It makes sense."

"What do you mean?"

"You and Zander being friends," she said. "It makes perfect sense. I mean, you're both motorheads so you have tons to talk about. You speak his language."

"I speak his language?"

"Yeah. Totally. All he talks about are cars. You get him."

I nodded slowly. She made it sound as if we were aliens from another planet. I did get him. Sorta. But I didn't get the religion stuff he was so into and probably never would.

"Did you like youth group?" she asked.

I nodded. "Yeah."

She grinned. "Of course you did. You spent most of the time with Zander, and he's really cute."

I wished my cheeks wouldn't heat up at the mention of his name.

Her smile faded. "But seriously, did you like it, aside from Zander?"

"Yeah." I nodded. "The movie was good."

"Do you think it may help you cope?"

I shrugged. "I guess."

"Well, if you ever want to talk ..." Her voice trailed off.

"I'll keep that in mind," I said, even though I wasn't sure I'd ever want to open up to her.

"Well, good night." She started for the doorway and then stopped. "Would you like to borrow my Bible?"

Whitney read the Bible? I was stunned silent for a moment. "I have my mom's somewhere. I just haven't unpacked it yet."

"If you can't find it, just let me know. You can always borrow mine. Whenever I'm down, I read the Bible and certain verses help me feel better. It's not the same for everyone, but maybe some verses will speak to you too." She leaned on the doorframe. "Are you driving to school with me tomorrow?"

"Why wouldn't I?" I asked with surprise.

"If you and Zander are seeing each other then I figured you'd drive with him."

I rolled my eyes. "We're just *friends*, Whitney. Don't make more of it than it is, okay?"

She grinned as if she knew a secret that I didn't. "Sure, sure. Good night."

I sighed as she disappeared down the hall.

I turned toward the window and spotted Zander out in the garage, sitting on a stool while talking on his cell phone. I wondered if Andrew was on the other line. If he was, then was Zander telling him about me and our plan to fix the car? Would Zander make more of our discussion this evening as Whitney already had?

Probably not.

Another thought hit me. Why was Whitney so worried about me? Had I misread her since the funeral?

Pushing the thought away, I pulled out my journal and turned to a fresh page. I needed to share my feelings with Mom.

Thursday, September 1
Dear Mom,
Tonight I went with Whitney to youth group and had a better time than I expected. That might be because I spent the entire evening talking to Zander. He's really easy to talk to, and I found myself sharing some of my feelings about losing you. The only thing that bugs me about him is that he seems to have a really deep Christian faith, and it's kind of off-putting. I felt like he was preaching to me at times, and I don't think he understands my doubts. It was like he couldn't consider being angry with God or losing his ability to talk to God. If it wasn't for his witnessing to me, I'd probably be interested in dating him. Which tells you how much I like him. He's totally gorgeous and really nice. But I can't get past the religion issue.

But back to the good part of the night. Zander asked for my help with his car, and I agreed since it will get me out of my room and away from Darlene's nagging about my appearance and Dad's comments about the "chip on my shoulder." But I won't let Zander use me. I'm too smart to be used again.

Dad is acting strange. He met with the pastor tonight but won't share what they discussed. I don't understand his secrecy. I'm missing you too, so why can't we mourn together?

Whitney also is acting different from what I remember. She was the one who invited me to youth group, and she came to see me earlier to see if I needed to talk. She even offered to loan me her Bible. I wish I could find the comfort she and Zander seem to have. Last night I tried to pray again, and the words just didn't come.

I wish I could tell God how I'm feeling. How do I find my faith again, Mom? How do I find my ability to pray?

Even worse, what if I never find my way back to God? What will happen to me then?

I closed my journal and packed up my school books. Before stepping over to the bed, I glanced out the window and spotted Zander, still chatting on the phone.

Closing my eyes, I whispered, "God? Are you there?" I held my breath, hoping that I'd suddenly feel God's presence, but nothing came.

chapter nine

I awoke Saturday to knocking on my bedroom door.

"Emily?" Darlene called. "Are you up, dear? It's nearly ten."

Groaning, I rolled over and covered my head with my pillow. "Go away," I grumbled.

The door creaked open. "Emily," Darlene said. "Rise and shine, dear. Today is going to be a girls' day out."

I groaned again.

A hand on my back caused me to sit up with a start. I brushed back my mess of curls and found Darlene dressed and grinning at me.

"Good morning," she said, her hand on her slight hip. "Get showered and we'll head out."

I searched for an excuse not to go, but her all-business expression told me I was stuck. "Where are we going?" I asked.

"Whitney needs a new outfit for Kristin's party tonight," she said. "So I thought we'd make a day of it. We'll get breakfast, go to the mall, and then go see your grandmother. Doesn't that sound great?"

This can't be happening. I swallowed another groan and forced a smile. "Sounds fabulous," I mumbled.

"If we have time," she continued, counting off the places on her fingers, "we can stop by your dad's work too."

Then I can see Zander. The thought popped into my head before I could stop it. I hadn't talked to him since Thursday night, and I missed him.

"Chop-chop!" Darlene started for the door. "I'd like to be on the road in the next thirty minutes."

She closed the door, and I flopped back onto my pillow and stared at the ceiling fan above me. My dad had warned me that I might have to go see Grandma today, but I'd hoped he was playing some cruel joke on me.

I dragged myself out of bed and into the shower. Clad in denim shorts and a brown T-shirt with my curls pulled back in a ponytail, I jogged down the stairs and found my aunt and cousin sitting at the kitchen bar waiting for me. Whitney's eyes were glued on her phone while her fingers flitted over the keys in the middle of a text message.

Darlene was reading the paper and sipping her coffee. She glanced up, her eyes sweeping my attire, and I held my breath, awaiting her criticism. "Ready?" she asked.

No. "Sure." I shrugged my purse farther up on my shoulder.

"Let's go, ladies," Darlene said, placing her coffee cup in the sink. "Whitney, dear, please stop your texting."

Whitney snapped her phone shut and grinned at me. "Ready for some shopping?"

I forced a smile. "Can't wait."

We piled into Darlene's SUV, and I sat in the back. Whitney spent the entire ride to the Cameronville Toasty Inn giving a play-by-play report of last night's football game, including everything she and Kristin said to each other, every play Chad made, everything Chad said before and after the game, and everything said about Chad after the game.

While she jabbered on, I stared out the window, trying my best to tune her out and ignore the jealousy surging through me while she shared with her mother. I'd give anything to be able to share my day with mine. I turned my thoughts to my dad, wondering how he was doing at work. Then I pondered Zander, wondering how his day was going at the shop.

Whitney's football game discussion persisted during breakfast. I picked at my omelet and bacon while she continued on. I was studying my toast when I heard my name.

"Emily? Did you hear me?" Darlene asked.

I looked up at her. "I'm sorry. I was off in my own world. What did you say?"

"I asked if you attended football games at your previous high school." She lifted her coffee mug to her lips.

I shook my head. "Not often. I think I went once last year."

"You should come to one of our games," Whitney said after finishing a text. "I think they're fun, at least. Maybe you could go with Chelsea." She lowered her head again then clicked her tongue with disgust. "I hate this stupid phone. Kristin's is so much easier to text on."

I shook my head while nibbling on another piece of bacon. Whitney's priorities were so contrary to mine. A bad texting cell was better than no phone at all. I should know.

"Isn't it time for an upgrade?" Whitney glanced at her mother.

Darlene sighed. "I don't know, Whitney. Is it that important?"

"Totally." Whitney nodded, still texting. "I could get a new phone, and Emily could have one too. That way we can stay in touch and not have a repeat of Thursday night." Whitney gave me a dramatic wink.

I rolled my eyes and grabbed a piece of toast. "It's not that important."

"Whitney has a point," Darlene said. "We were worried about you Thursday. It's very inexpensive to add a line to our plan."

"I don't expect you to pay for my phone," I said. "I'll just get one once Dad and I get back on our feet."

"Nonsense." Darlene smiled. "I'm happy to do it for you."

"Maybe we should check with my dad first."

"Don't be silly. You're father will be fine with it." Darlene glanced at her watch. "We can stop by the cell phone store on our way to the mall."

Yay. I turned to Whitney, who was still texting on her "stupid" phone.

I roamed around the cell phone store, glancing at the selections and wondering why there were so many different phones. Some of them looked so complicated I assumed the user would need a degree in electrical engineering to figure the contraptions out.

"Emily!" Whitney called from the other side of the store. "Come help me choose a phone."

"Good grief," I mumbled, schlepping over to the counter where she stood examining two identical phones—one pink and one purple. Oh, the choices she had to make were just so difficult.

"Should I get the pink or the purple?" she asked.

I squashed the urge to roll my eyes. "What color does Kristin have?"

"She got the purple."

"So get the pink." I glanced around the counter, looking for a low-cost, nonpink, nonpurple phone. I'd want to get one that was plainer than Whitney's and durable. Something that could withstand being dropped accidentally on the garage floor and would be easy to wipe grease off.

"Did you make a choice?" Darlene asked, sidling up to Whitney.

"Emily thinks this one is best, and I like it too," Whitney said, lifting the pink phone, examining it further.

"Good." Darlene called the salesman over, and I disappeared by the accessories, examining the prices and shaking my head with disgust. I then took a seat on a stool by the window and people watched for a while.

"Emily!" Darlene called.

I joined them at the counter, and Darlene held out the sequined phone.

"What's this?" I asked.

Darlene smiled triumphantly. "Your new phone."

I swallowed my shock at being offered Whitney's castoff. "I really don't think—"

"Just take it," Whitney said, looking uncomfortable. She barely looked up from her new phone, texting yet again. Did she ever run out of things to type?

Darlene set the phone into my hand, her smile becoming stiff. "You can change the cover to something less girly."

"What kind of skin would you like?" the salesman asked.

"Anything but pastel or sequins," I said.

I walked out of the store with a camouflaged phone. During the ride to the mall, Whitney gave me a detailed lesson on the device, including everything from programming in contacts to changing the ringer to, of course, texting. She programmed her number into the phone and told me to text her. I forced a smiled and told her I would, even though I couldn't even imagine sending her a message. I did, however, send a quick text to Megan and Chelsea.

I played with the phone while Whitney tried on outfit after outfit at the mall. Since the technician didn't have to change the SIM card in the phone, all of Whitney's contacts remained. I scrolled through the numbers, deleting some and also adding some from back home. I stopped when I came to Zander's home and cell number, and considered sending him a text message. But I stopped, not wanting to come off as a clingy girl by texting him.

"You should go try on some jeans," Darlene said while we stood outside the dressing room at an overpriced department store. "Cold weather will be here before you know it."

"That's okay," I said, studying the phone. "My jeans from last year still fit."

Darlene squeezed my arm. "Emily, you've had a rough year. You deserve some new clothes. Think of it as an early birthday present."

I bit my bottom lip, considering my answer. I didn't want to be her charity case twice in one day.

"Emily, I think you'd look lovely in one of those green sweaters over there." She nodded toward a rack across from the dressing room. "Green is your color, thanks to those eyes you inherited from your mother."

I turned toward the sweaters, and I had to admit to myself that they were gorgeous. But I didn't need clothes. Or, more specifically, I didn't want her buying them for me.

"They are nice," I began, "but I don't feel right spending your money. The phone was already too much."

"Oh, please." She waved off my comment with a laugh. "It's just money." She nudged me toward the rack. "Go on. Pick out a few things. Whitney will probably be awhile, so take advantage and get yourself a few things. Don't worry about the price tags."

An hour later, Whitney carried her five bags to the SUV while I carried my two, containing three pairs of jeans and two sweaters. I'd suffered heart palpitations when the three-digit price rang up on the register, but Darlene never blinked an eye when she swiped her card. I couldn't help but wonder what it felt like to be able to buy anything you ever wanted without hesitating. It must be liberating.

When we parked in front of the Cameronville Assisted Living Center, the heart palpitations began anew. I hadn't seen my grandmother since the funeral, and the last visit was anything but pleasant. She'd jumped onto the "let's give Emily a makeover" bandwagon with Darlene. Her weekly phone calls since then had consisted of nothing but what I called the Whitney Report, and I couldn't imagine enduring the Whitney Report in person.

"Emily," Darlene called, standing on the curb. "Are you coming? Your grandmother is very excited to see you."

"You're confusing me with the other granddaughter," I growled, climbing from the backseat.

"What was that, dear?" Darlene asked.

"Nothing," I groused, slamming the door. I followed Darlene and Whitney through the maze of hallways to a door with "Jean Curtis" written on a plaque.

Darlene gave me a serious expression. "I don't want to alarm you, but Grandma has slowed down quite a bit in the past couple of months. Don't get upset if she seems a bit lethargic."

I followed them through the door to where my grandmother sat in an easy chair in front of the television. She looked the same as I remembered. Her graying blonde hair was cut short, and her brown eyes were bright. She resembled an older version of Darlene: tall, thin, and attractive.

Her eyes lit up when she spotted my cousin. "Whitney!" Grandma reached for her, and Whitney kissed her cheek. "How are you, sweetie?"

"Fine." Whitney gestured toward me. "Emily's here."

Whitney and Darlene sank into a love seat, and I sat across from them on a wing chair.

Grandma glanced toward me and smiled. "Why, Emily. I thought you weren't going to come and see me. I called your daddy the other day and asked him if he still loved me. I can't believe you've been in town two weeks and haven't come by."

Still the master of guilt. I grimaced. "It's good to see you too, Grandma." I hoped my tone didn't come across as bitter as I felt. I cleared my throat, hoping Whitney would jump in and give Grandma the play-by-play of the football game while I disappeared into the chair cushion. "How have you been?"

"I'm having some trouble with my knee." She pointed to her right leg. "The doctor says it's osteoarthritis, but the pain is simply unbearable some days."

"I'm sorry to hear that," I said.

"What have you done to your hair?" Grandma asked, squinting her eyes to get a better look. "It looks a bit frizzier than the last time I saw you." She pointed at Whitney. "You should try some of the new shampoo Whitney has. What's the name of it, dear?"

Whitney gave me an apologetic look, which shocked me. I wondered if she could feel my pain on the other side of the room.

"I got it at the salon," Whitney said quickly. "I'll let her borrow it. So, how was bingo yesterday, Grandma? You always go on Fridays, right?"

Way to steer the conversation, Whitney! I bit back a cheer.

While Grandma prattled on about bingo and her aches and pains, I turned my cell phone over repeatedly in my hands and glanced around the apartment, taking in the knickknacks, books, decorative pillows, doilies, and framed photographs.

Pictures of Whitney at all ages and poses peppered the walls. A few of Logan and me were also mixed in, but there were more than double the number of photos of Whitney. I couldn't imagine her favoritism being any more blatant.

One photograph in particular drew my stare like a magnetic force: the last formal portrait my parents and I had made before my mother became gravely ill. It had been taken for our church directory two years ago. I studied it, taking in my mother's beautiful face and dazzling smile. It made my heart ache. If Mom were here, she'd brag to Grandma about all of my accomplishments, making a point to have Grandma acknowledge me as more than the second-best granddaughter.

"What about you, Emily?" Grandma asked, yanking me back to reality.

"I'm sorry," I said, meeting her stare. "I didn't hear you."

"Are you going to join the cheerleading squad with Whitney or maybe the honor society?" Grandma asked.

I couldn't stop my bark of laughter, and the sound caused Grandma to wince, surprised. "I don't think they'd want me on the cheerleading squad, Grandma," I said. "I'm about as flexible as a steel rod."

"Yes, but you're a beautiful girl," my grandma said, her expression serious. "You'd be a nice addition to the team."

Grandma thinks I'm beautiful? I nearly fell off my chair at the compliment.

"You just need to do something with that mess of curls on your head and wear some makeup," she continued. "You looked radiant at your mother's funeral, dear. Did you keep that makeup Darlene bought for you?"

My mouth fell open. Leave it to Grandma to ruin the compliment. Not only did she insult my hair, but she told me I looked radiant at my mother's funeral—the ultimate irony.

"Emily joined our church youth group," Whitney chimed in. "She had a great time on Thursday."

I turned to Whitney and found the apologetic expression again. Was she defending me?

"That's nice, dear," Grandma said. "Darlene, how is Chuck's job going? Is he still very busy at the bank? I heard on the news that the market was picking up some."

By the time we got back to the SUV, I'd heard the details of

Chuck's daily work schedule and more about Grandma's aches and pains than I ever wanted to know.

During the ride to my dad's shop, I wondered if Whitney had deliberately taken our grandmother's focus off criticizing me. I glanced at her from the backseat, hoping to catch her eye, but she was busy wearing out the keypad on her new phone.

Within twenty minutes, we arrived at my dad's new shop. Cameronville Auto and Body was a typical collision repair center and much like my father's business back home. It was a cinder block building with a tiny office and waiting room off a huge garage, including stalls for the body technicians and mechanics, at least two dozen toolboxes, three paint booths, a frame machine, a lift, and a cleaning bay. Tools whirled and banged while loud voices shouted from within the garage. The smells in the air were comforting and familiar — dust, antifreeze, and grounded-up metal.

Darlene and I stepped into the office and found my dad sitting behind the small desk, talking on the phone. He looked up, smiled, and motioned for us to sit in the two chairs in front of the desk.

While he finished his conversation discussing parts and labor time, I fished my new phone from my pocket and examined it, scrolling through the contacts list and then the sent and received calls. I found I'd received a text message from Megan congratulating me on my new phone and asking how things were going.

"What have you ladies been up to today?" my dad asked, hanging up the phone.

"We've been shopping," Darlene announced, placing her purse on her lap. "Emily, show your dad what you got."

"I have a phone." I handed it to him. "Whitney upgraded, so I got her old one."

"Wow." My dad pushed a few buttons, looking impressed. "Very nice."

"It was very inexpensive to add her to our plan, so don't worry about anything," Darlene said.

He looked at his sister. "Thank you, Darlene. It's awfully generous of you to do this for Emily."

I studied my dad's expression, wondering if it was humiliating for him to accept handouts from his younger sister. It made me uncomfortable, but my dad looked happy. It totally baffled me. Didn't he resent her generosity like I did? And how come he readily accepted charity from his sister but wouldn't let me get a job to help out?

"We also went to the mall," Darlene continued. "The girls got some new clothes." She gestured at me. "Tell him what you got, Emily."

"Some jeans and two sweaters," I said, again feeling weird about the whole thing. I wondered if Darlene considered me one of those kids from third-world countries that you can adopt on television. *For fifty cents a day, the price of a cup of coffee, Darlene can give a poor, unstylish niece a makeover.*

My dad shook his head and smiled. "You've really gone above and beyond, Darlene. Someday I'll pay you back."

She waved off the comment. "Oh, don't be silly, Brad. We're family." She looped an arm around my shoulder and gave me a tight squeeze. "Emily's like my other daughter."

Yeah. Right. I resisted the urge to roll my eyes. Couldn't Dad see this was just a show for her? Her goal was to look good, not do good.

"We went to see Mom too," Darlene continued. "She told us to tell you hello."

"How's she doing?" he asked, leaning forward on the desk and folding his hands.

"She's doing all right." She shrugged. "She seems a little more forgetful than she has been, but overall her health is good. She repeated herself quite a bit while she talked."

I bit my lower lip and wished I could tell my dad the truth. *And she still thinks I'm a screwup with bad hair.*

My dad smiled at me. "I bet she was happy to see you."

I snorted and studied my phone, avoiding the warning look I was certain he was shooting my way.

"Oh, yes," Darlene said, ignoring my reaction. "I think Mom was very pleased to see both of her granddaughters." She stood. "So, do we get the twenty-five cent tour of your new shop, Brad?"

My dad stood and started for the door, gesturing for us to walk through. "There's not much to see. It's just your typical shop." He steered us through the large garage area, rattling off the names of machines and workers, speaking loudly over the noise of the hammers, tools, and the dozen technicians.

It occurred to me that Whitney hadn't followed us into the office, and I scanned the area, wondering if she was in the shop or back in the SUV texting her friends. I spotted her back on the other side of the shop gesturing and speaking to someone I couldn't see beyond a car.

I turned the corner and found Whitney chatting with Zander, who was leaning on a broom handle and laughing. Something that felt a whole lot like jealousy bubbled up inside me.

While I certainly didn't "own" Zander, it bugged me that Whitney was speaking to him with such animation. She flipped her hair off her shoulder and continued to tell her story, which seemed to be a laugh riot. I gritted my teeth and approached them, wondering why she had to hone in on a guy I liked when she had Chad, Mr. All-American Captain of the Football Team. Couldn't she leave the only motorhead in our neighborhood for me?

He was clad in dark-blue work trousers and a matching blue button-up shirt with the shop name on one side of his chest and "Zander" on the other. I'd seen plenty of mechanics and auto body technicians dressed in their uniforms, and, as corny as it sounded, I had to admit that some of them really looked good in them. Tyler was one, but Zander took the cake. He looked *really* handsome. I guess Mom was right when she once said there was something about a man in a uniform, and it didn't only apply to the military.

"Hey there!" Zander said, his eyes lighting up when he saw me. "What's going on?"

"Not much. Am I interrupting something?" I asked, hoping the question wasn't laced with the envy rioting within me.

"No." Zander shook his head. "Whitney was just telling me what the quarterback from the other team said to Chad last night."

"You should've been there," Whitney said, giving her hair another toss.

I'd heard the story twice so far today, once at breakfast and once in the car on the way to the shop, and it wasn't that interesting. In a lame attempt to start a fistfight, the quarterback from Ridge Park High had told Chad he threw like a girl. Big deal. As if guys didn't make cracks like that to each other every day.

In an effort to change the subject, I pointed at the broom. "I see you're putting your mechanical talent to good use."

Whitney guffawed. "Emily!" she squealed. "I had no idea you had a sarcastic edge."

"You obviously don't know your cousin," Zander said with a grin. "This isn't the first time she's put me in my place. She told me that if I want to fix my car, I should trade it for a Chevy."

Whitney snorted and covered her mouth.

I laughed, my cheeks heating with embarrassment. "He's right."

"And I'll have you know that I push this broom with pride." He moved the broom with a flourish. "Someone has to do the dirty work around here."

"In all seriousness," I began, "tell me that's not all they have you doing. You're way too talented to only do cleanup."

He leaned the broom against the wall. "They do let me do some real work too." He nodded toward a Ford pickup with primer on the quarter panel sitting in a stall across the shop. "I helped fix that one over there. It's waiting for paint." He pointed to a Chevrolet pickup on the opposite side of the shop. "That one over there belongs to one of the technicians. I helped him fix the AC earlier."

"Really?" I raised my eyebrows. "Was it a complicated AC problem?"

He shrugged. "Yeah, I guess."

"Would you consider helping me diagnose the problem with my dad's AC?" I asked.

"Hmm." He rubbed his chin. "I don't know. I'll have to see if I can work it into my schedule."

I clicked my tongue and shook my head. "Well, if you can't help me, then I don't think I can help you with your car."

He laughed. "Of course I'll help you. Let me know when you want to look at it." He gestured toward the phone in my hand. "I hear Whitney hooked you up with a phone today. Very cool."

"Yeah, I've got a phone." I held it up. "It has all of her old contacts, so you're in there."

"I like the camo theme better than the sequins. Can I see it?" He took if from my hand, hit a few buttons, and another phone began to play a song I'd heard on the radio. He fished the phone from his pocket, opened it up and started typing. Holding it up, I read "Chevy Girl" on the screen. "Now you're programmed in. I can send you texts telling you my Dodge can outrun your Chevy."

I laughed. "I'll have to change your contact name to Mr. Mopar."

Whitney shook her head. "You guys are two peas in a pod."

My cheeks burned again.

"Are you going to Kristin's party tonight?" Whitney asked. "Should be a really great time."

I studied my phone, and started to answer Megan's text from earlier.

"Hello?" Whitney asked. "Did you hear me?"

"Huh?" I looked up. "Were you talking to me?"

"Yeah!" She shook her head. "Who did you think I was talking to?"

"Zander." I pointed at him.

"I'm not sure." He ran his hand through his hair, obviously stalling or fabricating an excuse to not attend. "I have some stuff I need to get done at the house."

"You can work on that stupid car any time," Whitney said, jamming a hand on her small hip. "This party is going to be a blast, and everyone will be there."

He folded his arms across his chest. "I'll see. I'm not sure yet."

She looked at me. "What about you?"

"I'm not sure," I said. "I was hoping to go to the movies with Chelsea." It was the truth, and I had texted her earlier. I just hadn't heard back from her yet.

She blew out a sigh. "Why do I even bother asking you two?"

"Girls!" Darlene called from the bay door leading to the parking lot. "Let's go!"

"See ya," Whitney said, marching across toward her mother.

"I guess we're leaving," I said.

"See ya later," he said. "Maybe I'll call you."

I grinned. "And maybe I'll answer."

He laughed in response. As I started toward my dad, my heart fluttered.

chapter ten

My dad stood in the doorway of my room later that evening. "Why didn't you go to the party with Whitney?"

I closed my journal and placed it next to me on the window seat. "I didn't want to." I shrugged. "I was hoping to go to the movies with Chelsea, but I haven't heard back from her yet."

He lowered himself onto the edge of the bed. "You should call her and see if she wants to go out. Don't sit in here by yourself." Apparently, even if I spent an entire day out with Darlene and Whitney, I was still in danger of becoming a hermit.

I glanced down at my flip-flops and then at my phone sitting on the dresser. It wasn't worth a fight. "Okay. I'll send her another text. Does that make up for blowing off the party at Kristin's house?"

To my surprise, my dad smiled. "Yes, that works."

"Fine." I retrieved my phone. "I'll call her now."

"Great!" My dad stood. "I just want you happy, Emily. That's my goal. We all need some happiness after the year we had."

After he was gone, I texted Chelsea:

Hi. Did you get my text? Want to go to a movie 2nite?

While I waited for her reply, I went back to writing in my journal:

Saturday, September 3
Dear Mom,

*I endured a "girls' day out" with Darlene and Whitney
today. It actually wasn't as bad as you'd think. Grandma was
critical of me, as usual, but Whitney came to my defense. I'm
starting to feel like I could be friends with Whitney, and it's
kind of nice. For some reason, I have a good feeling—a better
feeling about things. I don't know if it's because of Zander or
something else. I just think things may get better. I just wish I
could find my faith in God again.*

My phone pinged and I opened it to find a return text:

Hey Em. Glad you got phone. At Dads for wkend. C U Tues.
Hope you njoy holiday. Chels.

The holiday! I'd forgotten Monday was Labor Day, and
Chelsea went to her father's house for every holiday weekend.

I needed another avenue to get my dad off my back about
missing the party. I glanced out the window and spotted Zander
walking over to the garage. He punched the keypad, and the
door lifted.

Perfect!

I checked my hair in the mirror and then felt silly for the effort.
Why was I worried about my appearance? I knew the answer—I
liked Zander. Really *liked* him. But I wondered if he and I would
make a good couple. Yes, we had a lot in common, but our little
talk about faith during youth group still bothered me. I couldn't
endure it if he preached to me every time I expressed a doubt.

I made my way down the stairs and past my dad, who
was watching a show featuring a guy building a souped-up
motorcycle.

"Are you and Chelsea going to the movies?" he asked as I
passed him.

"Nope. She's at her dad's." I stopped in the doorway. "I'm going to see Zander in his garage. Does that qualify as a social engagement?"

"Yes," he called after me. "I'll accept that."

I shook my head. "Glad you approve," I deadpanned. "See you later."

Zander was perched on a stool and studying a car manual when I entered the garage.

"So, let me get this straight," I began. "You work on cars and push a broom all day for a living and then you come home and work on cars for pleasure."

Grinning, he closed the manual and placed it on the counter beside him. "Being a fellow motorhead, I figured you of all people would understand that."

I leaned against the car and crossed my arms over my shirt. "Yeah, I do actually. I could work on them twenty-four seven, if I was able." I pointed toward the door. "That keypad you have outside, I see you use it all the time."

"I know what you're going to ask." He gestured toward the Jeep. "I lost the remote control for the door. I actually managed to lose a total of four, and I'm sick of paying for new ones. So I have to use the keypad. I had each controller on the visor in my Jeep with the convertible top off. It doesn't take a rocket scientist to figure out how I lost them."

I tried in vain to stifle a laugh.

He gestured toward the side door. "I also managed to mis-place the key for the side door, so I can't use that door either."

Without warning, I guffawed.

"It's okay." He shrugged. "You can laugh. I did. If you ever need to get in here, I'll tell you the secret code. Although it's really not much of a secret. Just hit zero, six, zero, seven, and then enter. Although, sometimes you have to hit enter twice."

"Zero six zero seven?" I asked.

He smiled. "Yeah. My birthday."

"June seventh?"

He nodded. "That's right."

"Cool." *Now I know your birthday.*

"When's your birthday?" he asked.

"November twenty-fourth," I said. "This year it's Thanksgiving."

"Cool," he said.

"I guess so." I shrugged, not wanting to admit how much of a double whammy it would be to experience my first birthday and Thanksgiving without my mom all rolled into the same day. "So why didn't you go to Kristin's party?"

He hopped down from the stool and crossed to the refrigerator. "I had more important things to do. Why aren't you there?" He returned with two cans of Coke and tossed one to me.

"I had much more important things to do—specifically, avoid overcrowded parties with people I barely know. I'd planned to go to the movies with Chelsea, but she's at her dad's. I forgot she goes to see him every holiday weekend." I opened the can, which popped and fizzed loudly. "Thanks for the drink."

"You're welcome." He dragged over a stool and set it in front of me. "Have a seat. So I'm your second choice for the evening. Wait a minute." He pretended to count off on his fingers. "I'm your *third* choice since you considered the party and then Chelsea before you came over here."

"That's not necessarily true." I grinned. "I'd considered staying in my room too."

He laughed. "You're never short on comebacks are you?"

"Nope. How was your day?" I hopped up onto the stool.

He took a long drink of soda and then shrugged. "It was the usual. Lots of sweeping, some real car work. Not exciting but good just the same."

"How's the new boss?"

Zander nodded. "The new boss is good. Your dad knows what he's doing, and I think the other guys like him too."

I held my finger over the edge of the can. "His old employees liked him a whole lot. He ran a good shop."

"Can I ask what happened?"

"Mom's cancer," I whispered, studying the Coke logo. "It took everything from us—the business, our money, our house, and most importantly, Mom."

"I'm truly sorry," he said.

I glanced up and found his eyes full of sympathy, and it was almost overwhelming. "Thank you."

"So, how was your day?" he asked, lifting the can again.

I snorted. "Not as good as yours."

He raised an eyebrow. "No? You got a cell phone, right? That was good."

"Yeah. I got Whitney's hand-me-down." I sighed. "I feel like a charity case. It makes me crazy. Like I'll always be less than her, you know?"

He shook his head and seemed contemplative. "No, I don't see that at all."

"Well, here's an example." I set the can on the trunk of the car behind me. "We went to see our grandma—my dad's mom, who obviously is also Darlene's mom. Everything with Grandma has always been about Whitney. She even would call my house back home and brag about Whitney."

He snorted. "You're kidding, right?"

"I'm so *not* kidding," I said, gesturing with my hands. "Grandma would call every Sunday night and tell us everything Whitney was doing: her straight As, her cheerleading, her volunteer work with the youth group, on and on. So today we go see Grandma, and it's the first time I've seen her since the funeral. She immediately criticizes my hair."

"Your hair?" Zander looked surprised. "What's wrong with your hair?"

I pursed my lips. "*Everything* is wrong with my hair. Darlene asks me all the time if I want her help to straighten it."

"Why would you straighten it?"

"Beats me. Darlene even dragged me to a salon to have my hair straightened and my makeup and nails done the day of the funeral." I pulled a strand of curls over my shoulder and held it up for emphasis. "She hates my hair. Today my grandma suggested I borrow Whitney's shampoo to lessen the frizz."

Zander shook his head, staring at my hair. I wished I could read his mind to see if he thought I was insane or just overreacting.

"There's nothing wrong with your hair," he said. "In fact, I like your hair."

"You do?"

"Yeah." He shrugged. "It's, well, nice."

"Nice?" I repeated slowly, wondering what it meant. Did he find my hair as captivating as I found his eyes?

He laughed. "Does that somehow make me not manly or something? Believe me, I'm a guy. I'm just saying that your hair is part of what makes you ... you."

"Wow," I said, flabbergasted by his words. Had I finally met someone who accepted me for who I was without trying to make me into something I'm not?

I grasped my can in my hands. "Grandma even asked me if I was going to join cheerleading with Whitney. My dad, of all people, asked me that the night we moved in. *They* are both off their rockers."

He sipped his Coke and then shook his head. "I know what that's like to try to be something you're not, and it doesn't work out. That's how I messed up my knee."

"What do you mean?"

"I was trying so hard to be like my brother in order to win my dad's approval, and I wound up pushing myself too hard and having knee surgery for the effort." He glanced down at his leg. "All I ever heard was what a great athlete and student Andrew was. So, to shut my dad up, I went out for football and didn't even make it through the season. I made some great friends during my time on the team, but Andrew's life wasn't for me."

He gestured around the garage. "This is where I want to be, not on the football field or in medical school. I finally got tired of fighting with my dad. I talked to Pastor Keith about it, prayed about it, and then I finally told my dad that I have to be me. He was angry for a while, but the arguments finally stopped."

"That helped you?" I asked.

He looked surprised at my response. "Absolutely. Hey, have you thought more about what I said during youth group? I mean, you're talking to God now, right?"

I studied my soda can. "Yeah, sure. Of course I am." I was too embarrassed to admit the trouble I'd had praying, or that God wasn't exactly talking to me either. I was also hoping Zander would drop the subject.

"You don't have to lie to me," he said softly.

Looking up I found his curious eyes watching me. Was he reading my thoughts? "I'm not lying," I insisted, my cheeks heating. My eyes were drawn to the cross around his neck. His faith was intimidating and intriguing all at once. Like it had been for my mom, it seemed so easy for him. I wished I could harness it and make some of it my own, but I didn't know how. All I knew was faith had to come from your heart, and mine was only filled with doubt.

"Are you going to church tomorrow?" he asked.

"I guess." I shrugged.

"Church might make you feel better about things." He placed the can on the workbench beside him. "I've found that whenever I'm really down, I'll read my Bible or pray, and it lifts me up."

He sounded just like Whitney. I studied his eyes, trying to picture him curled up on the sofa with the Bible in his lap. Somehow, I could see it. I could almost imagine him nodding in agreement with the verses and smiling as he turned the page.

But that was Zander, not me. I hadn't been able to crack open a Bible since last year, and I couldn't see myself doing it now. I wouldn't even know what chapter to read.

Zander was a better person than I ever would be. If he knew the extent of the doubt that was in my heart, he would never want to spend time with me. For sure he'd call me a heretic or an atheist and send me on my way.

"Are you okay?" he asked, pushing up from the stool and standing. "You look worried about something."

"Not at all." I popped up from my stool, determined to take the focus away from my anxiety. I needed to change the subject quickly. I really liked him and didn't want to see this issue come between us.

"Are we going to stand around all day talking or are we going to get this Dodge running?" I walked around to the front of the car and surveyed the engine. "Do you want my help or not?"

He grinned. "I love it when a woman takes charge." He gestured toward the toolboxes behind me. "Have at it."

I started fishing through the drawers in a toolbox behind me. "Watch and learn."

He laughed. "Yes, ma'am."

chapter eleven

The following morning, I slipped into the seat next to Logan at the end of the church pew. My father, Darlene, and Chuck were on the other side of Logan, and Whitney was in the back on the other side of the church with her friends. Cupping my hand to my mouth, I yawned. Zander and I had worked on his car until after midnight.

By the time I'd left to go home last night, we had the engine completely torn apart, but it would take quite a bit of time to rebuild it. The subject of God and faith didn't come up while we worked on the car. Instead, we'd talked about less intimidating stuff—transmissions, music, movies, books, and school. It was a fun and easy discussion. I'd felt so at ease with him, as if I could say anything—except admit that I wasn't sure I believed in God anymore. That was the one thing about Zander that kept me from completely opening up to him. I was sure he didn't understand my doubts and would just keep giving me more advice that felt like empty platitudes. Thankfully, the key to steering clear of the topic of religion was to keep a wrench in Zander's hands. I could handle that.

But I was paying for our time in the garage. This morning I'd had to drag myself out of bed and into the shower after Darlene knocked on my door. I considered feigning a headache and going back to sleep, but, truthfully, I'd come to church for one reason—to see Zander again.

How sacrilegious was that?

Pushing thoughts of Zander away, I busied myself with reviewing the bulletin for the service. I was studying it when I felt eyes staring at me. Glancing up, I found Zander smiling down at me. He wore a green collared shirt and tan Dockers.

"Hi," I said, pushing a lock of hair behind my ear. I absently smoothed the skirt of the blue sundress Whitney had insisted I borrow from her.

"Is this seat taken?" he asked, gesturing toward the vacant spot next to me.

"No." I pushed over, closer to Logan. "Sit."

"Thanks." He slipped in beside me, his leg brushing mine. He leaned over me and greeted Logan, my dad, and Whitney's parents, all delighted to see him join us. "How are you?" he asked, turning back to me.

"Tired," I admitted with a smile.

He chuckled. "You're a master mechanic."

"You're just saying that because you want me to rebuild the engine," I teased.

"Yeah, you're right. You're better at this stuff than I am."

I waved the thought off. "Please. I'm sure you've been doing it longer than I have."

"I think I was a little older when my grandfather put a wrench in my hand." He flipped through the bulletin.

It suddenly occurred to me that I'd never asked him who'd taught him about cars. If his father was pushing him to go to medical school, than it couldn't have been Dr. Stewart. There'd had to have been someone else, but Zander had never shared that information. "Your grandfather taught you?" I asked.

He looked up at me and nodded.

I opened my mouth to ask him more about his grandfather, but Pastor Keith began the service by welcoming everyone.

Throughout the service, I was very aware of Zander beside me. The aroma of his musky cologne filled my senses, and his leg and arm brushed against me a couple of times. While I tried to concentrate on the pastor's words, my eyes would steal occasional glances of Zander, and he would smile, looking genuinely happy to be sharing church with me, and it made me feel guilty. I hoped he didn't get a false impression.

When the service was over, we filed out of the sanctuary and followed the crowd to Fellowship Hall for coffee hour. I stood between my dad and Zander and ate chocolate chip cookies while they discussed how nice the service had been and then chatted about work.

"Would it be okay if we went to J2A together and then I'll give Emily a lift home?" Zander asked my dad between bites of an oatmeal raisin cookie. He quickly explained to my dad what J2A was.

I raised an eyebrow and studied Zander. Did he really think I wanted to go?

I gave a sigh of defeat. Who was I kidding? Of course I would succumb to another hour at church if it meant being with Zander.

"Sure." My dad shrugged. "Does that sound okay to you?"

"Yeah," I said. "Sounds fine."

Zander and I sat at the back of the classroom, the same room where the movie had been shown. I spotted Whitney up front with her friends, and when she saw me, she waved. I waved back and then scanned the room, recognizing some of the faces from youth group Thursday evening. Jenna, the youth director, came in from the hallway and smiled at me.

"Good morning, everyone," Jenna said, stepping to the front

of the room. "It's good to see you all here." She looked at me. "I'm excited to see new faces here. Welcome, Emily."

I nodded, and when all eyes turned to me I slumped a little in my seat.

"Today we'll continue our Bible verse discussion. We'll pick a verse and discuss what it means to us." Jenna held up a basket filled with slips of paper. "Who would like to pick today?"

"Emily should pick," Whitney announced, smiling at me.

Thanks a lot, cuz. I shook my head. "That's okay. Someone else can."

Jenna looked pleased. "No, I think it's a great idea." She made her way back to me and placed the basket on my table. "Go ahead. Pick a verse and read it aloud."

I hesitated.

"It's okay," Zander said softly. "I'll read it if you'd like me to."

"I can do it," I said, sitting up straight. Far be it from me to be a helpless female. I snatched a slip of paper from the basket.

Jenna moved to the front of the room and sat on a table. "Read it when you're ready."

My eyes scanned the paper, and my heart thumped. The paper read *Deuteronomy 31:6: Be strong and courageous. Do not be afraid or terrified because of them, for the* LORD *your God goes with you; he will never leave you nor forsake you.*

How could I ever read this out loud?

"Sure you don't want me to read it?" Zander asked.

I was really tired of him reading my mind. How was it that this guy could detect my every insecurity?

"No, thanks," I snapped with a bit more force than I'd planned. "Really, I can do it." I cleared my throat and read the verse, trying in vain to fight the quaver in my voice.

"What does that verse mean to you, Emily?" Jenna asked. "Or how does it make you feel?"

I blanched, a lump forming in my throat. Was she trying to make me cry in front of these staring faces?

"I don't know," I whispered, lying through my teeth.

The verse had hit me right in the chest. It was as if someone was speaking to me, but I couldn't put my finger on whether it was God or my mom. Maybe it was both. No matter who it was, I suddenly felt like I did the day the congregation sang "Beautiful Savior." I wanted to run and hide, but I couldn't make a spectacle of myself again.

"Anyone else?" Jenna asked, scanning the class.

Mindy, the girl who'd shared her popcorn with me Thursday, raised her hand and prattled on about God's love and protection while Zander leaned close to me.

"You okay?" he whispered, placing his hand on my arm. His palm was warm and soft, despite the Gojo he'd used to clean off the grease last night after we'd worked on the car. I absently wondered if he'd used a lot of hand lotion before going to bed.

"Yeah," I said, clearing my throat and wiping my eyes. "I'm fine."

"You don't look fine," he said, still leaning so close that his cologne tickled my nose. "You want to go?"

"No." I forced a smile. "I just have something in my eye."

"Something in your eye," he repeated. "Right."

For the rest of class, I held the verse in my right hand while fingering my cross with my left. I couldn't stop thoughts of my mom from flooding my mind. I wondered again how my mother had kept her faith alive during her illness. How could she pray through everything that was happening to her? I know she read the Bible nearly every night, and she insisted we all accompany her to church on Sunday and even some Wednesday nights before she became too ill to travel out of our little house much. My mother's faith baffled me. She knew she wasn't going to make it, but she still believed until the very end.

My mother was still in the forefront of my mind when Zander and I stepped out into the hallway after class. He gave me a smile and started to say something but was interrupted by Whitney.

"I'll go find Logan and meet you at the car, okay?" she asked me.

"Actually, we have plans," Zander said.

"Really?" Whitney's eyebrows careened to her hairline.

"We have to discuss my car," he said with a smile. "Right?"

"Right," I said. "We still have to make a plan of attack for the rebuild."

"Oh." Whitney looked between us and shrugged. "You kids go and have fun. I'll see you later."

Zander and I fell in step on our way down the hallway, and he held the door open for me.

"Did you really want to talk about the car?" I asked on our way to his Jeep.

"Not necessarily. I just didn't want her and Logan to join us for lunch," he said, wrenching the door open for me.

"We're going to lunch?" I asked.

"Yup." He nodded toward the seat. "Hop in."

I sat across from Zander in the booth at the Cameronville Diner. The restaurant was bustling with the lunchtime crowd. Families dressed in their Sunday best clogged the booths and tables while servers weaved through the sea of chairs, delivering food. The aroma of burgers and fries filled the air.

"What's good?" I asked, perusing the menu.

"They make a mean burger," Zander said, placing his menu on the table.

"Hence the delicious smells?" I asked, looking up and seeing his smile.

He grinned. "Yup."

The server stopped by, and we both ordered burgers and fries. She returned a few minutes later with our Cokes.

"Tell me about your grandfather," I said once the server was gone.

Zander swished the straw around in his glass. "He was the most amazing mechanic that ever lived. Or so I always believed."

"Oh, he's gone," I whispered, internally kicking myself for bringing up a sad subject after my own emotional J2A class. "I'm sorry."

"It's okay." Zander took a long drink and then settled back in the seat. "He passed away about two years ago, but he lived a good, long life. He was almost ninety. My mom is the youngest of five, and my grandpa was in his forties when she was born."

"Did he live here?" I asked.

He nodded. "He worked at the shop where your dad and I work. In fact, he was the original owner — Jack bought him out a few years ago."

"So that's why you said your family has known the owner for years."

"Exactly. My grandpa was a mechanic all his life. He started teaching me about cars when I was around six or seven, I guess. He always had a project car in his garage, and he and I would tinker." Zander glanced out the window toward the traffic rushing by on Highway 29. "My dad used to tell me it was a good hobby but not something I should pursue full-time."

"Sounds like Chuck," I said, lifting my glass. "He told Logan the same thing."

"I asked my dad once why it was good enough for Grandpa and not me, and he said that Grandpa didn't have options. Back when Grandpa was growing up, he didn't have the money for college, so he did the only thing he knew, which was cars."

Zander shook his head. "Dad doesn't understand having a passion for cars. He could never accept that my grandfather was happy with his choices in life."

I sipped my drink. "My dad is happy too. I mean, of course there are things he wishes he could change, but I don't think he ever regrets his career choice."

There was a pause, and Zander's expression turned serious. "Was J2A too much for you today?"

"No," I said quickly. Where were some tools when I needed them? "It was okay."

"You don't have to lie to me. I could tell that you were ..." He paused, as if choosing his words. "You were upset."

I studied his expression, wishing I could read his mind. "No, I wasn't."

He smiled, and my heart fluttered. How corny was that?

"You may be able to hide it from others, but you can't hide it from me. I think I know you pretty well."

No, you don't. "You do, huh?" I gave him a challenging smile. "So what am I thinking about right now?"

The server appeared with our burgers.

"Lunch," he said with a laugh.

"Bingo," I agreed, snatching a fry from my plate.

"So, what's your dream car?" Zander asked as he steered the Jeep into the driveway later that afternoon.

"My dream car?" I asked, twirling a lock of hair around my finger.

"Yeah." He threw the truck in neutral and jammed the emergency brake before killing the engine. "What one car do you wish you could build? Of course, money isn't a factor. Pretend it's free."

"Oh," I said with a sigh. "That's easy. A sixty-nine Camaro."

He raised his eyebrows. "From the sound of that sigh, I'd guess you came close to your dream."

"I did. But that went bye-bye along with everything else we had to sell." I glanced toward my dad's Suburban parked by the detached garage and thought back to the day Dad had a buyer. I'd seen tears in his eyes when he told me. I knew why it killed him to let it go—he knew how much it meant to me.

"Was it an SS?" he asked, pulling the keys from the ignition.

"No." I gathered my purse from the floorboard. "I never could've afforded an SS. It was just a plain-Jane sixty-nine that needed some TLC. Dad got it cheap off a customer because it needed so much work. I had gotten it back running, and a guy bought it off us just a few months ago. I was going to ask my dad's friend to paint it metallic purple when it was done, but I never got that far. I did hear it run once, and I actually drove it around the block. That was about it." I leaned back in the seat and smiled. "I have to say it sounded pretty good too. I did a good job with the rebuild."

"I bet you did. We'll have to find you another one someday."

I blinked at his words. They sounded so long-term. Like a commitment to ... something. I didn't know what, but I kind of liked the sound of it.

"Thanks for hanging out with me today." He pushed his door open and climbed from the Jeep.

I climbed out and met him at the front end. "It was fun."

"My dad said something about going away for one night to our place at the beach since tomorrow's a holiday. He wanted to leave yesterday, but he was called in to work for an emergency. My mom insisted we get away since she thinks my dad's a workaholic." He shook his head. "It seems silly to go away overnight, but my mom always says we need more family time. If I protest, it turns into a huge argument."

"Oh." I tried my best to hide my disappointment. I had

assumed we'd spend the rest of the holiday weekend working on his car. "Well, have fun."

"I'd rather be here working on the car." He pointed toward the garage. "But I guess the car will be here when I get back. We can start on it Tuesday night if you feel like it."

"Sure," I said, adjusting my purse on my shoulder. An awkward silence fell between us. I felt like he was expecting something. Should I hug him? Did he think we were a couple now? I thought we were just friends, but what did I know?

He smiled. "I guess I'll see you Tuesday."

"Have a good trip. Be safe." I started toward the gate.

"One more thing." He trotted over to me.

"Yes?" I held my breath, wondering if he was going to kiss me or hug me. The sheer idea of a hug or a kiss from Zander Stewart made my insides warm.

"About J2A," he began. "I know you were upset by that verse. Don't stop yourself from listening to the meaning."

"Huh?" I grimaced, trying to decipher what he was saying.

He grinned, revealing that adorable dimple. "What I mean is, don't give up on God. If you feel like he's trying to tell you something, open up your heart and listen."

"Oh." I stared at him, dumbfounded. "Okay."

"See you Tuesday." He turned and headed for the house.

As he walked away, I shook my head. Dating him was so *not* an option. I couldn't stand being his mission project.

Later that evening, I stood in the kitchen and pulled the folded slip of paper containing the verse from my purse. I stared at it, rolling the words over again and again in my mind. What did they mean? Was God trying to talk to me? If so, what was he truly saying?

Deuteronomy 31:6: Be strong and courageous. Do not be

afraid or terrified because of them, for the LORD *your God goes with you; he will never leave you nor forsake you.*

I pulled the words apart and then put them back together in my mind. Glancing out the sliding glass doors, I stared at Zander's garage. The garage was always my solace, the place I'd gone to think and to escape the stress of my mom's illness.

Gnawing my lower lip, I debated going to his garage and working on the car without him. He'd given me the code and said I could go in there. It was an invitation. It was permission. And at that moment I needed to go there.

Folding the piece of paper, I shoved it in my pocket and opened the sliding glass door with a whoosh. I passed through the gate to his garage, where I punched in the code, opening the door.

As I stepped into the garage, a calmness rained down on me. It was as if I'd come home. At least, it felt more like home than Whitney's house.

I ran my fingers along his row of toolboxes, opening the drawers and glancing through his collection of basic tools he needed for projects. I stepped past the car and over to the workbench covered in engine parts that we had stripped down.

After sliding on Zander's thick gloves, which were huge on my hands and covered my arms past my elbows, I pulled a respirator, and I spent the next hour washing parts. I scrubbed them with a wire brush and the chore was cathartic. I let my mind wander, contemplating my feelings for Zander along with that Bible verse.

At one point, I closed my eyes and tried to pray. I tried reciting the Lord's Prayer, but the words felt rushed and empty. I still felt a distance between God and me. Was it me? Was I doing something wrong?

After a while, I'd washed a few of the pieces but I felt as if my soul had taken a bubble bath. Although I hadn't been able to talk to God, I felt like I'd accomplished something. I felt different, but I didn't know why. I locked up the garage and made my way into the house and back up to my room.

After taking a long shower, I fished the Bible verse from my pocket, plucked the Scotch tape from the bookshelf, and taped the piece of paper to a blank page in my journal. Then I began to write.

Sunday September 4
Dear Mom,
Church was different today. I didn't cry, but I did get emotional. And it was all because of a verse I picked from a basket during J2A, which is what they call Sunday school here. The verse seemed to speak to me personally. I guess that sounds crazy, but I keep thinking that it was meant for me. There was a reason why Jenna handed that basket to me and not one of the other kids. And when I read the verse, I almost felt like I did the night you died, but it wasn't exactly the same. But it was powerful, so very powerful.

After church, Zander took me to lunch at his favorite diner, and he told me about how he lost his grandfather, who taught him about cars. They were close, so it had to be difficult for him. It seems that the way he dealt with losing his grandpa was to turn to God and lean on him. I wish I could do that. I wish I could open up to God. But I can't seem to reach him. I'm going to ask Zander how he got through his grandpa's death—not just trite phrases, but something real. Maybe he can tell me something that will help me, Mom. Maybe he can unlock something inside me that will help me work through my grief.

Zander went to his beach house with his parents, so I went out and worked on the car a little bit. I felt stirred to go after reading the verse I attached to this page. Working on the car

*helped me clear my head, but it didn't help me reach out to
God. I was sure I'd be able to reach him in the garage. What
am I doing wrong? Is something wrong with me, Mom?*

*I tried reciting the Lord's Prayer—nothing like starting
with the basics—and it felt forced. But I felt something while
I was in the garage. I'm not sure what it was, but it felt good.
Still, that verse changed something inside me. I don't know
what it is, but it's something.*

Yawning, I closed the journal and placed it on the nightstand. Snuggling down under the covers, I wondered if Zander
was having fun with his parents at their beach house. I couldn't
imagine how it felt to have two houses, two addresses, two
places to call home.

I rolled onto my side, and the verse from J2A seeped through
my mind again. Closing my hand over my mother's cross, I
wondered what verses were her favorites. With that thought on
my mind, I fell asleep.

chapter twelve

So you had fun at your dad's?" I asked, sinking into the seat across from Chelsea and pulling out my lunch bag.

Chelsea shrugged. "I guess so. The sad thing is I missed the twins. My mom said she had a hard time putting them to bed at night, so she thinks they missed me too."

I shook my head and fished my sandwich from the bag. "Wow. That's cool that you're so close to them. I bet they'll always feel like your sons rather than your brothers."

She popped a fry into her mouth. "Probably. I guess that sounds weird, huh?"

"Not really. I mean, there's a huge age difference, so it really makes sense." I opened my bottle of water.

"What did you do this weekend?" Chelsea asked.

"Not much," I began. "I just hung around—"

Before I could complete my sentence, the chair kitty-corner to me spun around with a whoosh and a body appeared in it. "Hey," Zander said, leaning on his elbows on the table. "How's it going?"

Chelsea and I exchanged stunned expressions.

"Are you slumming, Stewart?" Chelsea asked. "Or are you lost?"

"Neither, Morris." He snatched two fries from her tray and stuffed them into his mouth. "I was just wondering what Curtis is having for lunch, but yours looks much more appetizing."

Chelsea gave me a grin so wide I wondered if her pearly white teeth would fall from her mouth.

He took another fry and looked at me. "Your lunch is boring."

"She has that every day: turkey sandwich, apple, and a bottle of water. Sometimes she substitutes a pear for the apple." Chelsea scrunched her nose. "It's very boring. The only color is in the red apple."

"You're right. It's not a very exciting lunch," he agreed, taking another fry off Chelsea's tray.

"Would you two please not talk about me as if I'm not here?" I said. "You sound like my grandmother."

Zander reached for another fry, and Chelsea swatted his hand. "Go get your own, Stewart!"

"Fine, fine." Zander stood. "I'll be right back." He looked between us. "Want anything?"

"No thanks," I said.

"Get me more fries," Chelsea said.

"I'll be back." He took off toward the kitchen.

Once he was out of earshot, Chelsea leaned over the table and smiled. "You've been holding out on me, Emily!"

"No, I haven't." I was certain my blushing cheeks told otherwise. Why did I always have to blush? It was impossible to hide my embarrassment when my cheeks were the color of cherries!

"I want info and I want it now!" She smacked the table with impatience. "What's the deal? Did you guys get cozy while I was gone?"

"We spent some time together," I said with a shrug, hoping to be nonchalant. "We worked on his car a little, sat together in church, and went to lunch. No biggie."

"Are you kidding? That's huge!" Chelsea's eyes were wide with excitement. "So are you dating?"

"No. We're just friends. That's it." I bit into my apple.

"That's more than friends if he spent that much time with you," Chelsea said. "I think he likes you. I mean, *likes* likes you, Emily."

"Change the subject *now*," I hissed as he approached.

He sank into the chair next to me and placed his tray, covered with fries, a cheeseburger, and a container of chocolate milk, in front of him. He placed an extra order of fries on Chelsea's tray.

"I never knew chocolate milk went with a burger and fries," Chelsea quipped, smothering her fries in more ketchup.

"You should try it." He shook his milk and then opened it. "What were you ladies discussing while I was gone? You looked engrossed in an intense conversation."

"Nothing," I said, swiping a fry from his tray. "How was the beach?"

He shrugged. "Boring as usual."

"Boring?" I asked, nonplussed. "How can the beach be boring?"

"It's boring when there's no one there your age to hang out with, your dad controls the only TV and watches the news incessantly, your mom complains constantly that he watches too much TV instead of talking to her, and your cell phone doesn't get a signal unless you drive twenty minutes away to town." He bit into the burger. "Someday I'll drag you down to our beach house. You'll agree with me—it's boring."

Out of the corner of my eye, I saw Chelsea give me a knowing smile. I glanced past her and found the crowd at Whitney's table watching us, probably trying to figure out why Zander was sitting with Chelsea and me. I was certain they echoed Chelsea's earlier comment about Zander's slumming.

"Don't get me wrong," he said, wiping his chin. "The house is nice, and I appreciate that we have it. But I don't understand why my parents insist I join them for every trip. I'm going to be eighteen in June. Doesn't that make me old enough to stay home alone without setting the house on fire?"

I snickered, lifting my bottle of water. "You have a point there."

"It's a family thing," Chelsea said, waving a fry for emphasis. "They're trying to get as much time with you as possible before you run off to college next year and leave them with an empty nest."

Zander frowned.

"What's that frown for?" I asked.

"College is a sore subject." He chewed a fry.

Chelsea and I exchanged curious expressions.

"How's your sister?" he asked her.

Chelsea swiped a napkin across her mouth. "She's doing well. She's getting straight As and dating some guy who makes her happy."

"Cool." He ate another fry. "Is she going to law school next?"

"Oh, yeah." Chelsea smiled. "Christina's brilliant. I'm sure she'll be a big-time lawyer. How's Andrew?"

"Doing great," he said. "Same as Christina—straight As, nice girlfriend. My parents are pleased as punch."

I studied him, wondering what he meant about college being a sore subject. He was going, right?

"And your little brothers?" he asked.

She laughed. "They're fine too. Now you have the Morris family update."

I looked past Chelsea and found some of the members of Whitney's table still watching us. "I think your friends miss you."

He turned toward the other table and waved, causing his friends to nod before quickly looking away. "They'll get over it."

I felt a sharp pain in my shin as Chelsea kicked me under the table. I shot her an evil look and she cupped her hand over her mouth to stop her laughter.

"So, are we on for tonight?" he asked me, moving a few fries through the lake of ketchup on his plate.

"For ...?" I asked.

"Hanging out in the garage. I'm going to drop the heads off at the machine shop today. I thought we could start cleaning the parts." He lifted his burger and grinned at me. "Or if you don't want to get your pretty hands dirty, you can keep me company while *I* start cleaning parts."

I narrowed my eyes. "You did *not* just call me a girly-girl, did you?"

He shrugged. "I don't know. Did I?"

"Those are fighting words, Stewart." I swiped one of his fries and poised it, ready to fling it at his head. "Take it back or I'm going to bean you with this."

"Okay, okay." He held his hands up in mock surrender. "I take it back. I'm not calling you a girly-girl. You're a worthy mechanic who can fix my car all by herself."

I bit into the fry. "Don't overdo it. I'm not going to fix your car all by myself."

"That's fine," he said. "We can fix your dad's AC after we finish my car. Fair is fair."

"That sounds like a good plan," I said, ignoring Chelsea's grin out of the corner of my eye.

"Are you riding home with me?" he asked. "I'll even let you come to the machine shop if you're nice."

"Oh, boy. You'll even let me go to the machine shop?" I fluttered my eyelashes. "What a dream come true."

He wagged a fry in my direction. "Only if you're nice."

"I'll ride home with you, but I can't guarantee I'll be nice," I said. "It depends on my mood."

Chelsea looked between us, her eyes wide. I couldn't even imagine the comments she would have to share with me when Zander was gone.

The bell blasted through the cafeteria, and we stood, packing up our trash. Zander piled up Chelsea's tray, his tray, and my trash and then headed for the can.

"He's totally smitten with you, Em," Chelsea said with a grin. "You guys are such a cute couple."

"We're just friends." I hoisted my book bag onto my shoulder. "Please don't start any rumors."

She nodded toward Whitney's table. "I'm pretty sure the rumors have already started without my help."

I groaned.

"Why are you upset?" Chelsea asked as we started toward the exit. "The hottest guy at school offered to give you a ride home. You should be celebrating."

"We're friends, Chels," I whispered as he approached. "Just friends."

"I guess I'll meet you in the parking lot after class?" he asked, falling into step with us.

"Absolutely," I said.

"Excellent. See you ladies later," he said before disappearing into the sea of bodies in the crowded hallway.

Thursday night, I kicked off my flip-flops and jogged up the stairs. The past couple of days had flown by with a strange turn of events. Zander had driven me to and from school and had joined Chelsea and me for lunch. Both Tuesday and Wednesday night we'd spent more than two hours in his garage, talking and laughing while washing off parts of the Dodge's engine. He never said anything about the parts I'd washed while he was out of town. Apparently he hadn't noticed that I'd been in the garage while he was gone or he'd noticed and it didn't bother him.

Tonight, we'd ridden to youth group together and stood side by side while preparing toiletry kits for the local battered women's shelter. Although Chelsea insisted Zander and I were dating, I felt a very close friendship forming. Instead of discussing only cars, we'd moved on to music, television shows, and movies, and I was surprised to find that we had similar interests there too.

When I got home, I popped my head into Logan's room and said hello and then continued on to my dad's door. I tapped lightly, and after receiving an invitation I stepped into his room and found him sitting on the sofa, watching the evening news.

"Hey," Dad said, patting the cushion next to him. "How was youth group?"

"Good," I said, sitting down next to him. "How was your session with Pastor?"

He shrugged. "It was okay. He said it was productive, so I guess it was."

I studied his brown eyes, wishing he would open up to me. "So what does that mean really?"

"It means we talked about a lot of stuff, and I felt relieved after the session." He gripped the remote and began channel surfing.

"What does that really mean, Dad?" I pressed on. "What are you discussing with Pastor Keith?"

"Stuff," he said, his eyes trained on the television. "It's really not that exciting."

"Why don't you share it with me and let me decide if it's exciting or not?" I bit my bottom lip while he flipped through the channels, settling on a channel displaying two men fishing. I would never understand how watching two men sitting in a boat was entertainment.

After a minute or two, my father glanced at me. "How was youth group?"

"I already told you it was good." Anger flared inside me. "Why are you changing the subject?" I snapped. "I asked you about your counseling session and you won't answer me. Does that mean you spent the hour complaining about me and what a lousy daughter I am?"

He winced. "Why would you even think that?"

"Because you won't talk to me!" I stood, jamming my hands on my hips. "Why are you so secretive, Dad? What are you hiding from me?"

"Hiding from you?" He laughed. "You can't possibly be serious."

"What else am I supposed to think?" I threw my hands up in frustration. "You won't tell me anything about your sessions."

"I haven't told you because it's not about you." He pointed to his chest. "It's about me and what I'm going through. It's about my grief and my broken heart."

Tears filled my eyes. "I lost her too, Dad. Maybe I need to hear you talk about your grief so I can figure out mine." I sat on the arm of the sofa and wiped my eyes.

"I'm sorry, Emily," he said softly, touching my knee. "I'm not good at expressing my feelings." He hit a button on the remote, killing the television. "I can tell him things and not worry about his judgment. With you, I worry too much about what you think of me."

"That's ridiculous. I couldn't ever think badly of you." My voice quavered and I cleared my throat. "You're my family. We're in this together, right?"

He nodded. "Maybe you need to talk to someone."

I shook my head. "I'm doing okay."

"But you're spending all of your time with Zander," Dad

said. "Don't get me wrong, I'm glad you two get along, but you need to be with girls your age too."

I blinked, taking in his words. "Are you serious? First you criticize me for spending too much time in my room. Now you're going to complain that I'm not spending time with the right people. You've got to be kidding me, Dad. I can't seem to do anything right when it comes to getting out." I stood. "I can't believe we're having this conversation again. I'm going to bed."

"Emily," he called.

I ignored him and opened the door.

"Emily Claire!" he snapped.

Sighing, I closed the door and scowled at him. "What?"

His expression softened to concern. "I worry that you'll get hurt again."

I folded my arms across my chest. "Is this about Tyler?"

He nodded. "Yeah, I guess it is."

"Well, I'm a big girl and I can handle my friendships." I gripped the doorknob. "Zander and I are just friends. We have a lot in common, and we enjoy each other's company. I don't think we'll ever be more than friends, so you can rest assured that I'll be fine."

He shook his head. "Emily, you're my daughter. I worry about you. All I'm saying is I think you need to be around girls too. Spending all of your time with a guy could get you hurt."

"I don't just spend time with him. I also spend time with Chelsea and I'm in youth group. What more do you want from me?"

"Emily—"

"Why is this turning into a lecture about my social life?" I asked, getting angrier by the second. "I asked you about your counseling session, and you give me the third degree about my friends. This is stupid." I yanked the door open. "Good night."

"Emily!" he called after me.

Ignoring him, I continued down the hall and locked myself in my room. Dropping to the floor, I pulled my knees up to my chest and fought back the tears flooding my eyes. Questions swirled through my head. Why wouldn't my dad talk to me? What was so secretive about his grief?

I lost Mom too!

More than ever, I wished I could talk to her face-to-face, tell her how I was feeling and ask her how to get Dad to talk to me. I felt a mixture of guilt and anger—guilt for being nasty to my dad but also anger with him for not sharing his thoughts and feelings with me. I should be the one he talked to, not a pastor who hardly knew us. Dad and I were family. We should be holding each other up.

Tears streamed down my cheeks, and I glanced toward my bed, spotting an unfamiliar box underneath it. When I'd moved in, I'd slipped a few boxes under the bed without checking the contents.

Intrigued by the box marked "Claire," I yanked it out. I grabbed a pair of scissors and slit the packing tape from the corners.

I opened the box and found some of my mother's belongings: her favorite novels, a purple scarf she wore after her hair had fallen out, a framed photograph of her and my father standing at the altar after their small wedding, and an album filled with her favorite family photos.

With tears streaming down my cheeks, I held the scarf to my nose and breathed in, hoping to find a whiff of her scent remaining on the thin fabric. The slightest scent of her perfume filled my nostrils, and I closed my eyes, trying to uncover my last memory of her. I dug deep into the depth of my mind, struggling to remember the sound of her voice saying my name.

And it came to me—her tiny voice croaking from the hospital bed, "Emily, I love you. Always remember I love you. Forever."

Looping the scarf over my shoulders, I swallowed a sob and rooted through the box, looking for something, anything, to make me feel closer to Mom again. Something to hold close to my heart.

I fished through books and CDs until I pulled out her Bible. The brown leather cover was cracked and faded, evidence of how often she poured through it. I unzipped it and flipped through the pages, finding page after page highlighted with faded yellow ink. My eyes glanced through the many verses she had marked, and I couldn't help but wonder if she had marked them for herself or for me.

I gasped when I found one in particular that she had marked—underlined in pen and then highlighted in yellow: Deuteronomy 31:6.

"You liked that verse too, Mom," I whispered.

Is this a sign?

I poured through more, each verse touching my heart and filling my mind with something that felt a whole lot like hope. Was this what faith was? Is this what Zander meant by opening my heart and listening to what God had to say?

Then the strangest thought hit me like a ton of bricks—*Did God send me Zander since I can talk to him about everything in my heart, at the same time I can't get my father to communicate with me?*

Pushing the thought aside, I flipped through more pages, taking in more verses. When I reached the back of the Bible, a slip of paper fell to the floor. I unfolded it and blew out a surprised breath when I found my mother's handwriting. I sucked in a breath and then read the letter.

My Dearest Emily,
    Writing this letter is the most difficult task I've ever had to do. How can I possibly express my hope and

*love for you for the last time? I've started this letter
over and over, probably two dozen times. However,
I've finally decided I need to just tell you how I feel
and trust that the Lord will guide my words.*

*You are everything to me. You're my life. You're
my breath. You're my heart. The day you were born
was the happiest day of my life. Your father and I had
dreamt of having a child, but we tried in vain for nearly
five years. Since we couldn't afford any of those fancy
fertility treatments, we waited and prayed—often. I'll
never forget the day we found out we were going to
have you. Your father and I rejoiced. And when you
arrived, you were perfect—so beautiful. All of my
dreams came true the day you came into our lives.*

*And now, fifteen short years later, I have to say
good-bye. It breaks my heart that I will miss so many
milestones in your life. But I take heart that you will be
okay. Yes, you'll miss me, but you have your wonderful
father. Hold onto your dad. Let him guide you. I know
he makes you crazy sometimes, but always remember
he loves you more than life itself.*

*It's difficult for me to decide what words to impart
to you when there's so much I want to say. Growing
up can be painful, and it will be even more difficult for
you since you won't have me by your side. But I need
you to remember I'll always be with you in your heart.
You can talk to me anytime. If you need me, find a
quiet place and just talk.*

*I'm leaving you my precious Bible, which has
helped me through my darkest hours and given me the
strength I've needed to endure this terrible disease.
Please read it often. Read and listen to my favorite
verses, which I've marked for you.*

I'm tired and my eyes are closing, so I must end this note for now. Emily, always remember to be true to yourself. You're a beautiful young lady, both inside and out. Don't ever feel you have to change in order to fit into some mold dictated by your peers or even a boyfriend. You're special. Don't ever let anyone change you.

Never forget that I'll always love you. We'll never understand why God chose to end my life so quickly, but I'll never doubt why I was put here on this earth— to be a child of God, your mother, and Bradley Curtis's wife. I know I've served my purpose and my life was not wasted on this earth. I know this for certain because I had you, and my spirit will live on through you and the deeds you accomplish during your life.

Most importantly, Emily Claire, never ever doubt God's love for you. He'll always be with you, loving you and guiding you. Don't be afraid to turn your burdens and your sorrow over to him. He will be the most important source of strength you have.

I'll leave you with one of my favorite verses—

Isaiah 41:10: So do not fear, for I am with you; do not be dismayed, for I am your God. I will strengthen you and help you; I will uphold you with my righteous right hand.

My love to you forever and ever,
Mom

With tears streaming down my hot cheeks, I studied the letter, reading it over and over until I had it committed to memory. Then I changed into my nightshirt and sweatpants and curled up into bed and read the letter over and over again until I fell asleep.

chapter thirteen

Zander and I walked side by side on our way from Fellowship Hall to the classrooms. I'd made it through the service without tearing up once, even though my mother's letter was still fresh in my mind three days later. I almost felt as if she was with me today.

Last night I'd dreamt that she was in my room, sitting on the edge of the bed while chatting with me and reciting the words from the letter. I could hear her voice and see her bright, green eyes. In my dream, my mother's curly brown hair had grown back and fell to her shoulders in the bob style she'd worn since I was a little girl. She wore a white, flowing nightgown, and her skin was pink and shiny. She'd looked like an angel.

I could still hear her parting words: "Forgive your father, Emily. He's coping the best way he knows how. Remember he loves you. And God loves you, Emily. God loves you."

"Emily?" a voice asked, wrenching me from my thoughts.

I turned and found Pastor Keith standing by his open office door. "Hi, Pastor," I said, pushing a lock of hair behind my ear. I'd worn my hair down today, and it flowed to the middle of my back. It had driven me crazy during church, falling in my face at inopportune times when I was trying to follow along with the readings and hymns. I made a mental note to pull it up when I got home.

Pastor glanced at Zander. "Good morning."

"Hi, Pastor." Zander gave a slight wave and smiled, his dimple appearing.

Pastor looked back at me. "I was wondering if you had a moment to talk."

"Oh." I twirled a curl around my finger, wondering what to say. Why would the pastor want to talk to me? I felt like a delinquent who'd been sent to the principal's office. Was I in trouble?

Zander touched my arm. "I'll come get you after J2A, and we can go out for an awesome burger."

"Okay." I watched him disappear into the crowd of kids heading to class and then I turned back to Pastor.

"Come on in." He gestured for me to enter his office.

"Thanks." I sat in a chair across from the pastor's desk and expected him to sit behind the desk in a formal sort of way.

Instead, Pastor Keith sat across from me and smiled. He was a handsome man, with a kind face, dark hair, and warm brown eyes.

"So," he began, clasping his hands together. "How are you doing?"

"Fine." I shrugged and smoothed my jean skirt.

"How's school?" he asked, leaning back in the chair.

"Good." I glanced around the office, taking in the family photos showing his pretty blonde wife and two blonde girls. Framed photos with Bible verses and paintings of Jesus on the cross peppered the bright white walls. The office reminded me of Pastor Rob's office back home.

"Jenna mentioned you joined youth group and are going to J2A," he said, still smiling.

I nodded. "Yes, I am."

"That's good." He folded his hands in his lap. "Is there anything we can do for you at the church?"

I shook my head. "I don't think so." I wondered what this

was all leading to. Was he looking for volunteers for a commit-tee? Or was it more personal? Had my dad told him I needed counseling due to my lack of an appropriate social life and my snarky attitude?

Pastor's expression turned to concern. "How are you really doing, Emily?"

"Fine," I said, forcing a smile.

He raised his eyebrows. "Are you sure?"

"Yup." I nodded with emphasis.

"You know you can always talk to me. Or if you'd rather speak to someone closer to your age, you can talk to Jenna."

"Thanks, but I'm really fine." I cleared my throat and twirled a curl around my finger. I felt as if I were on display. I wanted to get out of the office and be a member of the J2A class — just another kid trying to find her faith. Then another ques-tion occurred to me — did other kids my age "lose" their faith? Would I be declared a heretic if I even admitted it out loud?

"I see you and Zander have become friends."

"Yeah, we have a lot in common," I said. "We both like to work on cars."

"I heard from your father that you're quite a car enthusiast. That's unusual for a girl your age." He leaned an arm on the edge of his desk. "I find it very interesting. My girls are five and nine, and they are all about dolls, clothes, and makeup."

"Yeah, I was never interested in that kind of thing," I said. "My mom told me that she wasn't much of a girly-girl either, so it must be in the genes. I had a few dolls when I was younger, but my toy boxes were mostly full of Matchboxes and Hot Wheels."

"Hmm." Pastor rubbed his chin, deep in thought. "How did you get into cars? I assume it was your father's influence, but how did *your* love of cars come about?"

"I don't know." I crossed my legs and settled back in the

chair, getting comfortable. "I always had an interest. I started handing my father tools when I was really little—about four, I think. Then as I got older, I graduated from handing him tools to actually putting the tools to use. I started working in my dad's shop when I was about twelve, and I was officially on the payroll at fourteen."

"Why cars?" he asked. "What I mean is—why did you choose cars instead of sewing or stamp collecting?"

"Stamp collecting?" I asked. He had to be joking.

He chuckled. "Your expression is priceless. The stamp collecting question was a joke. I'm just wondering why you love cars so much. What is it about working on a car that brings you joy?"

I shrugged. He was making something that was so simple way too complicated. "Cars are easy."

"Easy?" He rubbed his chin again. "I can tell you that when I tried to fix the radiator on my wife's van last year, it wasn't easy. It was hard and also expensive when I had to pay a mechanic to fix my mess."

"To me, cars are simple because they just are what they are." I gestured with my hands as if I were pointing to an engine. "Cars are basic. They all pretty much have the same parts. They're just in different places if you're working on a Ford instead of a Chevy. They're kind of like a big puzzle, and I love trying to figure out how to solve it."

"Your dad mentioned you'd worked at his shop before your mom passed." His face became sympathetic. "How are you doing without your mom, by the way?"

So this is why he called me in here. This must be Dad's doing. "I'm okay." I shrugged.

"What helps you cope?" he asked.

I paused, not sure what to say, because truthfully, I didn't know the answer. "I guess being with friends."

"Like Zander?" he prodded, his smile back.

"Yes," I said, twirling a curl again. "Zander and I have been working on his car, and that's a lot of fun. I also spend time with my friend Chelsea."

"What else helps?"

"Staying busy. School is a good distraction."

"Do you ever talk to God?" he asked.

I blanched, feeling as if I'd been caught doing something terrible, like shoplifting. How could I possibly lie to a pastor? That would get me a ticket to hell for certain. "No," I whispered.

"You know his door is always open," Pastor said. "He'll listen to you any time. You can say anything to him, anything that's in your heart or on your mind."

I nodded.

"Are you afraid to talk to him?" he asked, his expression gentle, full of understanding.

"No." Deep down, I knew my answer wasn't the whole truth. Fear was only one part of it.

"Sometimes we're afraid to share our thoughts and feelings because we think he won't approve, but I can assure you nothing is off-limits when it comes to sharing with God," he said. "No problem or concern is too big or small for Jesus." He checked his watch and then stood. "I better get you out in the hallway before Zander thinks you left for lunch without him."

I followed him to the door and out into the hall, where a group of kids hurried by, talking excitedly.

"Thank you for visiting," Pastor Keith said. "Feel free to come by anytime to chat. My door is always open."

"Thank you," I said.

"Have a good week," Pastor said.

"You too."

I looked down the hallway toward our classroom just as Zander and Whitney approached. "How was class?"

"Good," Zander said. "How was your session with Pastor?"

"Good," I said.

"Are you guys going out for your car session again?" Whitney asked.

"That's right." Zander looped an arm around my shoulders.

Whitney smiled. "Have fun."

We started to step away, and Whitney gently pulled me back.

"Are you doing okay?" she asked.

"Yeah." I shrugged. "Why?"

She looked concerned. "Zander said you were meeting with Pastor Keith, so I wanted to make sure you were all right. I haven't had a chance to talk to you."

I twirled a lock of hair again. "I'm fine."

"If you need to talk," she began, "I'm here."

"Thanks," I said.

"Go have fun." She gestured to Zander, who was chatting with another boy while he waited for me.

"Okay. See you later." I turned to Zander, and an overwhelming feeling enveloped me. There were people around me who seemed to really care — Zander, Pastor Keith, and even Whitney. Come to think of it, my former church was the same way when Mom got sick, reaching out when I needed them most.

I stepped over to Zander, and he steered me out to the Jeep with his arm once again around my shoulder. I wondered if he enjoyed being close to me as much as I enjoyed his proximity, and worked to suppress a smile.

At the diner, we sat at a corner booth by the window and ordered cheeseburgers, fries, and Cokes. Once the server walked away, I leaned in and studied Zander's eyes, summoning all of my emotional strength to ask him the question that had been haunting me since I found the letter from my mother.

"You look like you're going to burst if you don't say what's on your mind," Zander said with a smile.

I sighed. "There you go again, reading my mind."

He laughed. "Just say it. You can speak freely with me. We're friends."

I took a deep breath. "When you lost your grandfather," I began slowly, "how did you deal with it?"

He sipped his Coke and ran his finger over the condensation on the glass. "It wasn't easy. We were close. He was like my best buddy, you know?"

I knew exactly what he meant. My mom was more than just the woman who'd given birth to me. She was my best friend, my confidante. I shared everything with her. When Tyler broke up with me, I cried—mostly because I couldn't share my heartache with her and hear her say, "Emily, he wasn't worth your time. You'll meet someone someday who will cherish you and treat you right," like she'd told me when Bobby Matthews broke up with me.

"I would say that God got me through it," Zander continued. "I still miss my grandpa, and sometimes I'll see something that reminds me of him. But I hold onto my favorite Bible verses, and they help more than anything."

I sipped my Coke and thought about the letter I'd found a few nights ago. I wanted to share it with Zander, but I was afraid it was too personal. Would he think I was weird for sharing it?

"Is there something else on your mind?" he asked, running his fingers over the table.

I paused, trying to find the words. "I found something a few nights ago while I was going through boxes."

"What was it?"

I swirled the straw in my drink. "First I found my mother's Bible. All of her favorite verses were highlighted in it."

"That's really cool."

"There's more." I glanced up and found his warm expression encouraging me, giving me the strength to share what was in my heart. "A letter was in the back of the Bible. It was addressed to me."

"Wow." His eyes widened.

I shared some of what the letter said, including the verse she quoted at the end. When I was finished, my eyes were full of tears and my voice was thick. I cleared my throat and wiped my eyes.

"That's powerful," he whispered. "It's as if she and God were speaking directly to you."

"I looked through the Bible and that verse I read in J2A last week was highlighted too." I sipped my Coke, hoping the carbonation would help me reclaim my voice.

He shook his head. "That's incredible. God's really speaking to you. Remember what I told you: Open your heart. Don't stop listening."

The server brought our food. We ate in silence for a few minutes, and I let Zander's words soak through me. While I understood his words about God speaking to me, I wasn't certain I agreed, at least not completely. I *was* certain I didn't want to push it and get into an argument. As I continued to ponder things, another question I'd been wondering about occurred to me, and I decided to ask it in order to change the subject.

"The other day at school," I began, "you made a comment about college being a sore subject. What did that mean?"

He grunted while finishing a fry. "It's a sore subject with my father. We have different ideas about my future."

"Med school?" I asked.

"Well, we've come to an understanding on that. I'm not going to med school, and he needs to stop pushing. My grades last semester established that." He took a bite of burger and was silent while he chewed. "Now he's pushing about what kind of college I go to."

"What do you mean?" I asked, pushing a few fries through the blob of ketchup on my plate.

"He wants me to go to the local university, but I want to go somewhere else."

"Where do you want to go?" I asked, wondering why he was hesitating to tell me.

"Promise you won't laugh?" He gave an apologetic smile.

Now I was truly intrigued. Did he want to be a minister? Is that why Whitney made that comment about Zander being the most harmless guy at Cameronville High?

"It's a technical school." He studied the burger on his plate. "It's to learn how to build racecars and stuff."

"You mean Motorsports Tech in Spencerville?" I asked, a smile growing on my lips. "I've heard of that place. It's very cool."

He shrugged. "Yeah, it is."

I leaned forward, even more intrigued than before. "Why were you afraid to tell me that?"

"My dad and my brother think it's a stupid dream. I guess I thought you might too."

"Are you kidding me?" I laughed. "Why would I think it's stupid? You know I'm into that kind of stuff."

"Yeah, but how is building racecars a career?"

"How is it not a career?" I shook my head, wondering why Zander would think I wouldn't support that decision. Then another thought hit me: Why was he so worried about my opinion? Did my opinion truly matter to him?

"So, what about you?" he asked, lifting his glass. "Where do you want to go to college?"

I shook my head. "I have no idea. There's no money for college."

"There's always scholarship money," he said. "I imagine you're smart and will get some of it."

"My grades are okay, but they're not really honor-roll worthy. I'm pretty much a straight B kind of girl."

"Straight Bs are nothing to sneeze at," he said. "It's way better than me. School was never my thing. I find it an extremely tedious waste of time that could be better spent in the garage."

"I agree there." I glanced out the window, thinking about what my plans had been before we lost Mom.

"What's going through your mind now?" Zander asked.

"Where do you see yourself in five years?" I asked.

He laughed. "I have no idea."

"Sure you do." I shrugged. "We all have hopes and dreams."

He blew out a sigh. "I guess I see myself graduating from some type of mechanical school and maybe running a shop or working on a race team. How about you?"

"Before my mom died, I always thought I'd get a degree in business and then help my dad run his shop. Now, I just don't know. I don't even know where I'll be living next year, but hopefully it won't be in Whitney's house."

"Is it that bad?" he asked, his expression sympathetic.

"No," I said with a grin. "I guess I don't mind the guy next door with the cool garage."

"So, you're using me for my garage."

"Yeah. Pretty much."

He cupped his hand over his heart and feigned a dramatic sigh. "You got me right here in the heart."

I laughed and tossed my napkin at him.

chapter fourteen

I waved to Zander across the cafeteria, and he grinned and waved back while taking his place at the end of the food line. He gestured to ask if I wanted a drink, and I nodded before sinking into the seat across from Chelsea.

"So, are you guys, like, officially dating yet?" Chelsea asked, shaking her container of chocolate milk.

"No." I pulled my sandwich and pear from my bag.

Chelsea's eyes studied me. "Has he confessed his feelings yet?"

"No." I shook my head and unwrapped my sandwich. "We're friends. That's it." Although lately, I wasn't entirely sure.

Chelsea's eyes probed my face, and a grin turned up her lips. "Has he kissed you?"

"No!" My cheeks flushed. "We're friends, Chelsea. How many times do I have to tell you that? We're *just friends*."

"Yeah. Right." She rolled her eyes. "For more than a month now you've been riding to and from school with him. You spend nearly every night in his garage helping him rebuild his car or working on your dad's truck. You're riding to and from church and youth group with him. If that isn't a relationship, then I don't know what is." She sipped her chocolate milk.

"It's a really good friendship." I bit my sandwich. "Okay, so maybe it's more like a best friendship since we talk about nearly everything."

Chelsea grimaced with frustration. "Emily, are you blind? You guys are the perfect couple."

"No, we're not. We're very different." I polished my pear with a napkin. "We just like some of the same things, like cars, movies, and music."

She rolled her eyes. "Don't you see? He really likes you."

"Yes, he does." I tapped the table for emphasis. "As a *friend*. If he liked me more than that, then he would've kissed me by now." I wished she were right. Oh, how I'd love to be kissed by Zander ...

"He won't kiss you if you're giving him mixed signals. You probably haven't shown him that you *want* to be kissed." She bit into her club sandwich.

My stomach flip-flopped at the thought. I did want to show Zander how I felt, but the idea of confessing that I had really strong feelings for him scared me, especially when I wasn't exactly certain what I felt. I liked him as more than a friend, but it was much more complicated than that. There was no way I could even put that into words.

I spotted Zander approaching with a tray full of food and two bottles of tea. He grinned and my heart fluttered. Perhaps Chelsea was right, and Zander wanted to date me. And that thought terrified me. Was I willing to risk our friendship?

While I was scared about getting hurt again, I was more scared of losing Zander for good. It wasn't ever possible to go back to being friends after dating a guy. Once it was over, it was over for good. I would've rather been his friend and secretly wished for more than risk losing his friendship all together.

Another broken heart would be too much.

"Good afternoon, ladies," Zander said, handing me an iced tea and sitting in the chair to my right "How's your day going?"

"Thanks," I said, shaking the bottle. "The day is going well. Chels?"

"Just fine." She smirked at me and I shot her a warning glance.

"What are you doing this weekend?" Zander asked me, unwrapping his sub sandwich. He opened a packet of mustard and squeezed it over the ham and cheese.

I shrugged. "I don't know. I was planning to work on the Dodge or finish the AC in my dad's truck."

"I think I know something even more fun that we can do," he said, lifting the sandwich.

"What's that?" I looked at Chelsea, who was grinning again. I kicked her under the table and she grumbled and glared at me in response.

"It's Halloween," he said.

"Huh?" I said. "Halloween is Monday."

"Right, but we're invited to a costume party on Saturday." He turned to Chelsea. "You're invited too."

"Thanks for the invitation, but I can't make it." She lifted a potato chip. "I promised my mom I'd babysit so she and my stepdad can go to a party. She never gets to go out alone with my stepdad."

"Where's your party?" I asked Zander.

"Kristin's house." He nodded toward Whitney's table, where Whitney and her group were talking and laughing loudly. They'd stopped staring at us a few weeks ago; I assumed they'd realized Zander had taken up permanent lunchtime residence at my table, and they simply had to accept it.

"Kristin's, huh?" I frowned, contemplating the idea of spending Halloween with Whitney's friends.

"Is that a problem?" Zander lifted his eyebrows.

"No," I said quickly, lifting my bottle of tea.

"It'll be fun," he said. "Kristin's parties are never dull."

"You should go," Chelsea said. "Trust me, you'll enjoy it."

"Whoops," Zander said, standing. "I forgot mayo. You guys need anything?"

Chelsea and I shook our heads.

"I'll be right back." Zander sauntered back toward the kitchen area, and I silently admired his tight jeans.

Snapping out of my trance, I looked at Chelsea. "I can't go to that party without you," I said. "There's no way."

"Don't be silly." She waved off the comment. "You can do anything with Zander by your side. You'll be the envy of the party."

I shook my head. "Too much pressure."

"Do you trust me?" Chelsea's smile was wide.

"I don't know ... Should I?"

"Yes." She placed her sandwich on the tray. "I have the *perfect* costume for you. We used it last year at the community theater. I can make you so beautiful that Zander Stewart will fall head over heels for you and kiss you Saturday night."

I grimaced. "I don't think that's a good idea."

"Trust me, Emily." Chelsea's eyes were bright with excitement. "I'll come over early Saturday night and do your hair and makeup. You'll be the belle of the ball."

I grimaced. "It's just a Halloween party."

"Just trust me, Emily. You'll thank me later." She winked. "You'll get your first kiss from Zander—guaranteed."

"I don't see how a costume—"

"Just trust me, Emily. *Please*." She folded her hands, pleading. "Please let me dress you up. You won't regret it."

"This better not be something really over the top. You know I hate makeup." Something about the gleam in Chelsea's eye had me worried.

"Just let me dress you up this one time. Then I promise I won't do it again until your wedding."

"Wedding?" I rolled my eyes. "Chelsea, please."

Zander approached the table. "What were you two talking about?" He sat down beside me and opened the mayonnaise packet.

"The perfect costume for Emily," Chelsea said, looking proud. "I'm going to make her up Saturday night."

"Cool." He smiled. "So we're going, right?"

"I'm warning you, I don't do Halloween parties." I bit into the pear.

"She'll be there. I'll make sure of that," Chelsea said with a smile.

I inwardly groaned. What was I getting into?

Saturday night I sat on a chair in front of Chelsea and blinked my eyes. "Are you almost done?" I whined. "My eyes are so itchy. I don't think I can stand it with all of this junk on my eyelids."

"Quit moving," she hissed. "You're going to make my hand slip, and you'll wind up with eyeliner on your nose."

I groaned. "This is excruciating."

"You should try it from my point of view. You're a terrible client." She bit her bottom lip and continued painting my face with who-knows-what.

"When I'm done with you, Zander is going to fall head over heels for you," she said with a grin. "He won't know what to do when he sees you."

"He might run in the other direction," I grumbled. "I appreciate what you're doing, but he's used to an ordinary girl. He's not expecting a girl who's dressed up like a queen."

"Trust me," she said for the hundredth time since she'd shown up to help me dress. "This will all be worth it."

"What time is it?" I asked.

"We have a few minutes. Just relax. He had to run an errand, so I think it'll be a bit." She placed the eyeliner onto the dresser next to me and then grabbed something else from her bottomless makeup bag.

"How do you know he had to run an errand?"

"As I said," she sang, "trust me. You'll be excited."

"Are you almost finished?" I asked.

"Quit whining," she said, fishing through a small bag filled with lipstick tubes. "It's very unqueenlike."

I glanced across the room toward my mirror, and I didn't recognize myself. The makeup was perfect—bringing out the deep green of my eyes. Chelsea had spent nearly an hour piling my curls on top of my head. I was wearing a slip and pantyhose, as my costume still hung in a zipper bag in the closet. I didn't know exactly what the costume was, but Chelsea had been calling me Queen Emily since she'd shown up.

She stepped back, studied me, and then smiled. "Perfect." She crossed the room and opened the closet door. "Wait until you see this."

Outside I heard a big block engine roar, and I wondered what kind of car was driving through our neighborhood. It sounded as if it parked nearby, perhaps even next door.

Chelsea placed the garment bag on my bed and unzipped it, revealing a hunter green and gold dress.

My eyes widened with surprise. "What is it?"

"You're going to be Queen Elizabeth the First." She pulled a few accessories from a tote bag, including a sequined gold crown and a large white collar.

I cupped my hand over my mouth. The costume was so unlike me, but it was so captivating that excitement surged through me. "I can't wear this. It's too beautiful."

She laughed. "You're so silly. You don't even realize that the dress is more you than you know."

"What do you mean?" I ran my fingers over the velvety soft gown.

"You're a gorgeous girl, Emily. This costume is actually perfect for you. Zander is going to flip." She lifted the gown and unzipped the back. "Let's get you dressed before he gets here."

I descended the stairs ten minutes later clad in the costume, complete with high heels and a crown, and nearly fell twice on my way down. In addition to my innate lack of coordination in anything but sneakers, the dress was awkward, probably weighing close to ten pounds with a huge crinoline underneath, giving the gown a distinctive bell shape. Chelsea followed close behind me, holding up the long skirt like my lady-in-waiting.

We stepped into the den, where my dad and Darlene greeted me, wide-eyed.

"Emily," my dad gasped, standing. "You're beautiful."

"No, Brad," Darlene said, holding up her camera. "She's stunning, breathtaking, and just plain gorgeous." She pointed toward the fireplace. "Let me get a few photos."

"Maybe we should wait for Zander," Chelsea said. "He should be here soon."

"Don't be silly." Darlene directed us to the fireplace and took several photos of Chelsea and me giving cheesy smiles. "The costume is beautiful." Darlene ran her hand over the sleeve. "Where did you find it, Chelsea?"

"We actually bought it last year for our community theater group." Chelsea placed her makeup bag on the floor. "I normally make the costumes, but we decided to buy this one at a shop. I tailored it for the actress, and she was shaped similar to Emily."

"It's just fabulous. Simply stunning." Darlene shook her head in awe. "Whitney will love this."

"Where is she?" I asked.

"She went over to Kristin's early to help her set up," Darlene said, examining the gold trim on the costume. "She was going to dress there."

"Zander!" Logan yelled from the kitchen. "You look so cool!"

My stomach somersaulted, and I grasped Chelsea's arm. "What if he doesn't like the costume?"

She laughed. "Emily, if only you could truly see yourself. He's going to be hypnotized by your beauty."

"She's right." My dad kissed my cheek. "You're stunning, Baby Doll, absolutely stunning."

I glanced at my reflection in the mirror above the fireplace and touched my face. I didn't recognize myself. I was pretty— or maybe glamorous was a more appropriate word. Chelsea had completely transformed me into a sixteenth-century monarch. I just hoped that Zander would approve. I spotted him in the doorway and took a deep breath.

Turning, I faced him and my eyes widened in surprise. He was clad in a black racing firesuit covered in various logos, including motor oil, tires, and fuel additives. The suit was snug with a zipper running up the length of it, bringing out his muscular frame. He looked positively gorgeous.

"You look amazing," I said.

Zander studied me, his eyes wide. His mouth gaped, but no sound came out. And my heart soared. So Chelsea had been right all along: he did like me. Maybe I would get that first kiss tonight ... My cheeks flushed even more at that thought.

My dad chuckled, smacking Zander's shoulder. "She looks good, huh?" he asked.

Zander cleared his throat. "Yes, she does." He smiled at me and bowed. "You look dazzling, Your Majesty."

"Thank you," I replied with a little curtsey.

Chelsea winked at me. "I need to run. My mom and stepdad are leaving soon for their party."

"Thank you," I said, hugging her. "I'll call you tomorrow," I whispered.

"You better," she said. She said good-bye to everyone and then exited through the kitchen.

Darlene directed us to the fireplace. "Let me get a few photos before you leave."

We posed for what felt like a hundred photos before Zander took my hand and led me through the kitchen to the back door.

"I have a surprise for you," he said, squeezing my hand slightly. "I guess you could say it goes with my costume."

"Oh?" As we walked the short path to the fence dividing our yards, my heart turned over in my chest yet again. He looked so handsome that I couldn't take my eyes off him.

"Close your eyes," he said, taking both of my hands in his and walking backward while leading me the rest of the way.

I followed instructions, a smile growing on my lips. I couldn't even imagine what he had in store for me.

"Okay, open them!" he said.

My eyes flew open, spotting a shiny, dark metallic blue '69 Camaro, and I blew out a surprised breath, cupping my hands to my mouth.

"Where ...? How ...?" I stammered, the words floating through my head but not forming sentences.

He laughed, tugging me toward the car. "When I told Jack my idea, he helped me find a Camaro SS." He held up the keys and jingled them. "I was going to let you drive, but I guess in that dress it won't be physically possible." He pointed to the skirt, which nearly stood up on its own.

"Wow." I ran my finger over the fender, marveling at the beautiful paint job. Peeking in the window, my jaw dropped. The black vinyl interior was perfect—clean and shiny. "Who owns this?"

"Some guy named Pete," he said, opening the passenger door. "He's good friends with Jack."

"How long did it take him to restore it?" I asked, lifting my skirt and climbing into the seat, trying to make the sea of material fit inside the car without revealing my slip and pantyhose beneath it.

"He told me it took him three years to get it perfect." Zander slammed the door and came around to the driver side.

While he got buckled in, I turned around and examined the car, shaking my head in amazement. The car was exactly the way I'd imagined mine would look after I'd finished my restoration, except that my car would've been purple instead of blue.

"It's nice, huh?" He turned the key and the car roared to life.

"Oh," I moaned, closing my eyes, taking in the purr of the engine. "That is the sound of heaven."

He laughed. "You really are a Chevy girl." He threw the car in gear and steered out of the driveway, the engine roaring with power. "He said I can keep it until Monday, so you can drive it tomorrow if you'd like."

When we came to a stop sign, I turned to him and smiled. "Thank you."

"No problemo," he said, negotiating a turn. "I thought we'd have fun tonight."

"Where'd you get the racing suit?"

"This belonged to Jack. He used to race in his younger days." He nodded toward the backseat. "The helmet's back there, but it's not very comfortable."

"Don't wear it. Then I wouldn't be able to see your face."

He steered down Kristin's street. "Isn't the point of Halloween to be unrecognizable?"

"I'm not wearing a mask," I said.

"I'm glad." He grinned. "It would be a crime to cover up your beautiful face."

My pulse skittered. This night was getting more perfect by the second—first he was speechless when he saw me, then he borrowed my dream car to escort me to the party, and now he told me I was beautiful. I couldn't imagine what would happen next. A kiss could make the night complete. My heart turned over at the thought.

A line of cars snaked down Kristin's street and music blasted from inside the house. He parked behind a red Toyota Prius, then came around the car and opened my door. I felt like Zander's prom date as he took my hand and helped me from the Camaro. Hand in hand, we walked up the driveway toward the front door. We stepped into the foyer and found a group of kids talking and laughing in the den.

Whitney, dressed as Dorothy from *The Wizard of Oz*, spotted me and screeched before coming over and taking my hands in hers. "You look awesome, Emily! Holy cow!"

She called her friends over, and they prattled on about how beautiful I looked, sounding like mother hens. The attention was actually kind of nice.

Out of the corner of my eye I saw Zander grinning, almost gloating over me. *Wow.*

Zander handed me a cup of punch, and I stood with Whitney and her friends, answering what felt like a zillion questions about my costume and who had fixed my hair and makeup. The conversation turned to gossip about people I didn't know, and I felt out of place. I silently wished Chelsea's parents had found a babysitter.

I glanced over at Zander standing with a group of guys near the entrance to the kitchen and he shot me a warm smile. I felt as if I were floating on a cloud.

I suddenly felt the urge to use the restroom and dreaded the thought of dealing with the crinoline and skirts. I leaned over to Whitney. "Where's the bathroom?"

"There's one off the kitchen and then two more upstairs," she said. "Want me to go with you?"

"I'll find my way. Thanks." Finding the kitchen bathroom occupied, I ventured upstairs, passing a group of girls who looked familiar from the cafeteria. I gave them a slight smile and steered through a large bedroom to a master bathroom.

On my way back through the bedroom, I stopped when I heard voices outside the door.

"She looks hot," one of the girls was saying. "I wonder where she got that costume."

"I'd kill for that hair," another said. "Most of the time it's frizzy, but someone did a great job styling it tonight. Perms never look right on me."

"I think her hair is naturally curly. You could never get a perm to do that," the first girl said.

They had to be talking about me. I leaned flat against the wall and held my breath. I wanted to go back into the bathroom to avoid hearing anything nasty, but I was stuck there, glued to the wall by the door, wondering what they would say next.

"I wonder what Zander sees in her," another said.

"What do you mean?" the first girl said. "She's really pretty."

"Yeah, but she's not, like, you know, in *our* group. It's hard to believe she's Whitney's cousin. They're so different."

"Yeah," the first said. "It's got to be weird for Whitney, you know? Imagine how awkward it is for her to see them together since she and Zander were pretty hot and heavy last summer."

I sucked in a deep breath.

"But that's ancient history, Monica. They broke up and now they're friends."

"Yeah, but she must still feel *something* for him," Monica said. "I mean, they, like, talk *all* the time."

"Yeah, that would be like your sister dating your ex-boyfriend. Awkward and weird."

"But Whitney's with Chad, and he's really hot."

"Not hotter than Zander. He's like a god."

"You got that right!"

They all giggled and someone suggested going down to check the food table.

I slid down the wall, sinking onto the floor, and hugged my arms around my stomach. I let the information seep into my mind: *Whitney had dated Zander.*

Now so much made sense. Now I understood why she'd said he was probably the most harmless guy at Cameronville High; she would know since she'd dated him. No wonder she said that all he talked about was cars. And now I knew why his numbers were programmed into her phone.

So why was he spending time with me?

I groaned, covering my face with my hands. Perhaps Whitney had asked him to spend time with me, and he was just seeing me as a favor to her. He was another hand-me-down—like the cell phone.

Then it hit me: This wasn't a favor for Whitney, this was about God. Ever since I'd confessed that I wasn't sure if I still believed in God, he'd been witnessing to me. He'd told me that he dealt with the grief of losing his grandfather by turning to God. Since I'd admitted I'd lost my faith, he'd tried at every opportunity to inject God into the conversation.

I was his witness project.

Our relationship had little to do with becoming boyfriend and girlfriend; it was about bringing me back to the faith.

How could I have been so stupid to believe that he liked me for me?

Humiliation coursed through me. I felt like a fool.

I had to get out of there before I lost it in front of everyone like I'd done in church. Standing, I checked my reflection in the mirror, making sure my eyeliner hadn't run, and then I marched down the stairs.

chapter fifteen

I found Zander standing in the kitchen with a group of friends. When he saw me, his smile transformed into a frown. He approached me and touched my arm, which I yanked back.

"What's wrong?" he asked, leaning close to my ear.

"I want to go home," I said, trying to keep my voice even.

He took my arm and pulled me over to a corner, away from the staring crowd behind us. "What's wrong?"

"I want to go home," I repeated, more forceful this time. "I don't belong here. These are your friends, not mine."

"If they're my friends, then they're yours too," he said, his eyes full of worry. "Did something happen? I noticed you were gone, and I couldn't find you."

"I told you, Zander. I don't belong here, and I want to go home. If you won't take me then I'll walk." I started for the foyer, weaved through the sea of costumes and curious looks, and made my way out the front door into the cool, falling raindrops.

"Wait up," he said, catching up with me. "What happened back there?"

"Just unlock the door." I hugged my arms to my chest as the raindrops soaked the dress. I wondered if it was a material that could withstand the rain. I climbed into the car and stared straight ahead while rubbing my arms.

Zander started the car and we drove in silence. I avoided his glances by studying the dashboard, wondering how many hours Pete had spent creating this masterpiece of a car. The rain drummed on the roof and beaded on the windshield, evidence that Pete had applied Rain-X to the glass.

Zander steered into his driveway and parked in front of the garage. I wrenched the door open and made an awkward dash for the gate, holding my skirts in my hands and hoping I didn't slip in the stupid heels. The rain soaked through my hair, which fell in wet curls past my chin.

"Wait!" Zander rushed over and grabbed my arm, pulling me to him. "You have to tell me what happened. Why are you so upset? Did I do something wrong tonight?"

I spat out vehemently, "Why didn't you tell me you dated Whitney?"

He blanched. "What?"

"Why, Zander?" I jammed my hands on my hips while the rain poured down on us.

"Why does it matter?" he asked.

"Because it matters to me." Glaring, I pointed to my chest. "Why didn't you tell me you guys had a hot and heavy romance last summer?"

"Hot and heavy?" He shook his head, bewildered. "I don't know who told you that, but it wasn't hot and heavy. We hung out for a couple of months and realized that we make better friends than boyfriend and girlfriend."

Tears filled my eyes and I felt like a total moron. But his relationship with my cousin wasn't the reason I was hurt, really hurt to my core. "What is it that we're doing, Zander?" I gestured between us. "What is this, you and me?"

He opened his mouth to speak, but I pressed on, cutting him off.

"Is our relationship a sham?" I asked, the tears flowing

down my cheeks along with the raindrops. "Are you hanging out with me as a favor to Whitney?"

He looked even more confused. "What are you talking about? How would being with you be a favor to Whitney?"

"Or is it more than that?" I asked, ignoring the rain running down my face. "Is this about God? Am I your witness tool? Will you earn extra points in J2A when you help me find the Lord again?"

"Whoa." He held his hands up. "I don't know where you got that idea from."

"You never miss a chance to preach to me," I continued, raising a finger at him for emphasis. "You're really good at reminding me that you turned to God when you lost your grandpa, and I should open my heart and listen to what he's trying to tell me."

He glowered and shook his head. "Why are you determined to make yourself miserable?"

I gasped. "What does *that* mean?"

"You're so focused on being miserable that you don't see what's around you." He gestured, the keys tinkling in his hands. "God is reaching out to you. You said yourself that you found the letter and Bible from your mother with verses highlighted for you." He pointed to my chest. "But you choose to turn the other way and insist that God forgot you."

I studied his face as a lump swelled in my throat. "How could you have any idea how I feel?" I pointed toward his house. "You have your mom and dad, and they're healthy. You live in this amazing house, and you have a huge garage that's all yours. You even have a beach house that bores you."

His expression turned to annoyance as he shook his head. "That's not—"

"You have opportunities," I continued, my body shaking with anger. "Money is no object for you. You can go to any school you want to after you graduate. The only problem you'll have is choosing which one you go to." My voice was thick, and I hoped I could hold back the threatening tears. "Whereas I live with relatives who took us in out of pity, and my mom is gone. You have no idea how that feels."

"Emily—"

"Let me finish," I hissed. "Your problem is that you're a spoiled rich kid who has no idea what it's like to struggle. Everything you've ever wanted was handed to you on a silver platter."

"That's not even *close* to the truth," he seethed. He pointed toward the garage. "I've worked my tail off for everything in that garage—every tool, every toolbox, every engine part was paid for by mowing lawns and working at the shop. *Nothing* was ever handed to me. My father *never* supported my car hobby. Ever."

His expression was pained, and I regretted my words for a nanosecond before more anger erupted inside me.

"That isn't real struggle," I growled. "You didn't have to witness your father bawl when he lost the love of his life. You've never seen your father go to pieces when the bank took the business that he spent years building by hand or when the bank foreclosed on your little house. Your biggest problem is having to deal with going to the beach house with your parents."

"You're just bitter," he retorted, his eyes smoldering.

"Bitter?" I asked, my voice high pitched, almost shrill. "Cancer stole my mother, and you think I'm bitter?"

"Yes." He blew out a frustrated sigh. "You're so focused on what's gone wrong in your life that you don't see how right things can be."

I wiped fresh tears from my eyes. "And how does that bring my mom back?"

"No one can bring your mom back," he said slowly. "But you can try to move past it. You have to. She would want you to live."

I shook my head. "You make it sound so easy."

He threw his hands up. "I just don't get you at all."

"I know. I thought you did get me, but I was so, so wrong," I said, my voice cracking. "Now I realize that you never understood me at all. You're just self-righteous and have no idea what it's like to lose everything. God has forgotten me and my dad."

"He hasn't forgotten you," he said, his own voice beginning to fracture. "You choose to live in this bubble where you close out everyone who cares about you and wants to help you. You'd rather wallow in self-pity than see how God is trying to reach out to you."

I let the words sink in, each one stinging my heart. "So you think that I wallow in self-pity and I want to be miserable," I whispered, tears splattering my already wet cheeks.

He ran a hand through his wet hair. "Yeah, I guess I do."

"And that's what you really think of me," I repeated.

He didn't answer. We stared at each other, and a suffocating silence fell over us while the rain continued to soak through my hair and my clothes.

"I guess I was wrong about you," I whispered, shivering due to the cold and the frost in his eyes.

"Apparently," he said. "You think I'm a spoiled brat."

"So, that's it," I said, swiping the tears and raindrops from my cheeks with the back of my hand. "Whatever we had is over."

"I guess so." He frowned, his eyes filled with pain.

With my heart breaking, I spun and stomped off through the gate and toward the deck.

I marched in through the kitchen and past my father sitting on the sofa watching television with Logan.

"You're home early," my dad called. "How was the party?"

"A blast," I muttered, stomping up the stairs to my room.

I locked my door and shucked the wet dress, hoping I hadn't ruined it by standing in the rain for so long.

Zander's words echoed through my mind and stung my soul. And I'd thought he liked me! I'd been wrong about so many things.

I changed into my pajamas and then yanked out my journal from my bag. Remembering Zander's retort, I grabbed my mother's Bible as well.

Wishing more than ever that Mom was here to talk to me, I reread the letter she'd written to me, hoping to find some comfort in her words. I then opened the Bible and read several passages, and my tears began to fall.

I needed to go into a garage and lose myself in a project. That was the only way I could think, but I had nowhere to go. I didn't dare go into Zander's garage. I didn't want to see him, and I wouldn't be welcome there anyway.

I opened my journal to a blank page and began to write.

Saturday, October 29
Dear Mom,
How can things go from being so right to so wrong in the matter of a few hours? I thought that when Zander and I went to the Halloween party tonight everything was going to be perfect. I was certain he cared about me and was even going to kiss me. I believed that by the end of the evening I would wind up his girlfriend, but now I'm not even his friend.

My heart is shattered, and I feel like a fool. He never wanted to date me at all, and though he denied it I feel like I was a conversion project to him. While we fought and said horrible things to each other, I told him he was a spoiled brat who had everything handed to him on a silver platter, and he told me that I'm bitter and determined to stay miserable.

Is he right about me, Mom? Am I holding onto this sadness and grief because I want to stay this way forever?

How can it be my fault that I've lost my faith in God, when I've been trying to reach out to him? I've tried to pray nearly every night, and I come up empty. Is it all my fault, Mom? You said God would be here to hold me and comfort me. So where is he? I open my heart and feel nothing.

And where are you, Mom? I don't feel your presence anymore.

All I feel is alone.

Closing my eyes, I tried to pray over and over again, but no words came to me. I didn't know what to say to God or what to ask for. Frustrated, I opened the Bible and read until my eyes burned with exhaustion. Curling up on my pillow, I fell asleep.

I awoke with a start and glanced at the clock, which read 1:18. A door slammed outside, followed by a male voice booming.

I slipped over to the window seat and threw the blinds up, seeing Whitney and Chad standing in the driveway in the rain, gesturing wildly. Feeling like a voyeur, I started to close the shade, but against my better judgment I opened the window instead.

The rain was a mist in the lights reflecting off Zander's garage.

"Whitney, you know I care about you," Chad was saying.

He looked like a pork sausage with his muscular physique jammed into a tight-fitting cheerleading uniform. Why did football players think it was unique to dress as their female counterparts on Halloween? It was so cliché that it was boring.

"That's why you're ending it?" Whitney's said in a shrill tone. "You care about me, so you're breaking up with me." Her voice was seeped with sarcasm. "Makes total sense, Chad." She turned and marched toward the deck, her red sequined shoes glittering in the low lights at the corner of the house.

A chill gripped me. The scene was familiar.

"Wait!" He ran after her.

She swatted his hand away. "Don't touch me!"

"I like you. You're a cool girl." Again, he held his hand out to her, but she folded hers across her blue Dorothy dress. "Look, we can still be friends."

She shook her head. "Whatever." Her voice trembled, and I could sense the threatening tears. "You just used me like you use every other girl. I should've listened to my friends. They were right about you." She stomped up the stairs to the deck and out of my sight.

"Whitney!" he yelled after her.

"Don't call me. Don't text me," she yelled.

The door opened and slammed, shaking my side of the house. I closed the shade and flipped off my light, rushing back to bed. When her footsteps sounded in the hallway, I held my breath, hoping she wouldn't stop by my room. I felt bad that she'd had a rough night, but I didn't want to share anything with her about my own incident.

"Whitney?" Darlene's tired voice sounded in the hallway. "Are you all right?"

"Mom," Whitney whined. "It was terrible."

"Oh, come here, sweetheart," Darlene cooed.

Footsteps echoed down the hallway and a door closed, and I rolled onto my side, hugging my extra pillow close while tears poured down my cheeks. I'd give anything to have someone who would dry my heartbroken tears.

"You sure you don't want to come with us?" My dad stood in the doorway the following morning dressed in his Sunday best—Dockers, a button-down blue shirt, and loafers.

"My stomach really hurts." Sitting up in bed, I hugged my

stomach for effect. I wasn't exactly lying; my stomach did hurt. But it was more the result of a night of crying than an illness. I'd been up half of the night thinking about Zander and wishing for my mom.

He studied me, and I braced myself for a lecture. Stepping into the room, he closed the door behind him. "Did something happen last night? You came home early and rushed upstairs in a huff."

I shook my head. "I just didn't feel well and wanted to come home."

His eyes continued to study mine, and I held my breath. *Please just leave, Dad. Please don't make me tell you the truth. You'll never understand how I feel.*

"Do you need anything?" he asked.

I breathed a sigh of relief. He bought it or decided to let it go. "No, thanks."

"What did you think of the Camaro Zander borrowed?" he asked.

"It was amazing. It was done just like I wanted to do mine."

He nodded. "He was really excited when he found one he could borrow for you."

I frowned, wondering if there was a hidden message in that comment. Was Dad trying to tell me that Zander really liked me? But how would he know Zander and I had an argument— unless he'd heard something last night. But he'd been watching TV with Logan, so I doubted that was possible.

A knocked sounded on the door, and my dad opened it.

"Are you ready, dear?" Darlene poked her head in. "Oh my. Are you sick, Emily?"

"She has a stomachache," my dad said.

"I'm sorry to hear that." She pointed down the hallway. "There's some Pepto in my medicine chest. Just help yourself." She looked at my dad. "Are you coming to church?"

He turned to me. "Do you need me to stay home?"

"Don't be silly." I waved toward the door. "Go on. I'll be fine."

He crossed to the bed and kissed my forehead. "I hope you feel better."

"Thanks," I whispered, overwhelmed by the gesture.

"You take care, dear," Darlene said. "Call us if you need anything." She turned toward the hallway. "Logan! Let's go! The car is leaving."

"See you later," my dad said. "Take it easy." He disappeared through the doorway, closing the door softly behind him.

The rumble of an engine drew my attention to the window. I sank onto the window seat just as the Camaro backed out of the driveway next door. I watched as my family left, Whitney and her parents in her mother's SUV and my dad and Logan in the Suburban. I crawled back in bed, yanked my book bag up next to me, and spent the morning finishing up homework.

While I worked, my phone chimed and rang, receiving three text messages from Chelsea asking me how the party was. I ignored the texts, deciding I would fill Chelsea in at school tomorrow. It would be easier to explain it in person.

Around lunchtime, I heard the back door slam followed by the echoing of footsteps and voices entering the kitchen.

Footsteps continued up the stairs, and I sat up straighter in bed, hoping that the sound would continue down the hallway. A light knock on the door destroyed my hopes.

"Come in," I said, finger combing my mess of curls.

Whitney appeared in the doorway. "Hey. Can I come in?"

"Sure." I motioned for her to sit on the bed.

She closed the door behind her and sat on the window seat across from me. "How are you feeling?"

I shrugged. "Okay, thanks. My stomach's a little better."

"I'm glad." She crossed her legs. "I guess last night was bad for all of us, huh?"

"Why do you say that?" I asked, not wanting to admit I heard part of her conversation with Chad.

She shook her head and glowered. "Chad and I broke up last night."

"Oh no." I frowned. "I'm sorry to hear that. What happened?"

She sniffed. "He said he has to concentrate on school or he won't get into college," she said.

Confused, I raised an eyebrow. "What does that have to do with you?"

"I'm a distraction." She threw her hands up. "Is that the flimsiest excuse you've ever heard? How can his bad grades be my fault?"

I nodded in agreement. "That's pretty lame."

"You want to know the kicker?" she asked, her eyes shining with fury.

"What?" I sat on the edge of the bed across from her.

"I saw him talking with Monica Barnes at the party, and they were getting pretty cozy." She blew out a frustrated sigh. "I feel so used."

I shook my head. "I know the feeling all too well."

"You do?" She looked intrigued.

"Yeah." I ran my hand over my bedspread. "When Tyler broke up with me, he said he wasn't attracted to me."

She gasped. "He didn't!"

"Oh yeah, he did." I scowled. "He said I was a cool girl, but he just wasn't attracted to me *that way*."

"No!" Whitney looked shocked. "He's an idiot. You're a gorgeous girl." She touched my arm. "Don't let that bring you down. Guys are stupid."

Surprised by Whitney's support, I laughed. "Thanks. And for the record, Chad's stupid too."

She smiled. "Thanks." She paused for a moment, and her smiled faded. "Zander wasn't at church today."

"Oh?" Frowning, I twirled a curl around my finger.

"Did you guys have a fight?" she asked. "I didn't see you leave the party, and Tiffany told me that you left in a hurry."

"My stomach hurt," I said quickly, not wanting to add fuel to any gossip spreading about Zander and me.

She paused. "You know, I think it's great that you and Zander are together."

"We're just friends." *At least we were friends until last night.*

"Oh, please." She waved the comment off with a laugh. "You guys are such a cute couple. He's crazy about you."

"Why do you say that?"

"It's obvious, Emily, by the way he looks at you." She glanced out the window, and I wondered if she saw him out there. "I can just tell. He's a nice guy."

I wanted to believe her, but still couldn't stop thinking that he was using me as his witnessing tool. Although I'd believed he cared for me, I couldn't get past his comments from last night about how I don't let God speak to me. He'd had no right to talk to me that way.

"J2A was fun today," Whitney said. "We started watching a movie, and we're going to discuss the parallels to Jesus' life."

"Cool," I said.

"Jenna asked about you," she said. "She said if you need anything, you can call her to chat."

"Thanks." Again, I felt overwhelmed by the compassion, and for a split second I wondered if Zander had been right, that I don't let people in.

Whitney stood. "Why don't you get dressed and come to the mall with Kristin and me? I need to do some serious shopping to get out of this funk Chad put me in."

"No, thanks." I pointed toward my bag. "I have a project due in History on Thursday." That was true, but I didn't mention that I had finished it earlier today.

"Are you sure? We'd love for you to come. You never join us when we go out." Whitney looked disappointed.

"Thanks, but I think I'll pass this time. Have fun."

She headed for the door. "Do you need anything?"

"No, thanks." I stood and stretched. "I think I may get dressed and clean the bathroom. It's my turn, right?"

She waved it off. "Forget the bathroom and come shopping. The bathroom can wait."

"No, I'm good," I said. "Have fun."

"See you later." She disappeared through the door, and I sighed. I knew she was trying to reach out to me. She'd definitely changed since the funeral.

Without thinking, I jumped up and hurried to the doorway. Glancing down the hall, I saw her stepping into her room. "Hey," I called.

She spun. "Yeah?"

"When are you leaving?" I asked.

"In about ten minutes. Why?" She looked hopeful.

"I'll come," I said. "I just have to throw some clothes on and do something with my frizzy hair."

"Awesome," she said with a grin. "Your hair looks fine. Just put on some shorts."

chapter sixteen

I sat down at the lunch table on Monday and unpacked my usual sandwich, bottle of water, and apple. I glanced toward the door and dreaded seeing Zander. I'd gotten up early and caught the bus in order to avoid riding with him or Whitney. While I'd actually had a good time shopping with Whitney and Kristin, I didn't want to admit to Whitney that Zander and I weren't speaking. I planned to take the bus home too.

I assumed Zander would corner me at lunch, but I didn't want to face him. I knew I'd said awful things to him, and I didn't know how to take them back. Besides, the accusations he'd thrown at me still stung, and I didn't know if he would ever apologize to me.

"Well?" Chelsea sat across from me and frowned. "You still haven't told me what happened."

I gnawed my bottom lip while debating how to tell her the truth. I'd avoided the subject in English and gym, and I knew Chelsea deserved an answer, especially since I'd never called her back. "I just don't want to go into it."

"Just tell me. I'm your friend, remember?" Chelsea said.

I sucked in a deep breath and gathered my thoughts. Then I hit the issue head on. "Why didn't you tell me that Zander had dated Whitney?" I asked.

Chelsea blinked, surprised. "I figured you knew. Besides, I didn't think it really mattered."

"I didn't know, and it does matter. A lot," I said. I started to tell her what I'd heard through the door at Kristin's house and what it had made me wonder, but stopped when I spotted him crossing the cafeteria, frowning. "Here he comes."

But instead of crossing to our table, he stood in the food line.

My shock must've registered on my face because Chelsea raised her eyebrows. "What?"

"He hasn't even looked at me," I said. "He got in the food line and didn't glance over here."

Chelsea grimaced. "That's not good." She shook her head. "I'm sorry I didn't mention that Whitney and Zander had dated. From what I heard, they didn't date very long." She moved a fry through the pool of ketchup on her plate.

"So their relationship wasn't a big deal?" I asked, looking toward the food line. Zander was nowhere to be seen, and I assumed that meant he'd moved into the kitchen to choose his meal.

Chelsea shook her head. "Not really. I mean, everyone knew they were a couple, but no one called them the homecoming king and queen or anything." She shook her chocolate milk. "I can't believe Whitney and Chad broke up. Everyone figured they'd be together forever."

"What do you think Monica meant when she said Zander and Whitney had been hot and heavy?" The question slipped from my lips before I could stop it.

"Monica's a witch," Chelsea quipped. "I wouldn't put stock in anything she said. She told my eighth grade history class that I practiced kissing my teddy bear for when I finally got a date."

"Yikes." I winced. "I bet you were teased for months."

"You have no idea." She rolled her eyes and sipped her milk.

"Zander said they were really more like friends than boy-friend and girlfriend," I continued.

"And you don't believe him?" she asked, reading my thoughts.

"It's more complicated than that." I looked over just as Zander crossed the cafeteria with a tray full of food. He nod-ded at the folks at Whitney's table and then kept walking out the door toward the courtyard. "Oh no," I gasped.

"What?" Chelsea's eyes widened.

"He bought his food and went outside to eat alone," I said, cupping a hand to my forehead. "I guess that's it. I lost him."

"Don't say that," Chelsea said. "He really cares about you."

I shook my head. "Too bad I never saw that. We had an awful argument after the party, and we both said some really nasty things to each other that we can't take back. It's over."

Chelsea gave a sympathetic look. "You can always apolo-gize, Em. It can't possibly be that bad."

I shook my head. "No, it was bad. I told him he was spoiled and had everything handed to him."

She scowled. "Ouch."

"Yeah," I said, staring at my uneaten turkey sandwich. "He told me I was bitter, among other things."

"Hey." Chelsea touched my hand, and I looked up. "You can always say you're sorry and you didn't mean it. We all make mistakes. And I still say he really cares about you. He may even love you."

I blinked, letting the words soak in. "Love me?"

"He gives you some pretty intense looks. Don't give up on love." She laughed. "Don't I sound like an old, experienced woman? What do I know about dating? I've never been out on a date, unless you count running to the grocery store with my neighbor." She chewed a fry. "Speaking of love, you need to give me advice sometime on how to get a guy's attention.

There's this really hot senior on the stage crew. I don't think he even knows my name. What should I do?"

"What do I know?" I asked. "I messed up what I had with Zander."

"I told you," she began with a huff, "you can fix that if you apologize."

"Sorry. So, tell me about this hot senior," I said, eager to change the subject. I bit into my sandwich.

We spent the rest of lunch discussing the senior she liked. She then filled me in on her weekend, telling me all about how she finished making matching pumpkin costumes for the twins. Her stories were background noise to the heartache that haunted me. I knew I'd messed up with Zander, but I didn't know how anything I could say would ever fix it.

The rest of the week, I felt as if I were walking through a fog. Although I took the bus to and from school, I passed Zander in the hallway several times and saw him in the cafeteria, and received a halfhearted nod or wave from him.

Thursday night, I rode to and from youth group with Whitney, and Zander didn't show up. She'd asked me what was going on, and I told her that we'd had an argument. She didn't ask for any details, and I was thankful.

Each night, I stayed awake, staring at the ceiling while contemplating what to do. While I couldn't take back the horrible words I'd said to him, I also couldn't go on with the silence. It was eating me alive inside.

Friday afternoon, I padded up the driveway from the bus stop and climbed the steps to the deck. Glancing next door, I spotted the Jeep in the driveway with the garage door up, and my stomach flip-flopped.

Entering the kitchen, I found Darlene standing at the counter while studying a cookbook. She smiled at me. "How was your day?"

"Pretty good," I said, dropping my backpack on the floor with a thump. I swiped an apple from the fruit bowl and bit into it. "How about yours?"

"Good," she said. "I did the grocery shopping and had a meeting at church." She turned toward the table, where a pile of books and a binder were spread out. "Would you do me a favor?"

"Sure." I said, biting into the apple.

"Would you go retrieve Logan from next door? He ran out of here when he heard Zander's Jeep pull up, and he needs to get back here and finish his homework." She frowned. "He's still grounded after getting a D on his math test. I let him go over there to say hi, but he knows he's supposed to get his homework done and study."

"Oh." I bit into the apple, trying to ignore the sick feeling that overcame me at the thought of going to face Zander.

"I would really appreciate it, dear," Darlene said while pulling some spices from the cabinet above her head.

"Okay." I tossed the apple core into the trash can, wiped my hands on a paper towel, and headed for the deck.

My heart thumped in my chest as I approached the garage. I wiped my sweaty palms on my jeans and then touched my headband to make sure it was still in place.

Standing at the open bay door, I found Logan sitting on a stool while Zander stood at the tool bench examining a carburetor that was in pieces before him.

"I told him that if he called me that again, I'd rearrange his face," Logan was saying.

"The best thing you can do with a bully is ignore him," Zander said. "That really makes them mad."

"Yeah, but—" Logan stopped speaking when he saw me. "Hey! It's Emily!"

Zander glanced over at me, and my stomach twisted. When he gave me a halfhearted nod, my heart sank. "Hi," he said.

I twirled my finger around a curl. "Hi."

I cleared my throat, trying to think of something to say. "You're having problems with a bully?" I asked Logan.

"Oh, it's no big deal," Logan said, waving it off. "I'm going to punch him out tomorrow."

"I think that will earn you a trip to the principal's office." I leaned against the rear end of the car. "I have a feeling your mom and dad wouldn't be too happy about that."

"I told him to ignore the kid," Zander said. "That will make the bully mad and keep Logan out of trouble."

"That's good advice." I smiled at Zander, and he looked down at the carburetor. In an effort to break the ice, I stepped over to him. "Doing a rebuild?"

"Yeah." He kept his eyes on the parts. "I figured I might as well since I have everything else rebuilt." He grabbed his gloves.

"Can I help?" I offered.

"That's okay," he said, avoiding my stare. "I'm good." He put safety glasses on and held the pieces over an oil pan while spraying them with carburetor cleaner.

Standing with my hands stuffed in my back pockets, I watched him, studying his handsome face and replaying our horrible fight. My heart was breaking in response to his silence. If we hadn't fought, I would've been standing beside him, probably laughing and teasing him while we cleaned the parts together.

"How've you been?" I asked, grasping for anything to say.

"Okay," Zander said, still not looking at me. "You?"

"What are you doing?" Logan asked, hopping down from the stool and stepping over to Zander.

Zander stopped spraying the parts. "I'm cleaning the parts with carb cleaner. Then I'm going to rebuild the carb, putting it back together with new gaskets."

"Wow." Logan rubbed his chin, deep in thought. "That sounds pretty hard."

Zander shrugged. "Not really. It's actually pretty easy."

I glanced toward the rebuilt engine on the stand. "Looks like you're pretty close to putting the engine back into the car."

"Yup," Zander said. "Pretty close."

"If you let me know when you're going to do it, my dad and I can help you," I offered with a weak smile.

"Sure," he said without facing me. "I'll let you know if I need help."

My heart sank. He knew as well as I did that he would need at least two people to help him get that motor back into the car. His statement meant one thing: he no longer wanted my help, and it crushed me.

"Logan James Richards!" Darlene's voice bellowed. "You better get back in here and finish your homework! *Now*, young man!"

"Uh oh," Zander said, grinning at Logan. "I think you're in trouble."

"Yeah," I said. "I was supposed to tell you to come home."

"Man," Logan whined. "I never get to do anything."

"Maybe if you do your homework, she'll let you come out after supper," I suggested.

"No," Logan said with a sigh. "She's still mad about my math test." He schlepped toward the door. "See you later."

"Bye, dude," Zander called.

"Bye, Zander," Logan called, heading toward the path.

I stood by the bench, running my fingers over the wood and wondering what to say. The silence between us hung like a dark, stifling fog. "Do you need any help?"

"Nope," he said, his eyes trained on the parts. "I'm fine. I've done this plenty of times."

Gnawing my bottom lip, I studied the engine. "I could bolt on the water pump for you."

He placed the cleaned parts on the counter. Removing his gloves and safety glasses, he turned to me, and I was glad to see his face, even though he didn't appear glad to see me.

"I think I got it under control," he said with a frown.

"Okay," I said quietly. "I just thought I would offer."

"I'm good," he said.

We stared at each other, and I wished I could think of the right thing to say. Although he frowned, I could see pain in his eyes. Was he feeling the same regret that I felt? Did he also wish he could say the right thing to fix what had broken between us?

"I guess I'll see you at school," I said.

"Take care, Emily," he said, turning back to the tool bench. It felt strange to hear him call me by my given name.

Feeling dismissed, I stepped out of the garage. Before I hit the path, I turned back once more and spotted him cleaning the parts without even looking up at me. It was then that I knew I'd really lost him, and my eyes filled with tears.

chapter seventeen

H appy birthday!"
    I awoke to my dad yelling and the warm smell of turkey roasting somewhere in the house. Yawning, I rolled onto my side and swept the curls from my face.

"Rise and shine!" he called, crossing my room with something shielded behind his back. "You're seventeen today. It's a very special Thanksgiving."

"Thanks, Dad." I sat up, stretched, and yawned again. "Happy Thanksgiving."

He sat on the edge of the bed and handed me a package wrapped in pink paper. "Happy birthday."

"Dad," I said, running my fingers over the paper. "You shouldn't have gotten me anything. I told you not to spend any money on me. We need to save to move out."

He ran his hand over my head. "You're my baby girl. Of course I had to get you something."

"Dad ..."

"Just open it," he whispered. "Please."

I unwrapped the package and found a brown photograph album with the word "Family" engraved on the front. I looked up at my dad, and he gave me a sad smile.

"Go ahead, Emily," he said. "Open it."

I flipped the album open and my eyes focused on a

photograph of my mother holding me in the hospital the day I was born. I sighed, tears filling my eyes. Turning the page, I found photos of my mother and me when I was a baby—her rocking me, giving me a bath, holding me the day I was baptized, and sitting on the porch wearing a yellow sun hat.

I kept turning pages, finding photograph after photograph of my mother and me. I laughed, remembering wonderful, special days, and tears streamed down my face as grief overwhelmed me.

"She was beautiful," I whispered, staring at a photograph of her and my father dressed up to go to their fifteenth high school reunion.

"She was," he whispered, wiping his eyes. "And you look just like her."

"No, I don't." I swiped my hands over my eyes. "She was much more beautiful."

"You don't see it, Emily, but you are too. You have her eyes, her hair, and her smile. I'm so proud of you, and I love you more than I can express."

"I love you too, Daddy," I whispered.

We flipped through more photos, sharing stories, laughing, and crying together. When I got to the last page, I studied one of my favorite photographs featuring the three of us sitting on our porch together the summer before we lost her. We were all so happy.

I ran my fingers over the album, marveling at the sentiment he'd put into the special gift. "This must have taken you forever to put together."

He shrugged. "I just worked on it every night when I was sure you were asleep."

"Thank you," I said, closing the album. "This is the most wonderful gift you could've ever given me." I wrapped my arms around him and kissed his cheek.

"Happy birthday," he whispered, holding onto me. "I love you."

"I love you too, Daddy," I said.

My phone began to ring, and my dad let go. "I'm sure your friends want to wish you a happy birthday too. Come down soon. Darlene has gifts for you."

"Thanks." Lifting my phone, I read Megan's name on the screen. I flopped back on the bed and answered it.

By the time I came downstairs, I'd spoken to Megan and Chelsea, taken a shower, and gotten dressed. I found Darlene and Whitney in the kitchen, cooking Thanksgiving dinner.

"Happy birthday!" Whitney said, hugging me.

"Happy birthday, dear," Darlene said. "Would you like your gifts now or when we have cake?"

"We can wait until later." I spotted my dad watching television in the den. "Where are Logan and Uncle Chuck?"

"They went to get Grandma," Whitney said.

"Oh." I stepped out onto the deck and shivered in the cold as I glanced over at Zander's house. We'd barely spoken over the past few weeks, and I missed him. He said hi to me in the halls at school and when I saw him at the house, but we barely spoke more than a lame greeting. Last week I'd retrieved Logan from Zander's garage, as usual, and Zander shared that he'd be away for the holiday. His mother had decided on a family Thanksgiving at the beach, and from my window I'd watched him leave last night. I wondered if he'd remembered today was my birthday and if he even cared. I missed his friendship so much that my heart ached.

A car pulled into the driveway and I inwardly groaned. *Just what I need now — Grandma.*

The SUV door opened, and Logan jogged up the steps to the back door. "Happy birthday, Emily!"

"Thanks," I said.

Uncle Chuck and Grandma approached, and I forced a smile. "Happy Thanksgiving, Grandma," I said.

"Oh, thank you, dear," she said, climbing the stairs. "My arthritis is giving me a fit. I may have to leave shortly after dinner. My recliner is the only place where I get relief."

"Oh, that's too bad," I said. She opened her arms, and I gave her a quick hug. "It's good to see you, Grandma."

"You too. I haven't seen you in a long while. Did you forget to come visit me?" she asked, her brown eyes full of scrutiny. "You've only come once since you moved here."

Does she practice these guilt trips?

"Oh, I'm sorry about that," I said. "I've been busy." *Where's Dad when I need him? He should take some of this flack.*

"How's school?" she asked.

"It's fine." I wondered if she forgot it was my birthday.

"That's good." She started toward the door. "Where's Whitney? I believe she had an advanced placement history test this past week. I bet she got an A."

As Grandma walked through the door, I turned toward Zander's garage. I considered sneaking in there later to get some peace and quiet. I wondered if Zander would mind if I went in there and worked on his car for him. He'd mentioned to me that he was close to getting the car running. Would he even care that I'd been in there?

"Happy birthday, Emily."

I'd forgotten Chuck was standing there until he spoke. I turned toward his smile.

"Thank you," I said.

"Your grandmother means well," he said. "She doesn't think before she speaks sometimes, but she has a good heart—deep down. Way deep down." He grinned. "Although it may not feel like it, she loves you. She's just a little thoughtless sometimes."

Stunned by his words, I blinked. "Thank you."

He opened the back door and then turned again. "Don't stay out here too long. There's a chill in the air."

I watched him go inside and looked back at Zander's garage. I hoped the day would go by quickly, so I could get back to what I missed and craved most for my birthday—working on his car.

"Logan, would you please say a prayer?" Darlene asked when we all sat down to Thanksgiving dinner a couple of hours later.

Logan rattled off his usual incomprehensible prayer, and then everyone began filling the special china plates.

"So, Whitney," Grandma said. "How did the history test go?"

"It went well," Whitney said with a smile. "I think I got an A."

"I'm sure you did," Grandma said with pride. "That's my girl."

Yup. That's your girl. I rolled my eyes and drenched my turkey in gravy.

"Everything is delicious, Darlene," my dad said.

"Yes, it's wonderful, Darlene," Grandma exclaimed. "You're such a good cook. I taught you well."

"Thank you." Darlene looked at me. "I got you an ice cream cake. Your dad said that was your favorite."

"Thank you," I said. "It is."

"Grandma," Whitney broke in. "Did you say happy birthday to Emily?"

I glanced at my cousin, and she winked at me. I couldn't help but smile in response.

"Oh, that's right," Grandma said. "Happy birthday, Emily." She glanced at Chuck. "Did you grab her card? It was on the table by the door."

"Yes," Chuck said. He gave me a half smile.

"Thanks," I said. *I bet it has my usual ten dollars from her in it.*

"Whitney," Grandma began. "Have you sent the invitations for your birthday party next week?"

"Yes, Grandma," Whitney said. "They went in the mail last week."

"All of the details are set?" Grandma persisted. "You reserved the activity center, right?"

"Yes," Darlene chimed in. "We also got the caterer and the DJ."

I glanced at my father, wondering if he agreed the birthday party Darlene had been planning for Whitney during the past month was over the top. He shrugged and grabbed the bowl of mashed potatoes.

"Did you get decorations?" Grandma asked.

"I got some balloons and little party favors," Darlene said, taking more turkey. "It's going to be lovely with the center-pieces and all."

I swallowed a groan. I couldn't even imagine what Whitney's wedding would be like if her birthdays were this extravagant. It would probably resemble something like a royal wedding with ten bridesmaids, a ton of flowers, and dresses costing thousands of dollars each.

The rest of dinner was spent discussing Whitney's upcoming party and the millions of details: appetizers, music, the cake, etc.

Once we were finished eating, I helped Darlene and Whitney with the dishes and then sat in the den with my dad, uncle, and Logan and watched football while the women continued planning Whitney's party.

My eyes were closed, and I was falling asleep when I heard someone calling my name.

"Emily," my dad said, nudging me. "I believe it's time to celebrate your birthday."

"Really?" I asked with a yawn. "I thought we were planning Whitney's party."

He gave me a sympathetic look. "I know that her party is a bit extravagant, but we have to endure it." He rubbed my arm. "We're guests here." Taking my hand in his, he led me into the kitchen, where an ice cream cake reading "Happy Birthday, Emily" and glowing with candles sat in the middle of the table.

Everyone began to sing to me, and I fought back tears when it hit me this was my first birthday and our first Thanksgiving without Mom. When they finished singing, I blew out the candles, and Darlene cut pieces of cake for everyone.

"Open my gift," Logan said, pushing a small box toward me.

"Thank you." I ripped it open and found a keychain with a Chevrolet logo on it. "It's perfect."

"You can use it when you get your own Chevy," Logan said.

I laughed. "I will. I promise."

"Here you go, dear." Darlene pushed an envelope toward me. "It's from your uncle and me."

"Thank you." I opened the envelope and pulled out a mushy card talking about how wonderful nieces are. Inside I found a $100 gift card for the Cameronville Mall. So over the top. Just like Darlene.

"Thank you," I said. "That's so generous."

Whitney handed me a small box and a card. "This is from me."

"Thanks," I said. I opened the box and found a pair of silver hoop earrings. I rarely wore earrings, but these were elegant and simple. Whitney did a good job figuring out what I'd like. "They're lovely. Thank you, Whitney."

"You're welcome." She smiled. "Maybe I can go with you to use that gift card. I had a blast when you went shopping with Kristin and me that time."

"Yeah," I said with a smile. "That would be cool."

Grandma handed me an envelope containing a card about

granddaughters and a ten-dollar bill. The usual. I couldn't help but snicker.

"What's so funny?" Grandma asked.

"Nothing," I said quickly. "Thank you, Grandma."

"You're welcome, sweetie. Enjoy," she said.

We finished our cake and then I retreated to my room, claiming I needed to rest, even though I planned to write in my journal. I flipped through my mom's Bible and then stepped over to the window. Sinking down into the window seat, I pulled open the shade and prepared to write, but instead my eyes wandered toward Zander's garage. The floodlights on the corner of the roof that automatically came on in the dark seemed to beckon me, inviting me to come over and enjoy the solitude.

I pulled on a sweatshirt and hurried down the stairs.

"Where are you going?" my dad asked from his place on the sofa.

"I'll be back," I said.

"I know you'll be back, but where are you going?" he called after me.

"For a walk," I said.

"But it's cold out," Chuck chimed in.

I stopped at the door and slipped on my boots. "I just need to clear my head. I'll be back soon."

Hugging my sweatshirt to my body, I jogged over to the keypad and mashed the digits for the code. After hitting "enter" twice, the door lifted. I stepped into the garage, turned on the lights, and hit the button to close the door. I felt like a burglar as I walked past the Dodge, running my fingers over the cool metal.

Standing at the front of the car, I examined Zander's work, wondering who had helped him get the engine in place. Although it stung that he'd continued his big project without me, I decided to help him get the motor hooked up.

I dropped my phone onto the bench, flipped on the small radio, and then went to work for the next two hours. Crawling under the car, I slid in the starter. I hooked up the engine brackets and then installed the power steering pump and alternator. Finally, I connected the wires for the starter, ignition, and alternator. When I was done, I was exhausted but somehow felt renewed, as if a weight had been lifted from my shoulders.

Since my hands were covered in grease, I stepped over to the sink and scrubbed them with Gojo. While I was washing them off, I heard my phone chirp. After drying my hands, I then lifted my phone from the bench.

When I glanced down at the screen, I gasped, finding a text message from Zander that said: Em—Happy Birthday—Z

I typed back: Thanks

He responded quickly with: And Happy Thanksgiving 2

My heart beat quickly as I typed back: U 2

Lowering myself onto a stool, I stared at the phone, hoping that he'd text again and say something like: *I miss you* or *I'm sorry* or, even a long shot of: *I love you.*

But no more messages came. I knew I should be happy that he'd even texted me since it was the first time in over a month. However, it still stung.

Closing my eyes, I concentrated, and for the first time in months, a prayer formed in my heart.

"God," I whispered, "I don't understand why things are going the way they are for me. I don't feel you in my life, and I need you. And I need Zander. Please, God, bring Zander back to me. Somehow. I need him."

I sat in silence for a few more minutes, trying to find the words to tell God how I felt about everything—losing my mom, moving to Whitney's house, arguing with my dad, facing the holidays without my mom. But I couldn't form the words. It was as if my short prayer about Zander was all my heart could handle.

But it was a start.

I glanced around the garage and yawned. It was time to go home.

After turning off the lights and radio, I locked up the garage and headed up our deck stairs. I was stepping through the door when a thought occurred to me: Zander had once mentioned that when he was at the beach house he had to drive twenty minutes into town to get a cell phone signal. Had he driven that far just to send me those few text messages? The idea eased my mind just a tad.

I showered and changed into my pajamas before climbing into bed. I was just opening my journal when a voice startled me.

"You okay?" Whitney asked from the doorway.

"Yeah," I said. "Just tired."

She stepped into the room. "Today had to be hard without your mom."

A lump swelled in my throat as I held up the album. "Would you like to see what my dad made for me?"

"Yeah." Whitney sat on the edge of the bed, and we flipped through the album, laughing and talking about photos. To my surprise, she even had tears in her eyes when she saw a few of the photographs.

"This is beautiful," she said, closing the album. "It's something you'll cherish forever." She looked up at me and frowned. "I'm sorry my party was the subject of the day."

I shrugged. "It's okay. It's going to be a big affair."

She sat on the edge of the bed and rolled her eyes. "My mom is really going to extremes. I tried to talk her out of it, but she insisted."

I couldn't help but snort. "Really? You don't love the attention?"

Shaking her head, she gave me a dark look. "Believe it or not, I don't want it all the time."

"And thanks for trying to bring the conversation to me," I said. "I appreciate it."

She nodded. "I hate how my mom and Grandma are so focused on me. They act like you don't exist sometimes."

"You noticed that?"

She snorted this time. "How could I not notice?" She looked serious again. "I saw you coming out of the garage. You miss him."

I sighed. "Is it that obvious?"

"I think he misses you too. He's hardly spoken to his friends. Everyone's noticed the change in him since you guys stopped talking."

My heart thumped.

"I don't know what happened, and you don't have to tell me, but I think you two need to talk."

"I've tried." My voice quavered and I cleared my throat. "He doesn't open up to me."

She pushed a lock of golden hair behind her ear. "Don't give up on him." She paused. "I think you two make a great couple, and you should try again."

I stared at her, shocked by her words.

"Hey, is that your mom's Bible?" she asked.

I grabbed it from my nightstand and held it up.

"Wow. I can't imagine how it must feel to have that." She paused for a second. "Emily, don't take this the wrong way, but I figured out awhile back that I can't take things on alone. I have to give my burdens to God. Don't try to do it all alone, okay?" She stood and started for the door. Before she opened it, she looked back at me. "Happy Birthday, cuz."

I smiled. "Thanks."

"Good night," she said, and made her way out of the room.

After she closed the door, I pulled out my journal and began to write:

Thanksgiving & My Birthday
Dear Mom,

To say that I miss you today would be an understatement. You always made my birthday the most special day of the year for me. But today was far from special.

I thought going into Zander's garage and working on his car alone would help, but the comfort it brought me was fleeting. I did manage to send up a short prayer tonight, however, and it felt good. I wasn't able to tell God everything in my heart, but it was a start. Maybe I'll figure this out, but it won't be easy without your help.

I wish you were here to tell me that everything is going to be all right. Truthfully, I'm not sure if it ever will be.

I wish I knew how to make things right with Zander. Whitney and Chelsea both told me that I should talk to him because they think he cares for me. He texted me to wish me a happy birthday, which shows he thought of me, but how do I know he cares if he won't talk to me? Okay, he speaks to me occasionally, but he only says "hello" and shares meaningless pleasantries. We don't really talk anymore, not about things that matter.

I feel like I'm an empty shell of the person I was before you died, Mom, stuck on some road I can't seem to find my way off of. I don't know how I'll ever feel whole again. If you can see this, Mom, would you somehow send me a sign? Can you tell me how to feel like myself again? Can you help me get Zander back?

More importantly, can you tell me how to reconnect with you and with God?

Can you show me how to pray?

With a lump in my throat, I closed my journal and curled up in bed. As I closed my eyes, I wondered if Zander had been partially right—I was completely miserable.

chapter eighteen

The heavy bass of alternative rock music thumped and vibrated off the walls as I walked with Chelsea into the Castleton Community Activity Room. The large banquet room was decorated with pink and white balloons emblazoned with "Happy 17th, Whitney" on each table, pink and white streamers, four long tables covered in food, and bowls of pink and white M&M'S also exclaiming "Happy Birthday, Whitney."

"You've got to be kidding me," Chelsea said, glancing around the decorated room. "This is for a birthday party? Are you sure it's not a graduation party or a wedding?"

"I hope I'm living in Europe or at least on the other side of the country when she gets married," I commented.

"I don't blame you," Chelsea said.

"This is *so* over the top," I said. "I got an ice cream cake on my birthday. Why does she need all this?"

"My guess would be this is as much for your aunt's social standing as Whitney's." Chelsea nodded toward Darlene, who stood laughing with a group of ladies as well dressed as she was.

"At least we could dress casually for this party. I don't know if I could take this in a frilly dress and heels," I responded.

"Maybe they're saving the full cotillion for her eighteenth birthday," Chelsea said with a laugh.

We moved to the drink table and helped ourselves to cups of pink punch. I sipped the overly sweet drink and scanned the crowd of faces. I recognized some of the kids from school. The adults were mostly strangers, except for a few familiar faces from church. "I don't see Chad. I guess they're not still friends after the breakup, huh?"

"I heard they had a big fight last week in the hallway after school," Chelsea said. "Apparently she saw him kissing Monica Barnes."

"Yikes," I said, grimacing. "So he didn't need less of a distraction from his school work. He just didn't want Whitney's distraction." I wondered why Whitney hadn't shared that with me. Maybe she was too embarrassed, which I understood since I'd been too embarrassed to share the details of my argument with Zander. I felt bad that I hadn't been there for her, though.

Chelsea's eyes were trained on something across the room. Following her stare, I spotted Zander talking with a group of jock-looking types. His eyes met mine and a tentative smile turned up the corners of his mouth.

"Have you talked to him?" Chelsea asked.

I gripped my cup. "Sorta. He said hi to me yesterday and asked how my birthday was. It was awkward at best."

"But it was something," Chelsea said.

"Yeah." I frowned. It may have been something, but it certainly wasn't enough. The pain of losing his friendship was nearly unbearable some days and it kept me awake every night.

Chelsea tapped my arm. "I've got to go to the little girl's room. I'll be right back."

"Okay." I stood by the punch table and scanned the crowd, continuing to search for familiar faces.

The music stopped abruptly and Chuck tapped on a microphone by the DJ. "Good evening." Chuck's voice boomed over the speakers. "Thank you all for coming to our very special party tonight. We're thankful that you've taken time out of your busy schedule to celebrate our little girl's day."

I refrained from rolling my eyes. *Despite what Whitney told me, this is completely insane.*

He motioned to Whitney, who sidled up to him with her mother and Logan in tow. "Tonight we celebrate Whitney's journey into another stage of her life," he continued. "She's a young woman who very soon will be graduating and leaving for college. We're so proud of all she's accomplished, making honor roll again this semester."

Everyone clapped and I reluctantly joined in without much enthusiasm.

"To celebrate this, Whitney," he said, looking at her, "your mother and I have a very special gift for you."

Darlene presented Whitney with a small box. Whitney opened it and squealed, holding up a key on a gold keychain.

"It's a key to a brand-new Jeep Compass," Chuck said. "It's parked outside." He pointed toward the exit doors.

I shook my head, trying not to get sick.

"Oh my gosh!" Whitney yelled into the microphone. "Thank you so much, Daddy!" She hugged her dad.

Darlene stepped over to the microphone and her eyes searched the crowd. "Where's Emily?" she asked.

"Oh no," I groaned.

Darlene located me by the punch table and pointed. "My niece, Emily, is standing over there. Dear, we're going to let you have Whitney's old Honda. I know you'd love to fix it up. That would be fun for you."

Everyone laughed, and I considered hiding under the punch table. Zander caught my eye and shot me a sympathetic look.

Can this get any more humiliating? I covered my face with

both hands as my cheeks burned. When I uncovered my eyes, I found a group of kids from school smirking at me and whispering, and I bolted for the nearest exit.

"Thank you everyone for coming," Whitney said into the microphone, her voice rushed. "Please enjoy some food."

I hurried out the door, marching out into the rain.

"Emily!" Whitney called. "Emily! Wait!"

With no destination in mind, I ignored her calls and kept going, stalking through the neighborhood, cutting through yards, and loping past Whitney's and Zander's houses.

I couldn't stop the anger and humiliation from swirling through me. Darlene had embarrassed me in front of nearly our whole school and church. But that was only the tip of the iceberg.

The cold December rain soaked through my sweatshirt and caused my curls to fall past my shoulders. I reached up to push my hair back and a lock of hair was stuck, twisted around my mother's chain.

My eyes fell on the cross, twinkling in the streetlights, and I sighed. Where was God when I needed him most? Why didn't I feel him in my life through this whole mess? It wasn't as if I hadn't been trying. I tried to pray over and over again, and I'd even had a small breakthrough in Zander's garage last week. I'd been reading my mother's Bible just about every night, but I still didn't feel God in my life. What was I doing wrong?

I needed someone to talk to. Someone objective who would listen without judgment and give advice without censoring himself or herself. I suddenly remembered the business card that Jenna had given me the day I'd met her. I yanked it from my wallet and dialed her number on my cell phone.

"Hello?" she asked.

"Hi, Jenna," I said. "This is Emily Curtis."

"Emily!" Jenna said. "How are you?"

"Well," I began, my voice trembling. "I was wondering if we could chat. You once told me that we could talk anytime."

"Of course," she said. "Would you like to meet somewhere?"

"That would be great," I said, dodging a puddle on the sidewalk.

"I'm actually driving by the Cameronville Coffee House," she said. "Would that work for you?"

"Yes," I said. "I can be there in a few minutes."

"Great," she said. "See you soon."

I reached the entrance to the neighborhood and crossed to a strip mall. As I approached the Cameronville Coffee House, I spotted Jenna walking in the parking lot.

"Emily!" she called, approaching me. "You're soaked! I would've picked you up."

"It's okay," I said, falling in step with her. "I was just trying to clear my head. Thanks for meeting me."

"I'm happy you called." Taking my arm, she led me into the coffee shop. "Let's get you out of the rain."

The warm aroma of coffee filled my senses.

"What would you like?" she asked, standing in line in front of the counter.

"How about a hot chocolate?" I asked.

"That sounds good. Are you hungry?"

"No, thanks." I was certain my stomach couldn't handle any food; it was still sour from Darlene's big, thoughtless mouth.

"You go find us a seat," she said, motioning toward the tables.

I weaved through the sea of tables occupied by couples, teenagers, and a few people sipping lattes while surfing the Internet on laptops.

I found a small table back in the corner and sat, staring out the window at the pouring rain. I couldn't stop my brain from replaying the scene of Whitney's gift, Darlene's comments, and then Zander staring at me from across the room. I wished I could turn off the hurt and humiliation that was surging through me.

Jenna came to the table and handed me a warm cup. "You look like you're carrying the weight of the world on your shoulders," she said, sinking into the seat across from me.

Feeling a lump swelling in my throat, I took a long drink.

Her expression was full of concern; her eyes were gentle. "Take your time," she said softly.

I stared down at my mother's cross, wondering where I'd gone wrong. "I feel so lost and alone," I said, my eyes still focused on the necklace.

"Why do you feel that way?" she asked.

"Everything is so easy for other kids."

"What's easier for them than for you?"

I looked up at her. "Everything—making friends, talking to God."

"I've seen you talk with plenty of kids in youth group and J2A." She sipped her coffee. "I can tell by how they interact with you that they like you. What makes you think they're not really your friends?"

I shrugged. "Sometimes I don't know what to say. I feel awkward."

"Why do you feel that way?"

I ran my fingers over my warm cup and inhaled the scent of the hot chocolate. "Most seventeen-year-old girls don't like working on cars like I do. Some may know how to check their oil, but that's about it."

She gave a knowing smile. "Did you know that Mindy Levine loves to play chess and Cassie Porter likes to build model trains?"

I shook my head. "I didn't know that."

"You're not the only teenage girl with an unusual hobby, but you won't find those things out until you talk to people and get to know them." She sipped more coffee.

I studied my cross, debating how much to share.

"What did you mean about having a hard time talking to God?" she asked.

"I think he's forgotten me," I whispered, tears filling my eyes. "When he took my mother, he abandoned me."

Jenna took my hand in hers. "God would never forget or abandon you."

"Then maybe I forgot how to talk to him, because I can't form the words." I wiped my eyes as the tears flowed. "I found my mother's Bible, and she highlighted verses and left me a letter, telling me to pray. She was one of the strongest Christians I've ever known, and that Bible was so ... helpful to her. I've tried so hard to follow her advice, and I've read that Bible until my eyes can't focus, but I can't form the words. Last week I finally was able to say something to him, but it wasn't much at all. It's like I've lost my voice when it comes to God, and I don't know what to do about it. It's so easy for others, like Zander and Whitney, but not me."

"God is always with you, Emily." She patted my hand. "In Isaiah forty-three, God tells us, 'When you pass through the waters, I will be with you; and when you pass through the rivers, they will not sweep over you. When you walk through the fire, you will not be burned; the flames will not set you ablaze.' "

"But I don't *feel* him," I whispered. "I read the Bible and I wear my mother's cross, but I don't feel his presence in my life like I did before she died."

"Maybe God's been there all along," she said. "You just haven't realized it."

I nodded, letting her words soak through me. *Was she right? Had I missed God all together?*

Jenna made small talk about school until we finished our

drinks. Throughout our conversation, I ignored the chiming of my phone, which rang several times.

Jenna stood and pulled on her coat. "Would you like a ride home?"

"No, thank you," I said, tossing our cups into the trash can. "I can run pretty fast."

Jenna smiled and rubbed my arm. "I'm glad you called me, Emily. Give me a call in a few days and let me know how you're doing."

"Thank you," I said as we headed for the door. "It was good talking to you."

I headed back through the rain toward the neighborhood in an attempt to clear my head. Trudging up the driveway, I spotted Whitney's new orange Jeep Compass and I rolled my eyes. I wondered where my hand-me-down car had wound up. Whitney had told me last week that she was having issues with the Accord, and from the way she described it, the Honda belonged in a transmission shop. Even after the car was fixed, I couldn't even imagine driving it to school and facing all of the people who'd heard Darlene's little speech about passing it down to me.

I faced the Stewart's driveway and was surprised to see that Zander's Jeep wasn't parked there. Glancing back toward Whitney's house, I found the lights blazing in the kitchen. Although the rain had increased, I wasn't ready to go into the house and face Darlene.

I craved some solace to calm my pounding heart.

Without much thought, I crossed to Zander's garage, punched in the code, and entered through the bay door. After flipping on the light and closing the door, I walked to the front of the car. I craned my neck and glanced under the hood of the Dodge and found that the gas lines weren't hooked up. I smiled. It was the perfect project for clearing my head.

Rolling up my sleeves, I set to hook the line from the gas tank to the fuel pump and then connected the fuel pump to the carburetor. While I worked, Jenna's words echoed through my mind, and suddenly I felt the urge to pray.

"God," I began out loud, "you might not be listening to me, but if you are, I'm here. I've been here, waiting to feel your presence in my life again. There's so much I don't understand, and it hurts, God. It hurts so much." Tears spilled from my eyes, and I wiped them with my arm.

Leaning over the engine, I continued attaching the lines. I thought I heard a noise on the other side of the car, but I kept working and praying, certain I'd imagined it.

"God," I continued, "Jenna says you've been here all along, and I've probably been shutting you out. But I feel so alone. I've lost everyone who mattered. First you took my mom, and I still don't understand why. Why did you let cancer steal her from Dad and me?" My tears began to flow in full force, but I kept talking, ignoring the quaver in my thick voice. "She was everything to us, God. Then you sent me Zander, and I thought things would be better. But I messed that up. I need him, God. I need your help to get his friendship back, God. Without him, I feel lost."

I couldn't stop the sobs when they started in full force. I lowered myself onto a stool behind me and wiped my eyes with my sleeves. I saw movement out of the corner of my eye. When I glanced up, I found Zander standing by the workbench, watching me with his arms folded across his chest and a tender expression on his handsome face.

"How long have you been standing there?" I asked, my voice croaking from the tears.

"A few minutes. I thought you might be in here, so I sort of snuck in through the side door. I actually found the key last week." He nodded toward the car. "This explains the visits from the engine fairy."

I cleared my throat and gave him a weak smile. "Surprise. Just call me Tinker Bell."

"How long have you been breaking into my garage and fixing my car?" he asked, his voice gentle instead of accusing.

"For a while." I grabbed a shop rag from the bench behind me and began to wipe the grease from my hands. "I should go." I stood. "I'm sorry for breaking in. I had no right to—"

"It's okay," he said, pulling up a stool next to me. "Please stay. We need to talk." He sat down.

"Yeah, we do." I felt the lump returning to my throat. I had to apologize, but I didn't know where to begin. I remembered Chelsea's and Whitney's advice: I just needed to say it.

"I'm sorry for all of those horrible things I said to you," I said, tears flooding my eyes again. "You're not spoiled, and you don't get everything handed to you." My voice quavered. "You're not self-righteous either."

He stood, opening his arms to me. "I'm sorry too."

With tears spilling down my hot cheeks, I stepped into his hug, enjoying the aroma of his musky scent and the feel of his muscular arms around me. I took deep breaths and willed myself to stop crying.

He blew out a deep sigh and rested his cheek on the top of my head. "I didn't mean it when I said you were bitter. I was just frustrated because I wanted to help you." He reached for something on the bench behind him. "I got you a birthday present."

I wiped the tears from my face and took the small box from him. "You didn't have to."

He smiled. "Yeah, I did. I'm a lousy friend, because I've actually had it awhile."

I opened the small box, pulling out a dainty silver bracelet with a cross charm on it. "Zander," I whispered. "It's beautiful." I lifted my wrist. "Will you put it on me?"

He took the bracelet and attached it to my wrist. "I'd

planned to give it to you and tell you that I thought this would help you find your way back to God. It was supposed to be a little reminder that God loves you." He shook his head. "But I went about showing you that in the wrong way."

I studied his eyes, stunned by his words. "What do you mean?"

He touched my arm. "Your faith journey is different than mine. When you said you lost your faith in God when your mom passed away, I thought I needed to push you back to him, but you needed to find your faith in your own way."

"You're right. I'm different from you." I gestured toward the car. "I realized tonight that this is the only way I really know how to cope. I worked on cars as a way to deal with my mom's illness, and I also needed the repair work to get me through my grief after her death. This is the only place where I can clear my head and reconnect with myself, and apparently with God." I shook my head. "It took me a long time to realize that, but when we moved here I lost my little sanctuary and I had no means of escaping until you invited me to share your garage."

"I'm glad you're coming over. You're always welcome here." His eyes were soft as he touched my shoulder. "I was so worried about you tonight."

"You were?" I whispered, my heart thumping against my rib cage due to his close proximity.

"I knew Darlene's stupid comment had hurt you," he said, his eyes narrowing. "I tried to stop you when you took off, but you left so fast. I'd been driving around trying to find you, but it was like you disappeared into thin air." He ran his thumb down my cheekbone. "I'm sorry for pushing you away. I assumed that faith had to be a certain way, but I've realized that we all experience it differently."

I swallowed, trying to stop my throat from going dry at his touch. "You were right when you said I built a wall up to keep people out. I was defensive and I overreacted to things, like when I heard you'd dated Whitney. I'm so sorry for hurting you, Zander."

Leaning forward, his lips brushed mine, sending the pit of my stomach into a wild swirl.

"I've missed you," he murmured against my ear.

"I've missed you too," I said, looking up into his eyes. "Let's never get into a fight like that again."

He smiled and wrapped his arms around my waist. "That sounds like a good plan."

He kissed me again and then nodded toward the clock, which read nearly 1 a.m. "I guess you better get home," he said, pushing my hair back behind my shoulder. "Your dad was really worried about you. We can talk more tomorrow when I get off work."

Looping his arm around my shoulder, we stepped toward the side door. "While I'm at work, you can finish hooking up the gas lines since you're an expert at breaking into my garage," he said with a laugh.

"Gee, thanks," I said.

We stepped out into the rain, and he kissed me again, causing my legs to wobble.

"Good night, Chevy Girl," he said. "I'll call you tomorrow."

"Good night," I said, smiling.

I felt as if I were floating as I headed toward the deck.

However, the floating feeling didn't last long. When I stepped through the sliding glass door and found my father sitting at the kitchen table and glaring at me, I quickly crashed to earth.

"Where have you been, Emily Claire?" he demanded. "You scared us to death."

Darlene stood frowning by the counter. "We were searching for you, and you didn't bother to answer your phone,"

I tossed my wet hair back from my cheeks. "I'm sorry I didn't answer my phone, but I needed time to sort through some things."

"What things were so important that you would scare your family like that?" Darlene asked.

"It's personal." I looked at my dad for help. I didn't want to talk about Darlene's stupid comment in front of her. "I needed some time alone, and so I went for a walk."

"For four hours?" Darlene asked.

"Yes," I said, even though I hadn't realized it had been that long.

"Emily, please sit," my father said.

"Actually, I think I need to go to bed." I started for the stairs. "I really want to get out of these wet clothes and head to—"

"Sit, Emily!" My father's booming voice caused me to jump. In my seventeen years of life, I'd heard my father yell a handful of times. He rarely lost his temper with me, and it was even rarer to hear him bellow like that. I knew by his tone that I was in for it.

I dropped into the chair and hugged my arms to my chest while my dad stood over me, glowering with such intensity that I winced.

I opened my mouth to defend myself, but my father cut me off.

"Emily, you're in deep trouble," he growled. "Consider yourself grounded until after New Year's."

"What?" My voice squeaked. "Are you serious?"

"I'm quite serious." He shook his head, scowling.

I jumped up from the chair. "I'm grounded because I needed to clear my head? This is outrageous!" I turned and started toward the door, but my father grabbed my arm and pulled me back.

"Sit down," he said. "We're not done. You're grounded because you took off without telling anyone where you were going and you—"

"I walked to the coffee shop and had a hot chocolate with Jenna, the youth pastor. Then I talked to Zander in his garage for a while. Is that really a crime?" I asked, leaning against the table. "I'm seventeen. I can come and go as I please."

"No, you cannot," he said, wagging a finger millimeters from my face. "That was irresponsible, and to make it even worse, you ignored our calls and texts to find you."

"I wanted to finish talking to Jenna," I said. "If I'd realized it was you—"

"And you worried us all," Darlene interjected. "We had to end Whitney's party early to look for you."

So that was it. In Darlene's eyes, I ruined Whitney's royal party.

I'd had enough of the way Darlene treated me. In that instant, I saw red, and I snapped.

"But *you're* the reason why I left the party," I said, pointing an accusing finger at her. "Didn't you realize that your comment about giving me the old hand-me-down car was humiliating? Don't you ever think about how you talk to me? How you put me down and criticize me?"

"Emily Claire!" My father's voice boomed again, causing the hair to stand up straight on the back of my neck. "Do not talk to your aunt like that. I don't care how angry you are. It's disrespectful, and I will *not* put up with it."

How could he betray me like this? Tears of anger welled up in my eyes as I looked between them.

"I humiliated you?" Darlene pointed to her chest. "But I'm giving you a car. That's humiliating? When I was your age, I could only dream of a car."

I shook my head and looked at my dad, hoping he would see

my side of things, but he just continued to look hurt, filling me with a mixture of outrage and guilt.

"She appreciates the car," my dad said quickly. "And I will pay you back for it."

"I don't want the stupid car," I said. "I'd rather take the bus." I started for the stairs.

"Emily!" my father bellowed. "Emily Claire!" He grabbed my arm and yanked me back, causing me to stumble. "You will not speak to your aunt that way and take off. You're going to apologize right now."

"Why? Because of all she's done for me?" I asked, my voice trembling as tears filled my eyes.

My father glared at me. "You have absolutely no respect or appreciation for all she's done for us. What about the roof over our heads? The clothes? The phone? How could you forget it all?"

"Oh, no," I snapped. "I remember it all." I pulled out the phone and stared at it. It was time for me to let it all out and tell her how I truly felt. I'd kept it bottled up for too long. "I appreciate the phone, but I despise being your charity case."

Darlene shook her head, her brown eyes glistening with tears. "I'm sorry you feel that way. I thought I was helping you. I gave you everything out of the goodness of my heart, not to make you feel bad."

"I'm also tired of being criticized," I continued, starting to feel confident. "I'm sick of hearing that you don't like how I dress or how I wear my hair. I'm not Whitney, and I never will be. I don't want to be a cheerleader, and I'll never be an honor student. Take me as I am or leave me alone."

"Emily," my dad hissed. "You better quit before you say something that you'll really regret."

I turned to him, irate tears spilling from my eyes. "You asked for the truth, and I'm going to give it you." My voice sounded foreign to me—too high and thick.

"I think it's time for you to apologize and then go to your room," he said.

"No." I shook my head, my voice quavering with hurt and anger. "I'm not finished." I raised a finger at him. I was on a roll. This was cathartic. "And I'm sick of trying to get you to talk to me. Why do you share your feelings with Pastor Keith and not me?"

I stood, my body shaking like a leaf in the wind. "You never ask me how I feel or how I'm coping. I lost Mom too. And neither of you," I began, looking between them, "asked me how it felt to have my first birthday without Mom. Whitney was the only one who bothered to see how I felt that night." I started for the door.

"Emily," Darlene called.

"Emily Claire!" my dad shouted.

Ignoring them, I raced up to my room, slamming and locking the door. I curled up on my bed and sobbed. I'd gone from flying high after kissing Zander to falling into a deep, suffocating abyss of despair.

A knock sounded at the door. "Emily?" Whitney asked.

"Go away," I grumbled, my voice barely a whisper.

"Do you want to talk?" she asked.

"Please," I said. "Not now."

"Whitney," Darlene's voice snapped outside the door. "Go to your room!"

"What did you do to her?" Whitney demanded, her voice moving away from the door.

I pulled my phone from my pocket and examined the missed call list, finding unanswered calls from my dad, Darlene, Whitney, Chelsea, and Zander. They were all worried about me, but that was still no reason for my dad and Darlene to go unhinged. There was one bar left on the battery indicator. I wondered if it was enough to text Zander and see if he could talk.

Glancing toward the window, I hoped Zander was still up. I texted: R U up? I need 2 talk.

Not receiving an answer, I sent the same text to Chelsea.

I tried to text Zander again, but the phone went dead. I smacked my forehead, wishing I'd brought the charger up from the kitchen. I hadn't heard my father's footsteps in the hallway, and I didn't want to risk running down to get it and seeing him again.

I snatched the framed photograph of my parents and me from two Christmases ago from the nightstand and stared at my mom's beautiful face.

"Why did you leave me, Mom?" I whispered, my voice choked back with sobs. "Why, Mom?"

The cross on my wrist twinkled in the light and I studied it, pondering what Jenna had said about God. How had I missed him?

I placed the photograph back on the nightstand and curled up on the bed. Closing my eyes, I opened my heart and I prayed.

"God," I whispered. "Are you there? I'm ready to tell you everything, beginning with how I felt when I lost Mom."

I talked to God until I ran out of words. And then I cried myself to sleep.

chapter nineteen

I awoke at noon the following day and noticed that the house was eerily quiet. Sitting up, I found myself clad in the wet clothes I'd worn the night before. The damp sweatshirt was zipped and clung to my body. My hair was a knot of curls hanging past my shoulders. I pushed them back, grabbed clean clothes, and headed toward the hallway, finding a note in my dad's handwriting taped to my door. I opened it and read:

> *Emily:*
> *I'm going to work. Whitney and her mother went*
> *Christmas shopping, and Uncle Chuck and Logan are headed*
> *to Logan's karate class. You're to stay home. We'll talk later.*
> *Dad*

I sighed as the events of last night played through my mind like some jumbled-up dream. My dad was still fuming, and I still had to face the consequences of going missing after the party and telling off my aunt. I felt somewhat at peace, however, which didn't make sense at all. What had changed since I'd gone to bed?

Then it hit me: I'd prayed. I'd finally been able to open my heart up to God.

Glancing down, I studied my bracelet and I thought of

Zander. I smiled as the warmth of those amazing kisses filled me. What did they mean? Were we finally a couple? Was I Zander Stewart's girlfriend?

Pushing the thoughts aside, I headed to the shower. When I got back to my room I was refreshed. I stood before my mirror and began the tedious task of combing out my curls and forcing them into a ponytail at the nape of my neck.

While running the pick through my hair, my eyes moved to two photographs stuck in the bottom of the mirror. Both were taken on Halloween and in the den; one featured Chelsea and me and the other Zander and me. I picked them up and studied them.

Then something Jenna had said last night echoed through my mind—maybe God's been there all along.

Movement in my peripheral vision drew my eyes to the window, where I spotted Zander's Jeep coming to a jerky stop in Whitney's driveway. He slammed on the emergency break and then leapt from the truck without closing his door, his face showing panic.

I moved to the window and watch as he took the deck stairs in one bound and then heard him banging on the back door and yelling my name.

"Emily!" he shouted. "Emily! It's an emergency. Emily!"

My heart racing, I dropped the photographs. As I ran down to the kitchen, Zander's voice echoed through the empty house.

"Emily!" he yelled, banging on the glass. "Open the door!"

My body shook with fear as I unlocked the sliding glass door and opened it with a whoosh. When I saw his eyes, icy fear prickled my back.

"Emily." He grasped my forearms. "I need you to come with me."

"What's going on?" I asked.

He took a deep breath. "There's been an accident."

"My dad?" I whispered.

He nodded, and my knees buckled. He caught me and leaned down over me, his eyes probing mine. "Emily, I need you to be strong. Get your coat. I'll drive you to the hospital."

I stared at him, trying to comprehend his words while tears flooded my eyes. "Is he ...? Is he ...?" I stammered.

"He's hurt, but I think he's going to be okay." He swiped away my tears with his fingertip. "I need you to get your coat, and I'll get you to the hospital as quick as I can, okay?"

I searched the kitchen, not remembering where I kept my coat. All I could think was that my dad was hurt, and he and I had fought last night. What if he ...? The thought trailed off as fresh tears streamed down my face.

"I don't know where my coat is," I blubbered like a moron.

He rubbed my arm. "It's going to be okay." He moved me to a chair and gestured for me to sit down. "You sit here and remember where your shoes are."

Shoes I could handle; they were always by the back door. I slipped on my boots while Zander disappeared into the hallway and came back with my coat. I shrugged into the coat, and we rushed to the Jeep.

Hugging my arms to my chest, I stared out the window while we drove in silence. A zillion thoughts assaulted my mind while worry and fear tangled within me. I wiped away my tears, trying in vain to be strong.

When Zander slowed to stop at a light, he covered my hand with his and the warmth of skin offered a little comfort amidst the panic.

I turned to him. "What happened?" I said softly, my voice trembling and thin.

Zander paused, and my heart thumped. *It has to be bad or he wouldn't have to filter his words.*

"We're slammed with work at the shop," he began, "so he

wanted to help out. He was sanding a car, and the grinder came apart."

Bile rose in my throat, and I gnawed my lower lip. I'd heard of that happening, where the disk with the sandpaper flew off like a Frisbee, a missile shredding anything in its path.

"How ...?" My voice trailed off.

"He was sanding a car and the disc got caught in the gap between two panels," he said slowly. "The grinding disc broke in half. With it spinning as fast as it was, it turned into a saw blade."

"And it sliced his left arm?" I asked, knowing that my dad was right handed and the disc would've flown toward his left.

"Yeah." He took my hand in his again as more tears flowed from my eyes.

A car horn blasted behind us. Letting go of my hand, Zander quickly put the Jeep in gear and accelerated though the intersection.

"Is it bad?" My voice was barely audible over the whining of the engine.

Zander kept his eyes on the road. "Yeah."

"How bad?" I asked. As grisly as it was, I needed to know if my dad was going to make it. I had to prepare myself for the worst.

"It was bad," he said, his voice trembling with emotion. He really cared, and it gave me comfort. "I think it was to the bone."

"Oh no." My tears flowed. I sniffed, hoping to get control of myself and stop my body from shaking.

"But we got him stabilized," Zander said quickly.

I looked at Zander's uniform shirt—really studied it—for the first time since he'd come to get me, and I saw dark splotches dotting the front it. Reaching over I touched it and then gasped.

"Is that my dad's blood?" My voice sounded distant.

He looked at me and his mouth was a thin line.

"You helped him?" I asked.

"Shawn, one of the auto body techs, is a certified EMT. He took his shirt off, and I helped him wrap the arm and apply pressure until the ambulance arrived. We had to stop the bleeding fast. Shawn said if we didn't, your dad could've ..."

He didn't have to finish the sentence. I already knew what he was going to say—my dad could've bled to death. "Thank you," I whispered. "You saved his life."

Zander shrugged and smacked on the turn signal. "I just did what Shawn told me to do while one of the other guys got on the phone and called for help." He merged onto Main Street. "As soon as the ambulance got there and they took over, I ran out the door to come get you. I wanted to get to you as soon as I could. I didn't want to call you because I thought I should tell you face-to-face." He gave me a sideways glance. "I got your text from last night. I don't know what time you sent it, but I must've been asleep. I'm sorry I missed it."

"Oh no!" I smacked my jeans pockets. "I don't have my phone! How am I going to call Darlene and Chuck?" But then I remembered—my phone was dead on my dresser.

"It's okay." He cradled my hand in his. "I have my phone."

As if on cue his cell phone began to ring from his pocket. He yanked it out and pressed it to his ear, while I stared out the window, questions and worry assaulting my brain. I silently prayed, begging God to not take my father.

I couldn't bear the thought of losing him. Not now. Please, not now. The anniversary of my mom's death was next week. I couldn't handle this right now. It was like some cruel joke.

"Yeah?" he asked, all business. "Okay. How is he? Right. Yeah, I got her. We're on our way now. We're just around the corner. She's holding it together okay. Yeah, I'm going to call them when we get there. All right. Thanks, Jack." He hung up and dropped the phone into the cup holder. "Jack's at the hospital."

I wanted to ask questions but was afraid my voice would betray me and my tears would take over.

Zander roared into the parking lot of Cameronville Memorial Hospital and steered to the drop-off in front of the emergency room. He brought the Jeep to a rough stop and I turned to him.

He's abandoning me? "You're just dropping me off?" I asked, my voice trembling.

"Are you serious?" he asked, looking stunned. "I thought it would be faster if I dropped you off while I go find a parking space."

"Oh!" Relief flooded me.

"I'll be back soon." He gave me a forced smile. "Everything will be okay. Your dad is in God's hands."

"Right," I said, climbing from the Jeep.

He waved me off. "Go on. I'll be back."

I slammed the door, and he motored through the parking lot. I rushed into the emergency room, finding a group of men dressed in the same uniform as Zander huddled together in a corner. I raced over to them and approached a man clad in jeans and a plain button-down shirt, assuming he was Jack since he wasn't wearing a work uniform.

"Jack?" I asked, hoping to sound confident.

His eyes lit up. "Emily?"

"How's my dad?" My voice betrayed my feigned confidence.

He sighed, and I bit my bottom lip, hoping to keep it from shaking. He placed a hand on my shoulder and led me away from the group. "He didn't look good when they loaded him into the ambulance, but the EMTs said he was in shock."

I sucked in a breath.

"Let's get you up to the desk and find the doctor," he said. With his hand on my back, he steered me up to the desk, where he told a woman that I was Bradley Curtis's daughter. We then stood together and stared at a flat-screen television on the wall while we waited. A man on the screen rambled on about the possibility of rain, but his words didn't register in my brain. All I could think about was my dad.

And I prayed.

I prayed he wasn't in pain. I prayed for the doctors. I prayed for myself, begging God to not take my only living parent.

The waiting room doors opened with a whoosh, and Zander entered with his phone pressed to his ear. "Right. Okay. Thanks." He hung up and approached me. "I called Whitney and Chelsea. They're on their way."

"Thank you." I wrung my hands, and Zander pulled me into his arms.

"He'll be just fine," he whispered into my ear.

"The family of Bradley Curtis," a female voice called.

Turning, I found a middle-aged female nurse wearing scrubs standing by the door leading back into the hospital. I hesitated, worry keeping me cemented in place.

Zander took my hand in his and gave me a hopeful smile. "I'll come with you." He led me to the nurse.

"Are you the family of Bradley Curtis?" she asked.

"Yes," I said. "Bradley is my father."

"What is your name?" she asked.

"Emily Curtis," I said. I touched Zander's chest. "This is my best friend, Alexander Stewart."

She gestured toward a small conference room off the waiting room. "Let's go talk in there."

I looked up at Zander, and he nodded, encouraging me to move. We followed her into the room and sat on a sofa across from her.

Her expression became grave. "Emily, your father is hurt badly."

Zander squeezed my hand.

"He was cut severely by that grinder," she said, her expression portraying sympathy. "It cut him almost to the bone, but the extent of the damage isn't known yet. There is a team of doctors with him now, and they've taken him in for emergency surgery so they can assess the damage and see what needs to be done. They're not certain yet if he severed muscles, nerves, blood vessels, or all three."

I blinked, letting the words permeate my mind.

"Is Dr. Michael Stewart on the team?" Zander asked.

The nurse looked surprised. "Yes, I think he is."

"That's my father," Zander said. He smiled at me. "Your dad is in the best hands, Emily. Have faith."

A glimmer of hope flickered in my mind—until the reality set in. "Is my dad going to lose his arm?"

"No," the nurse said with certainty. "Depending upon the damage, however, he may lose some function."

A whimper escaped from my throat without warning.

"Hey." Zander pulled me to him and I rested my head on his chest. "God is watching out for your dad. He's in control."

The nurse reached over and touched my hand. "Alexander is right. His father is an excellent orthopedic surgeon. In fact, he's the best at our hospital. Your father is in very good hands."

I wiped my eyes and nodded, unable to speak.

"Now, your dad will probably be in surgery for a few hours. I'll come out to give you updates." She squeezed my hand. "We're going to take good care of him."

Zander put an arm around my shoulders and led me back out to the waiting room, where he gave Jack and the rest of the crew from the body shop the update on my dad's condition.

I glanced at the uniforms in front of me until I spotted a man in a uniform shirt without his name sewn onto it. I guessed he was Shawn since Zander had said that the man who saved my dad had removed his shirt to stop the bleeding. He was a tall, lean man who looked to be about twenty-five or so. He had sandy blond hair and dark eyes.

I approached him and took a deep breath. "Are you Shawn?" I asked.

He stood. "Hi, Emily."

I wrapped my arms around him and hugged him tight as tears filled my eyes anew. "Thank you for saving my daddy."

He gave me a sad smile. "You're welcome, Emily. I think the world of your dad. I just pray he's okay."

Zander rubbed my back. "How about we go for a walk to get your mind off things?"

I nodded, wiping my eyes.

"We'll be back in a bit," Zander told Jack. "Have you met Brad's sister, Darlene?"

"Yeah," Jack said. "She stopped by the shop the other day."

"Would you keep a lookout for her?" Zander asked. "Also, could you look for Chelsea Morris? She's a redhead and our age."

"Sure thing," Jack said. "I'll text your cell when they get here."

With his arm around my shoulders, Zander led me down the hallway. "Are you hungry?"

As if on cue, my stomach growled, and I hugged my middle. "I haven't eaten anything since lunch yesterday."

"Let's get you something to eat."

I frowned. "I don't know if I could keep anything down."

"Don't be silly. Would you like a turkey sandwich?" he asked.

I shrugged. "Okay." Then I patted my pockets. "I don't have any money. I left my purse at the house."

"Please." He smiled, showing his dimple. "I think I can handle buying you something to eat. I do have a job, remember."

We found our way to the cafeteria, and Zander directed me to the tables before getting in line for food. I sat at a secluded table in a far corner and rested my head in my hands while I tried to make sense of everything that had happened since I'd walked out of Whitney's party last night. It had been a whirlwind of emotions—from a heart-to-heart talk with Jenna to the dreamy kisses from Zander. And then, without warning, my world came crashing down when I stepped into the kitchen and faced my father and aunt.

The conversation I'd had with Dad and Darlene played over and over again in my mind. It all seemed too surreal. I'd had the worst argument ever with my dad and now he was in surgery and would possibly lose function in his left arm forever. How was this possible?

The clatter of a tray brought me back to reality. I lifted my head and spotted two sandwiches, an order of fries, two pieces of chocolate cake, and two fountain drinks.

"Eat," Zander said, sitting across from me.

"Thanks." I unwrapped a sandwich and took a bite, followed by a long drink of Coke.

"Talk to me," he said. "You look as if you might explode if you don't."

I shook my head and breathed out a deep, ragged breath. "I feel like I'm stuck in a terrible nightmare that started last night."

"Were my kisses that bad?" he asked with a grin.

My cheeks burned. "Actually, your kisses were the only thing that went right last night."

Reaching over, he took my hand in his, and warmth shot through my veins at his touch. "Start from the beginning. I'm listening."

My eyes filled with tears. "After I talked to you last night," I began, "I had the biggest argument ever with my dad and

Darlene. I just can't bear the thought of losing him after the things I said." I sniffed and wiped my eyes.

"Look at me." His eyes were full of determination. "You're not going to lose your dad. The nurse said nothing about him dying, right?"

"Right," I murmured, wiping away fresh tears.

"Your father has the best orthopedic surgeon in this hospital working on him. Even the nurse confirmed that. Your dad is in very good hands, and he's not critical. The only question is whether or not he'll lose the function of his arm, but my dad will do everything he can to repair it." He squeezed my hand. "Right now you need to have faith that he's going to get better. Your job is to think about what you want to say to him when you see him in recovery."

"I just wish I could take back what I said to him last night," I whispered. "It was horrible."

"Do you want to talk about it?" Zander asked.

In between nibbles, I shared what happened when I entered the kitchen last night. He listened, his kind eyes focused on me. When I finished the story, I took a long drink of soda.

Zander stuffed a fry in his mouth, and I waited for him to speak.

"I'm sure you have an opinion," I finally said. "You think I'm awful for what I said to Darlene."

"Why would you say that?" he asked.

"Because you are everyone's friend," I said. "You're practically perfect."

He snorted. "Is that really what you think of me?"

"You're everything I wish I could be," I said. "You never doubt God. You're not jealous of your brother, who is the apple of your father's eye. You're just happy-go-lucky and satisfied with everything that comes your way. I wish I had your strength."

"Are you finished eating?" he asked.

I glanced at the tray and my half-eaten sandwich. "I couldn't eat another bite if I tried."

"I want to show you something." He tossed the remnants of our lunch into the trash can and then took my hand in his. We walked back into the corridor and then he led me into a small chapel.

We sat together in the last row, and I was thankful that the chapel was empty. There were half a dozen rows of pews, and a small altar sat up front before a cross and paintings of Jesus on the wall.

"I spent a lot of time in here when my grandfather was in the hospital," he said. "Coming in here gave me comfort."

I stared at the cross and silently pleaded with God to watch over my dad.

"You may think I'm perfect, but I'm not," Zander said. "I've had my share of doubts, and I've had my share of screaming matches with my dad. I also used to resent my brother, but I finally made a decision that I wasn't going to live in his shadow anymore. I am who I am, no matter what my father thinks."

I twirled a curl around my finger and studied the thighs of my jeans while his words soaked through me.

"I'll never understand why you doubt yourself so much," he said while rubbing my back. "You don't see how amazing you truly are."

I gnawed my lower lip and turned back to the cross, wondering how much was safe to share. Then something Zander had said to me when we argued on Halloween echoed in my mind: *You choose to live in this bubble where you close out everyone who cares about you and wants to help you. You'd rather wallow in self-pity than see how God is trying to reach out to you.*

A question surfaced in my mind: Was it time for me to let Zander in completely?

"I dated a boy before I moved here," I began, my words coming without much forethought. "It was Tyler, the guy who owned that Nova I fixed. He worked in my dad's shop. I thought we were in love, but I was wrong. Shortly before we moved he broke up with me. He said I was a really cool girl, but he wasn't attracted to me that way. He said we should just be friends."

"Ouch," Zander said with a grimace.

"I guess he sort of soured me on dating and trust," I said.

"I'm sorry he did that to you, but you can't let him hold you back from someone who cares for you." He touched my arm. "And, for the record, he's a total moron." A smile formed on his lips. "I think you're really cool, and I would like to be *more* than friends." He pushed an errant curl back behind my ear. "Would you be my girlfriend?"

My heart thumped in my chest. "Yes."

"Awesome." His lips brushed mine, and for a brief moment, all of my worries and problems evaporated. When he looked down at me, his eyes were filled with warmth and comfort. "Do you want to pray together?" he asked. "I mean, if you don't want to—"

"No, that would be nice," I said.

He took my hands in his, and we closed our eyes. Zander whispered a prayer asking God to watch over my dad, give the doctors wisdom and skill, and give me strength and faith.

Once he was finished, his phone chimed. He read the text and then stood, pulling me to my feet. "You have company in the waiting room."

chapter twenty

I entered the waiting room grasping Zander's hand. Scanning the room, my mouth gaped as I found my family, the guys from the body shop, Chelsea, Pastor Keith, Jenna, and a host of kids from school, including Chad, Monica, Tiffany, and Kristin. There were also kids from youth group—some of the faces familiar and others not.

"Why are all of these people here?" I whispered to Zander.

"Because they're worried about you and your dad," he said with a smile. "You don't realize how many people really care."

A mixture of emotions surged through me at the sight of so many people. Zander pulled me toward the group, and Darlene and Whitney approached us.

"Emily!" Darlene pulled me into her arms. "Oh, honey. We're so sorry about the accident. We got here as soon as we could." She cupped my face with her hands. "Are you all right?"

I studied her brown eyes, wondering if she was still miffed at me. I didn't see any sign of anger, but how would she feel about me when my father was better?

"Emily?" Dropping her hands from my face, she looked confused. "Are you all right? Do you need to sit?"

"I'm okay," I said. "I'm a bit shaken up, but I think I'll be okay." I grasped Zander's arm. "Zander's dad is one of the surgeons, so I believe my dad's in good hands."

"Good." Darlene gave a forced smile and patted my arm. "We've got to trust God now. He'll take care of everything."

Whitney pulled me into a hug, and I held onto her. "My mom's right, Em. God will watch out for your dad. From what I've heard, the accident could've been much worse."

Chelsea weaved through the crowd and hugged me next. "I'll stay with you all night if you need me to," she whispered in my ear.

"Thanks," I said. I stood in the same place for what seemed like an hour, accepting hugs and good wishes from friends, acquaintances, and total strangers who introduced themselves as members of my "church family."

Pastor Keith instructed us to form a circle. I stood between Chelsea and Zander and across from Darlene, Whitney, Logan, Chuck, and a host of friends and acquaintances. Once we were all holding hands, Pastor Keith said a prayer for my father and the doctors.

As the afternoon wore on, the nurse came out and gave an update, explaining that the doctors were sewing my dad up and it would take another hour or so before he was out of surgery. I sat between Zander and Chelsea on the sofa and stared at reruns of some old sitcom on the flat screen, wondering how long this day could possibly last.

After nearly two hours, the nurse appeared again. With a smile, she took my hand and pulled me to my feet. "Your father is in recovery. He made it through fine."

A cheer went up throughout the waiting room, and I hugged the nurse.

Turning, I found myself in Zander's warm embrace.

"I told you to trust God," he whispered.

Before I could respond to him, Darlene pulled me into a hug, followed by Chelsea and then Whitney.

Once the hugs were complete, I turned back to the nurse. "When can I see him?"

"It will be a little while," she said. "He just got to recovery and has to come out of the anesthesia." She squeezed my hand. "I'll come and get you as soon as it's time."

The crowd in the waiting room dissipated. Friends from school and youth group slowly left, promising to call or text later to see how he was doing. I thanked them all for coming and promised to keep them updated.

Zander, Chelsea, and I made a trip to the cafeteria around six and ate pizza. Chelsea kept my mind occupied by chatting about her current costume project and the cute boy on the stage crew, who now knew Chelsea's name and frequently made small talk with her.

Later, we sat in the waiting room and watched the news. I leaned against Zander and closed my eyes, hoping to catch a nap before going into my dad's room. Around seven, the nurse came back out and said family members could come back.

I hugged Chelsea. "You should go home," I said.

She shook her head. "You need me. I'm staying."

"Don't be silly. I'll be fine here." I motioned toward the door. "Go home and get some rest. You can come back and keep me company tomorrow. He'll probably be moved to a regular room, and you can sit with me and watch the news and old sitcoms for hours there."

She raised an eyebrow. "You sure?"

"Positive." I walked to the door with her. "Thank you. I couldn't have made it without you."

"I doubt that. You have Zander to keep you company," she whispered. "There's nothing like eye candy to keep up your spirits."

I felt my cheeks heat, and I chose to ignore her comment. "Get on home. I'll call you later. I have lots to tell you."

"Really?" she asked with a grin.

"Yes," I whispered. "He kissed me and asked me to be his girlfriend."

She squealed, and I shushed her. "I promise I'll call you later," I said.

"Promise?" she asked.

"Absolutely," I said.

She said good-bye and hurried through the doors to the parking lot.

I walked over to Zander. "I wish you could come back there with me."

"I'll wait here for you," he said, locking his eyes on mine. "I'll text my dad and see if he can get me permission to come back. He has some pull around here."

"Good." I took a deep breath.

"Go on," Zander said. "It's going to be okay. I promise you."

A warm hand took mine. "I'll come with you," Darlene said.

I gave Darlene an unsure expression.

"Come on," she said. "We need to let him know we're here."

Darlene and I followed the nurse through several doors and down two hallways to a small room. I found my dad in the bed, his left arm covered in a bandage. His skin was pale, almost gray, and his eyes were dull. My body began to tremble, and a lump swelled in my throat.

He gave us a forced smile. "Fancy meeting you here," he said, his voice a mere whisper.

I felt a glimmer of hope—my dad still had his wacky sense of humor. He was going to be okay.

"He's a little groggy from the anesthesia and the pain medicine," the nurse said quietly. "I'll be down the hall if you need me." She disappeared out of the room, closing the door behind her.

"We've been worried about you," Darlene said, standing over him. "How are you?"

"Oh, I've been better," he croaked. His eyes fell on me. "Baby Doll."

"Hey, Daddy." I rasped, tears trickling down my cheeks. "You scared me to death." I tried to smile, but my lips formed a thin line. "If you ever put me through anything like this again, I'll beat your behind."

He tried to laugh but coughed instead and then winced. "Wow," he mumbled, his voice gravely. "This scratch hurts a bit."

"You should take it easy," Darlene said, touching his good hand. "Don't work so hard to talk."

I lowered myself into a chair next to his bed and cleared my throat. Memories of sitting next to my mother's hospital bed a year ago flashed through my mind. Glancing down, I found my hands shaking and I hugged my arms to my chest, trying to force my body to calm down.

"I wonder how long I'll be stuck in this place," my dad said, his voice a little stronger. "I guess they don't send you home the same day when you slice open your arm like I did, huh?"

"I would imagine it will be a few days," Darlene said, sitting in a chair across from me. "You need to only worry about getting better."

His brown eyes studied me, and I wondered if he was still angry about everything I'd said last night. Guilt rained down on me, and I gnawed my bottom lip.

"So, how was your day?" he asked, but the mirth seemed forced.

I knew he was trying to lighten the mood, but nothing could hold back my tears. Once I started crying, I couldn't stop. The tears flooded my cheeks, trickling onto my coat. I cried for my dad, for losing my mom, and for myself. Everything I'd had pent up all day came out at once. I hugged my middle but couldn't quell my body from shaking.

He reached for me and then winced.

Darlene stood. "I'll give you two some time alone." She patted my back. "I'll be in the waiting room." She disappeared through the door, closing it gingerly behind her.

"Don't cry," he said. "I'm going to be fine."

I snatched a handful of tissues from the box by his bed and wiped my eyes and nose. Taking deep breaths, I willed myself to stop sobbing.

"You could've died today," I whispered. "And I never would've had a chance to say I was sorry."

"Shh," he said. "You need to stop worrying."

"I'm sorry for taking off without telling you where I was last night," I said. "I'm not sorry for what I said to Darlene, but I'm sorry about our fight."

"Let's not talk about this now," he said.

"I have to," I said, swiping the tissue across my cheeks. "I have to go home to that house tonight and so much is not settled."

He sighed. "Emily, we'll get through this, one day at a time."

I studied the metal bed railing, avoiding his stare. "I bet Darlene hates me."

"She doesn't hate you," he said. His voice was a little stronger, but he still didn't sound like himself. "Now you're just being ridiculous. I know that you have some issues with her, but you went about it all wrong by yelling at her last night. We could've sat down with her at another time and discussed it. I was upset that you went off on her and were so disrespectful."

"I shouldn't have gone off on her like that, but you both pushed me, and I snapped," I said. "Once I started unloading, I couldn't stop." My lip quivered. "I thought I was going to lose you today, like I lost Mom. I couldn't bear it if I lost you too." I leaned over and hugged him gently, the tears flowing again.

He ran his good hand through my hair. "It's okay, Baby Doll." His voice echoed in his chest with my ear resting next to it. "I'm going to be fine. We'll figure everything out when I get home. Right now I need you to be strong."

Sitting back down, I nodded.

"And you're still grounded for taking off and scaring me last night." He lifted his good finger and wagged it slightly. "Don't think this gets you out of your punishment."

I gave him a half smile. "You know, you're not good at the whole strict parent thing. Mom played that role much better than you."

"But I've been thinking about something you said," he told me. "You wanted to know if you could work. What if you worked on Saturdays, like Zander does?"

My eyes widened with surprise and excitement. "That would be great, Dad."

"I realized that I've accepted help from Darlene, but I've never let you contribute," he said. "Let's talk about the job when I get home, okay?"

"Absolutely."

"And also," he continued, "you were right about how I've suppressed my feelings about losing your mom. I need to open up to you more."

"Dad, please don't worry about that." I held his hand in mine. "You don't need to push yourself to open up to me. It was unfair of me to insist you talk to me."

"No, you were right." He gave me a weak smile. "We're in this together, Baby Doll."

A knock sounded at the door and Dr. Stewart stuck his head in the room.

I stood. "Hi, Dr. Stewart."

"Hello, Emily." He entered the room clutching a clipboard. "How are you feeling, Brad?"

"I've been better." My dad forced a smile. "I guess I messed up my arm a bit."

Dr. Stewart hugged the clipboard to his white coat. "That you did."

I studied his features, wondering if that was how Zander would look in twenty or so years.

"I did my best to put your arm back together. You severed some vessels and muscles." Dr. Stewart shook his head. "I'm not going to lie to you. You did some serious damage, but you should regain full function after some rehabilitation. It just might take some time."

"When can he come home?" I asked.

"It might be a few days," Dr. Stewart said, glanced through the pages on the clipboard. "We need to be sure he's on the right path with his healing."

I pushed my hair behind my ears and wondered what this would mean for our future. Would my dad be able to go back to work? Would we ever get to move into our own place? But at least he'd finally decided to let me work, so I could make a contribution. I had to trust it would be okay.

Dr. Stewart checked the bandage and listened to my dad's heart and lungs. He then started for the door. "My son wants to come back and see you. Would that be okay with you?"

"Of course," my dad said. "Your boy is family. Right, Emily?"

I nodded.

"I'll direct him back." Dr. Stewart gripped the doorknob. "I'm going to head out, but I'll be back to check on you tomorrow. Do you need more pain medication?"

My dad cupped his good hand to his forehead. "I think it's time. It's starting to throb."

"I'll send the nurse in. Good night." Dr. Stewart disappeared through the door and the nurse came in a few moments later with some pills, which my dad took with a small glass of water. After quickly eying his vitals, the nurse disappeared as well.

"Sorry to disappoint Zander, but these meds are potent. I think I'm going to close my eyes," my dad said, his voice soft and weak. "You should go home and rest."

"I want to stay for a while," I said. "I need to make sure you're okay."

"I'm going to be just fine," he said, his voice fading. Within minutes, he was asleep.

I found the remote control and flipped channels until I came to the evening news. I was watching a story about a robbery at a grocery store when Zander and Darlene came into the room.

Darlene waved me over, and we stood in the hallway. "I spoke with Dr. Stewart. It sounds like your dad is going to be in here a few days."

"Yeah, it does," I said, hugging my arms to my chest.

"He may have a long road of recovery ahead of him," she said, shaking her head. "He really did some damage."

"But it could've been a lot worse," Zander interjected.

I yawned and cupped my hand to my mouth.

"I think the stress is taking a toll on you, dear," Darlene said with a knowing look. "We should head home."

"No," I said. "I'm not ready to leave him."

"It's been a long day," she said. "You can come back tomorrow."

"What if I sat with her for a few minutes?" Zander said, looping an arm around my shoulders and pulling me to him. "I'll make sure she doesn't stay too late."

Darlene looked unconvinced.

"I promise I won't let her stay longer than an hour," he

offered. "We'll just make sure Mr. Curtis is resting okay and then we'll head home. You have my word."

She paused for a moment, considering it. "Fine," she said, holding up her finger up as a warning. "But only an hour, understood?"

"Yes, ma'am." He gave a deliberate nod. "I'll make sure of it."

"All right then." She touched my arm. "I'll see you at the house."

She disappeared down the hallway and I turned to Zander. "Thank you."

He shrugged. "No big deal. I knew you wanted more time."

"I don't know how I'm going to return to that house. I said some pretty awful things to her, and I can't take them back." I shook my head. "I know we have to talk it out, but it's going to be tough. Things are so messed up with her now."

He put his finger under my chin, forcing me to look into his eyes. "I think things are going to be just fine when you get home. She seems very supportive. Just talk things out with her."

We stepped into the room together and found my dad still sleeping. Zander frowned, his eyes studying the bandage.

I sank into the chair and Zander carried the extra chair over and sat beside me. We watched the news in silence. After an hour, I turned off the television before standing over my dad. I leaned down and kissed his cheek, and he stirred but didn't wake up.

Taking my hand, Zander led me from the room.

chapter twenty-one

I think he looked okay, considering the accident," Zander said as we drove out of the hospital parking lot.

The sky was dark, and the clock on the dashboard declared it was approaching ten. I was stunned by how quickly the day had flown by.

"I guess so. He looked really tired," I said, clasping my hands together. "Your dad seemed convinced my dad should regain full use of his arm, but he'll have to go through rehab for a while. It could be a long road back."

Zander put the Jeep in neutral, took my hand in his, and slowed to a stop at a stoplight.

"Thank you for everything," I said.

He shrugged. "It was nothing."

"No, it was everything," I said, shifting in my seat and facing him. "You saved his life, Zander. He could've bled to death."

"Like I said before, I just followed Shawn's orders." He seemed as nonchalant as if he were ordering a mocha latte at the coffeehouse.

"Without you, I wouldn't have made it through the day."

"That's not true," he said. "You had a waiting room full of people there for you."

"But you were the one who really saw me through it."

A horn blasted behind us, and Zander snickered while putting the truck in first. "We have to get better about paying attention at stoplights."

We drove in silence for a few minutes, and I sorted through my thoughts. There was so much I wanted to say, but I had to find a way to express them coherently and without crying again.

"It's been a long day." Zander steered into the neighborhood. "How are you handling it all?"

I stared out the windshield, watching the street signs fly by. "I can't explain it, but I'm kind of at peace. I feel like I learned a lot today."

"What do you mean?" He gave me a sideways glance.

"Last night when I left the party, I called Jenna and then walked up to the coffee shop and met her," I said. "She said something that made sense to me today."

"What was that?" Zander asked, pulling into his driveway.

"I told her I thought God had abandoned me, and she said that maybe God had been here all along."

Zander parked the Jeep in front of his garage and turned to me. "What do you mean?"

"I think I've missed that God has been here, and he's appeared to me through you, Chelsea, my family, and everyone who came to the waiting room." I touched his hand. "He's been watching out for me, and he's sent me wonderful friends to guide me. He sent Darlene and Chuck to take care of my dad and me too."

He smiled. "I think you're right."

"And there's something else I finally understand." I took a deep breath. "The night of the Halloween party when we fought, you said that I deliberately close out everyone who cares about me."

He shook his head. "I just meant—"

I touched my finger to his lips to stop him from speaking. "Zander, you were right. I built a wall up around myself when I lost my mom. I did it to shield myself from heartbreak, even though Tyler managed to break it anyway. But in the past twenty-four hours, I realized that I was keeping everyone out— including God and you." I paused, gathering my thoughts. "I owe you a thank you for showing me the way back to God." I lifted my bracelet and examined the cross. "You were right all along."

"I don't know how much I actually did, but I'm glad I could help you." He pushed his door open. "I think you need to get some sleep. We can talk more tomorrow."

I climbed from the Jeep and met him at the hood. I wrapped my arms around his neck and pulled him close. "Thank you, Zander. Thank you for everything."

"You're welcome." His lips brushed the top of my head. "See you tomorrow?"

I snorted. "I'm grounded until next year, remember? Literally. Even after nearly cutting his arm off and being all drugged up after surgery, my dad reminded me tonight."

He grinned, his adorable dimple appearing. "You have to go to the hospital, right?" He gestured toward the Jeep. "The guys won't be bringing your dad's truck home from the shop until tomorrow."

I smiled. "I guess you're right. I can't walk to the hospital, and my hand-me-down Honda needs some work. Whitney made some comments last week that make me think I'm in for some transmission work."

"Then I'll see you in the morning."

"I'll charge my phone and text you when I get up."

"Sounds like a plan." He leaned down and lightly brushed his lips against mine, sending liquid heat through my veins. "Sleep well," he murmured against my ear. "Your dad is going to be fine. It might take some time, but I believe he's going to be okay." Looking down at me, he winked. "See you tomorrow, my Chevy Girl."

I watched him saunter toward the house and I grinned. How ironic that despite all of the stress of the day, I finally was Zander Stewart's girlfriend. I headed toward the house and stopped dead in my tracks when I spotted Darlene on the deck.

"Emily," she said. "Let's talk for a moment."

It's now or never.

I took a deep, cleansing breath and climbed the deck stairs. "Yes, Aunt Darlene."

She sank into a chair at the table and motioned across from her. "Join me."

Sitting across from her, I suddenly felt the most overwhelming urge to apologize.

Her expression was contrite, but I could tell this moment was hard for her. "I've thought about what you said last night."

"Wait." I reached across and touched her hand. "Before you speak, I have to say something."

She raised an eyebrow. "What is it?"

"I'm sorry." My voice was beginning to thin. "I said some horrible things last night, and I'm truly sorry. You and Uncle Chuck were generous to take Dad and me in, and I'm sorry for not appreciating you. So, thank you."

She looked stunned. "You're welcome, dear. That's what family is for."

I folded my hands in front of me, wishing my voice would stop quavering. "I should've realized sooner how much of an effort you've made to help my dad and me—feeding us and letting us live here for free. I'm sorry for not appreciating it. Thank you also for the car, the phone, and the clothes. You've gone out of your way, and I've never really acknowledged it."

"It's okay." She touched my hand and then took a deep breath. "I need to apologize too. This morning when Whitney and I went shopping, she pointed out a lot of things I've been doing wrong lately."

My eyes widened with surprise. "She did?"

She cleared her throat and clasped her hands together. "She told me that I haven't been behaving like a Christian, and she's absolutely right. I was wrong to criticize how you wear your hair and how you dress. You're a beautiful girl, and nobody's perfect. Maybe I was wrong to make the comment about giving you the Honda in front of all of your friends at the party. Whitney said that it was horrifically embarrassing for you. I should've considered my words before opening my mouth."

I blinked, stunned speechless.

"So I too am very, very sorry." She took my hand in hers. "You're my niece, and I love you. I've treated you poorly."

"Aunt Darlene—" I began.

"Let me finish." She gave a weak smile. "Whitney has also pointed out that your grandmother and I ignore you when she's in the room. She told me that she's tired of being the center of attention, and she feels that you need to be recognized for how pretty, smart, and talented you are too. She said she's going to have a talk with Grandma about it next Saturday when we go visit her."

I gasped. *Go Whitney!*

"So even though I go to church and attend the women's meetings," Darlene continued, "I haven't been behaving the way I should. I'm very sorry for hurting you. We have some things to work through, but I hope you can forgive me as well."

"Of course I can," I whispered. "Thank you."

"Well, it's late." Darlene stood. "You need to get some sleep."

I stood, and she hugged me.

"Emily," she began. "You can rest easy, knowing that God is going to look out for your father. He has the best doctors in this area."

"Thank you," I said. "You're right. God has been taking care of us all along."

She headed for the door and then glanced back at me. "Are you coming in?"

"I think I'm going to stay out here for a few minutes and clear my head."

"Well, don't stay out here too long. It's cold, and you really do need to get some rest."

"Okay." I smiled. "Good night."

"Good night, dear." She disappeared into the house.

I lifted my gaze to the sky above, taking in the beautiful, twinkling stars, and I wrapped my fingers around my mother's cross. I finally understood how that little piece of gold gave my mother hope in her darkest hours.

"Thank you, God, for all of the wonderful people and blessings in my life," I whispered before heading into the house.

When I reached my room, I changed into my pajamas. Sitting on the window seat, I opened up my journal and started to write:

Saturday, December 3
Dear Mom,
The past twenty-four hours have been the most emotional I've faced since we lost you. To say it was a roller coaster would be an understatement. On one hand, I could've lost Dad in a terrible accident, but in a wild twist of events, I also became Zander's girlfriend.

When I found out Dad had been hurt, I was sure I was going to lose him like I lost you, and I felt so alone. But as horrible as it was today, it made me realize that I'm not alone, and I never was alone. God has been with me throughout this crazy journey. It's kind of like the "Footprints in the Sand" saying that you used to have hanging in your bedroom.

God was carrying me all along. He's been guiding me and leading me to people who care for me. He sent me Chuck, Darlene, Whitney, Zander, Chelsea, Pastor Keith, Jenna, and all of our friends at school and church. I'm so thankful for my friends, especially Chelsea. She's become the sister I never had, encouraging me through the rough spots.

Dr. Stewart said that Dad is going to have physical therapy when he gets out of the hospital, and he may have a long road to recovery. If he doesn't regain full use of his arm, will he be able to work and make enough money to move out? I'm not sure how it would feel to stay here and not have my own garage to tinker in.

But, on the other hand, I'm not so sure I want to move out either. It's sort of strange for me to say that, because I was so upset when Dad and I moved here. I thought my life was over, and I was humiliated to have to live with Darlene and Whitney. But moving here has turned out to be a blessing for me. Although I miss our house and my friends back home, having Zander next door, along with Whitney and Logan here, has actually been very cool.

I realized that Whitney's not who I thought she was back at the funeral. She's not the self-absorbed snob I believed her to be. She helped guide me back to God and also made her mother realize that she wasn't truly behaving like an example of Christ's love. I know I can learn a lot from Whitney about what it's like to be a Christian and show love and compassion. Besides, she's a fun person to go out shopping with sometimes.

And Zander ... What can I say about Mr. Mopar? He's my best friend and a really great kisser. He is also a great guy; I mean, he was trying to help me reclaim my faith, even when he barely knew me. We're experiencing different faith journeys, and hopefully we'll be able to help each other down those roads from now on. I'm so thankful that God brought us together, and I look forward to many hours working in his garage, joking around, and talking about everything from God to movies, music, and, of course, cars. Maybe we'll get that Dodge running and then someday build my Camaro.

Mom, you wrote in your letter to me that I need to remember that Dad loves me. I realized today that you're absolutely right. Just like my faith journey was different than Zander's, Dad's grieving process is different than mine. I was wrong to yell at him and demand he talk to me. I need to let him grieve in his own way, just like I need to go out in a garage and work in order to work through my grief. I have to be patient with him, and I promise I will.

I also know now that I experienced a crisis of faith because you were my spiritual rock. I thought faith had to be strong and unwavering, like yours seemed to be. (Mom, did you ever have doubts?) Now, I've come to realize that my faith is not a static thing. My relationship with God will continue to change, I think, but I know he'll always lead me and welcome me back when I seem to lose my way.

I may not know what's next for Dad and me, but there's one thing I do know for sure: I can face any of my problems with God's help.

I love you, Mom, and I miss you. Thank you for leading me.

Love,

Emily

Acknowledgments

This novel was the most challenging I've authored so far in my writing career, and I'm indebted to many people who have helped me craft this story.

From the bottom of my heart, I'm so very thankful to my amazing husband, Joe, for enduring my endless technical questions about cars, trucks, tools, and body shops. Thank you for answering each of my questions with patience, especially when I repeatedly asked you the same questions about rebuilding engines. You're my best friend and the love of my life. And I hope someday you can build me a metallic purple 1969 Camaro so we can cruise off into the sunset together.

Of course, I'm grateful to my mother, Lola Goebelbecker for her love, patience, and guidance with all of my writing. Mom, you're still my best plotting partner! Thank you also for keeping the boys busy while I'm writing. I could never meet my crazy deadlines without your dedicated and unwavering assistance. I appreciate you more than words can express. Love you, Mom!

Zac and Matt, my amazing sons, are an inspiration in my life. Thank you both for your laughter, hugs, and kisses. You make every day rewarding. I'm honored to be your mom.

My critique partners deserve special recognition for their loyalty and guidance—Lauran Rodriguez and Sue McKlveen.

I'm especially thankful for Sue's suggestions with the faith element in the book and Lauran's help with the diary entries.

Youth director Liz Fisher was vital in helping me craft Emily's faith journey. Thank you so much for your time and guidance with the youth ministry component of the story. I wish you joy in your new career. You're a blessing to the children's lives you touch!

I appreciate Teresa and Cosmo Gigante's advice on the little details of the book.

Thank you to William G. Larsen, M.D., of Northwest Family Physicians, in Charlotte, North Carolina, who helped me with the medical aspects in the story.

I'm grateful to John Smith, Auto Body Technician with Wilburn Auto Body and Emergency Medical Technician, for his guidance and suggestions.

Mary Sue Seymour is the best agent in the world!

Thank you to my editor, Jacque Alberta, for believing in this book and helping me grow as a writer. I also appreciate the rest of the Zondervan team who made this book a reality.

Thank you most of all to God for giving me the opportunity and privilege to spread his Word through my books.

Roadside Assistance
discussion questions

1. Emily lost not only her mom, but her house, her friends, and a lot of her freedom. If you were in her situation, what would you miss the most? How would you cope?

2. Emily journals and writes letters to her mother as a way to work through her emotions and vent frustrations. What do you do to help you deal with difficult situations?

3. Humiliated and lost after Whitney's party, Emily was feeling pretty down. Thankfully she knew she could call Jenna. Who do you talk to when you're feeling low?

4. After Whitney's birthday party, Emily loses her temper. Was there a better way for Emily to vent her frustration? Do you think she was justified in yelling at her dad and aunt? Or would you have handled the situation in a different way?

5. After losing her mom, and almost every other constant and familiar thing in her life, Emily loses her connection with God as well. Have you ever doubted God? What do you do to build your relationship back up?

6. Zander, Chelsea, and Whitney all try to help Emily cope during a difficult time in her life. If you were Emily's friend, how would you try to help her? What could you do or say to make her feel better?

7. Tyler, Emily's ex-boyfriend, breaks up with her because he wasn't attracted her "that way." Emily thinks it's because

her knowledge of cars can be intimidating and oftentimes emasculating to guys. Yet despite the disparaging comment, Emily doesn't try to change who she is and her interest in cars never wanes. Is there an aspect of your life that you feel this passionate about?

8. Both Aunt Darlene and Emily's grandmother criticize her for the way she dresses and how little effort she puts into her appearance. If you were in Emily's shoes, how could you handle the pressure to be something you're not?

9. Emily uses cars as an escape, as a means to clear her head. Do you have an activity that helps you when you're feeling down?

10. Zander admits to Emily that college is a sore subject in his family because Zander's dad thinks working on cars is a hobby, and not a career choice. If you were Zander, how could you convince your dad otherwise? Have you thought about what you want to do after high school?

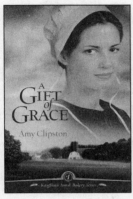

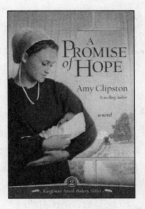

Talk It Up!

Want free books?
First looks at the best new fiction?
Awesome exclusive merchandise?

We want to hear from you!

Give us your opinions on titles, covers, and stories.
Join the Z Street Team.

Email us at zstreetteam@zondervan.com
to sign up today!

Also—Friend us on Facebook!

www.facebook.com/goodteenreads

- Video Trailers
- Connect with your favorite authors
- Sneak peeks at new releases
- Giveaways
- Fun discussions
- And much more!